CP/4'

Brad Kessler's work has appeared in the *New Yorker*, the *New York Times Magazine*, *Doubletake*, the *Nation* and the *Village Voice*. A former editor at *Interview* magazine, he is the author of several award-winning children's books. He lives in Vermont and New York City.

LICK CREEK

Emily has lived in the small rural town of Lick Creek for her entire life. Bereaved of the men in her life following a mining disaster, she struggles to support herself and her mother. After construction begins on the new electrical power lines, Emily blames the intruders for everything that has gone awry. But when Joseph, a charismatic electrical worker, is struck by lightning, and her mother takes him in, Emily is seduced by his past — the world of Jewish immigrants forced to flee persecution. A passionate love affair begins, but Emily knows she has to take revenge upon another man whose violent act still haunts her . . .

BRAD KESSLER

LICK CREEK

Complete and Unabridged

ULVERSCROFT
Leicester

First published in 2001 in Great Britain by
Abacus
London

First Large Print Edition
published 2003
by arrangement with
Time Warner Books UK
London

British Library CIP Data

Kessler, Brad
    Lick creek.—Large print ed.—
    Ulverscroft large print series: general fiction
    1. Appalachian Mountains—Fiction
    2. Love stories 3. Large type books
    I. Title
    813.6 [F]

    ISBN 0–7089–4773–5

Published by
F. A. Thorpe (Publishing)
Anstey, Leicestershire

Set by Words & Graphics Ltd.
Anstey, Leicestershire
Printed and bound in Great Britain by
T. J. International Ltd., Padstow, Cornwall

This book is printed on acid-free paper

Amber stones are yellow and translucent and look somewhat like old teeth. They are the fosilized resin from an extinct variety of pine. The ancient Greeks realized that amber, when rubbed, drew small objects to itself like paper, silk, or hair. They stuck amber on the bobbins of their spinning wheels and fashioned jewelry from it for their lovers and wives. Amber routes spread from the Baltic to the Mediterranean and Africa. In some measure it was desire — or even love — that moved amber from one end of the known earth to the other. The Greeks called amber and its powers of attraction *elektron*. It is the root of the English word *electricity*.

To Dona

1

She wakes in winter to the scrape of iron in the stove, her mother bringing embers back to life from their night's dying. She watches later through frosted panes her father and brother lean into darkened snow, each with his own tin bucket, the two like cutouts of each other, one smaller but with the same stooped back. Their lanterns swing into dark. In April, when the mornings warm, she blankets the pony and trails them from a distance downhollow, all the way where the Lick Creek Road meets the Two Mile Road. She paces the pony so they won't see her behind, and she watches them descend the talus toward the coal camp, and there she'll wait in a copse of poplars, looking down at the rows of homes with men filing from them. She tries to keep track of her father and brother, but they become lost with other lanterns, flitting and wheeling through trees, like a procession of pilgrims carrying candles toward the mouth of the mine.

★ ★ ★

She found her hollow once on a map of West Virginia. Lick Creek was the thinnest scribble of blue, a crack in a porcelain cup. Nothing like the cold waters and salted boulders she knew or the spring water that tasted of sulfur. On the map in the schoolhouse, she traced the creek with a finger as it fed thicker rivers, spidered south, then west. She memorized the names of the rivers it became and on April nights, lying awake in the dark, she whispered the words like a prayer: *The Greenbrier, the New, the Ohio, the Mississippi,* traveling them all in a trance, half-asleep, slipping past Baton Rouge, New Orleans, and down the Delta into the Gulf of Mexico. When she woke again in the night, she could taste ocean on her tongue.

★ ★ ★

She first met Gianni when she went to buy the goat with her father. Gianni Fermini, his name was like a noodle in her mouth; it kept slipping out. They argued about the kid. He called it a *capro*. She said, Huh-uh, he's a goat. The hair on Gianni's head was black as a raven, so iridescent she wanted to touch it. He was wearing no shirt, holding the kid in his bare arms, the white wool against his brown chest as if they belonged together. Her

4

father stood back and surveyed the kid, sucked his teeth and rubbed his chin and changed positions to get a better view. His father pushed out his lips and said, 'He be a good one for the ladies.'

Her father nodded noncommittally and checked the hooves, held open its mouth and studied the small teeth. He stood back again and they both looked at the sky, talked weather, then came back to the goat, circling the deal like dogs before lying down. While they were bargaining, Emily said to Gianni:

'You're an Injun, ain't you?'

'No,' he said, shaking his head, his lids half-closed. 'Italian.'

Emily didn't like his confidence, the way he was handling the kid as if he still owned it.

'You're holding him all wrong,' she said, and grabbed the goat from his arms, so it nayed, and gathered it under her chin and said, 'See you're supposed to hold'm like this.'

He was four years older. He smelled of dried grass. She called him John.

'No,' he corrected her, 'Jee-ah-nee.'

'Bye,' she said as she was leaving, 'John.'

★ ★ ★

A few years later she'd steal down to the coal camp with its cluttered new houses painted

5

impossible colors — greens, blues, and yellows. A town of secrets and foreign tongues, where she always felt illicit, observed, a stranger in her own country. Gianni's parents owned a Victrola they kept polished and oiled, the rosewood so shiny she could see herself in it. On Sunday afternoons, while his family sat on folding chairs in the backyard, she and Gianni lay on the cool planks of the floor, listening to records. They were Italian mostly, the plates as thick as china, the sleeves yellowed and crisp with age. He taught her the popular tunes, the names of the great composers: Puccini, Rossini, Verdi. To her they sounded like a litany of flowers. She pictured Puccini as a moss rose, something delicate, a succulent that would last only a day. Verdi was hardy, a kind of vine. Donizetti, a day lily.

One afternoon, in his broken English, he tried to teach her the story of *La Traviata*. It was October, the trees changing in the hollow. Outside, his parents were drinking jugs of wine. The recording was scratched and noisy. The music sounded rich to her, like brocade or lush curtains, something plush and prohibited, an odd religion. It made the new hairs along her legs tingle. The sun was scuffed in the windows, shafting the bare boards of the house, and Gianni was acting out parts for her. He tried to explain

6

Violetta, the prostitution part, but couldn't find the correct word in English.

'*Prostituta*,' he said. 'You know . . .'

He hiked his pants and pretended a garter belt and batted his eyes.

She didn't understand. The family was laughing through the screen door. Glasses clinking. The music was too much, suddenly suffocating, and she was seized with the urge to run.

'Wait, wait, listen,' he said, and closed his eyes. A woman was singing:

Addio, del passato bei sogni ridenti . . .

★ ★ ★

Afterward, as she walked home on the Two Mile Road, the music was still about her. The first leaves were shredding from the chestnuts, the evening beveled in the branches. She had no idea what the opera was about, but the music clung to her like a washcloth, something warm she couldn't shed. She heard it in the alders and the larch; she heard a whippoorwill whistle in the forest; she remembered Gianni's face, singing, and she hugged her shoulders and began, suddenly, to shiver.

★ ★ ★

Gianni and her brother, Delmar, both work the mines. They enter at the same time and leave at the same time, but each works with his own father on a different face in a different part of the mine. When they do see each other, it is with Emily, and they argue about everything.

'America,' Gianni says, 'is Italian.'

'Horseshit,' says Delmar.

Her brother is moonfaced and pale, a scratch of mustache above his lip. His name means 'of the ocean,' though he seems to Emily of the earth, white and loamy. Standing next to her brother, Gianni looks as sharp as a knife.

'You are named after an Italian,' Gianni tries again.

'To hell I am.'

'Amerigo Vespucci, he was Italian. *He* is America.'

Delmar rolls his eyes and spits. 'Sure, chief. Whatever you say.'

★   ★   ★

One Saturday they all went swimming in the pond below the high pasture. Thunderheads had been stacking all morning, and by afternoon the sky turned slate and lowered and the first drops emptied over the pond.

Emily and Delmar climbed from the water and toweled themselves and waited for Gianni. He was still making loops in the pond.

'Come on, John,' Emily yelled. 'Lightning's coming.'

He was treading water, smiling. 'It's okay,' he yelled, waving to her.

The rain picked up, swung over the pond. She and Delmar covered themselves with a blanket, holding it above their heads, like two tent posts.

'What the hell's he doing?' Delmar said, and laughed, but didn't know why. The thunder was nearing; they could hear it cracking downhollow, working its way along the ridgetops. She yelled to him again.

'It's not okay! Come on in!'

He swam in a circle, fountained water from his mouth, grinned. She pleaded with him. She knew he was doing this for her sake.

'See, it's all right,' he yelled, lifting his arms. 'No problem.'

They watched Gianni in the water, incredulous, Delmar muttering 'Dumb shit' over and over and Gianni with his hair slicked and creased and the bones of his shoulders popping above the water like two brown buoys that followed him wherever he went.

The thunder was now overhead. Rain

misted the water, and Gianni was small and blurred, a black dot surrounded by dropping silver. A wire of lightning crashed above and the air jumped and brightened and Emily screamed. They could feel something electric crawl their skin. She peered at the pond but couldn't see Gianni anymore. His head was gone, the pond empty, the surface stuccoed with rain. She hid her face in the blanket, yelling. The thunder rolled back into the hills.

When she opened her eyes again, he was climbing out the far end of the pond, hunched in the rain, lank and panting, his black hair hanging in a wedge.

'See,' he said when he reached her, 'it was okay.' He was smiling triumphantly, water pebbled on his chin.

'Idiot,' she muttered.

Delmar shook his head in disgust and left the blanket and headed up the trail for home. The rain was slackening, passing to the south. She gathered the ends of the blanket about her shoulders and left, too, Gianni trailing behind.

They walked single file up the slope past huddled cows. No one talked. The wind was sharp, harrowing the wet pasture grass and trembling the cottonwood trees. Gianni's teeth were chattering, his arms bracing the bones of his chest, trying to warm.

When they reached the Lick Creek Road, Gianni turned toward the coal camp.

'Come,' he said to Emily. 'Kiss to make up.'

'I hope you get struck by lightning.'

He flicked the hair from his face and grinned. 'Come on,' he said. 'You got scared, didn't you?'

Delmar had gone ahead and was waiting in the road, etching something in the mud with a stick.

'Come on, say you were scared for me.' He said it with his chin, provoking.

'Jackass,' she said.

Before she could turn to go, he grabbed her elbow and pecked her on the cheek and said, 'There, now we are friends.'

Emily colored and swung around and belted him in the stomach. He tried to laugh but couldn't catch his breath. Up the road, Delmar was smiling.

* * *

On the way home he said, 'I told you them I-talians are all dumber'n shithouse rats. Don't even have sense enough to come in out'a the rain.'

He struck a tree branch with his stick, knocking crystals on the road. 'Why, they'd rather climb a tree and tell a lie than stand on

11

the ground and speak the truth.'

'Hush,' Emily said.

'They're all half muscle, and the other half's fool.'

'Hush.'

'Why, that boy's dumber'n a bucket of hair,' he said. 'Dumber'n — '

She didn't let him finish. Before she was aware of what she was doing, she hauled back and belted him. The disbelief equal on their faces, he falling in the road, his nose already blossoming a rosette of blood.

★ ★ ★

A kettle bottom is the stump of an old tree, petrified millions of years ago. It sits in seams of coal, suspended like a loose fossil in the soft bituminous rock. Kettle bottoms can drop from a ceiling seam unexpectedly when undercut. They weigh about five hundred pounds, and when they fall they crush men. The miners call them widow makers.

Emily has never seen a kettle bottom but is haunted by them. She's learned of them through Delmar. He tries to make the mines seem romantic, so she's jealous.

'Do you know what it's like being under a mountain?' he asks.

'Just on top.'

12

'Below,' he says, 'is even better.'

Every mountain has a secret, he says. Fossils, bones of old animals, ores, a vein of crystal quartz. No one on top would ever know this, he says. There's a power inside the earth, he says. You and the mountain. One million tons of weight above you. The coal hasn't seen light in 250 million years. You are the first to discover it. You are its savior.

She watches him say this and knows he's picked it up from some old miner he's overheard and is trying it out on her like a new pair of trousers. Still, she is jealous. She imagines the kettle bottoms, the crosshatchings and tunnels, the ribbing of poplar buttresses, the headway and gob pile where the miners meet for lunch. Each face like a room in a palace, this place underground where they sit and work, the earth with chambers of its own no one but the miners know.

He's told her about the mules they lower into the shafts half-crazed, their legs lashed so they won't snap and their eyes blinkered. How the first nights of April are always the worst, when the odor of green onions blows through the brattices and the mules kick and scratch to get outside, and how the mule boss has to beat them back, and the mad ones are shot. After one season in the

13

mines, they usually die.

Emily imagines Gianni down there as well, left alone to handle the insides of the earth. He himself with pick and shovel, in a room he can claim his own. A kingdom of coal. He's brought her fossils from there. Trilobites. Tracings of ancient ferns, beetles carved in traprock. Treasures from the deep where he is a diver. She knows the instruments he works with inside the planet, the pickax, breast auger, the black powder, the shovel. He's lit his lamp for her, popped the acetylene in his palm, and placed it upon her head, yet the life there remains a mystery, full of rumor and darkness, like the way she turns over rocks and finds insects she's never known before or how, in her dreams, she opens a door to a closet and discovers an ocean or a room in a city in a country she never knew existed. She know she'll never see his world, for the taboo against women in the mine is too strong, and at Branton when a girl fled into the tunnels once, the miners wouldn't go back for months, afraid that ill fortune would follow them ever after. All she knows, then, are the edges of things, the way Gianni smells in the evenings before washing, an odor of damp from his body, like her brother's, only sweeter. Their fingernails dyed with blackness. Gianni's told her the name of the people who used to own the mine and the coal camp but no longer do, the family from New York City. A funny name that sounds like laughter. They're called the Guggenheims.

She knows, too, that the limestone beneath her farm is like a cake of soap, soft, chalky, white as porcelain, with sinkholes here and there, places where the earth has opened like a lamprey and sucked everything in sight. Yet the limestone is relatively benign and brings forth musk mallow and cresses and trout lillies in early spring. She knows that farther downhollow the limestone becomes larded with anchors of coal, and the coal crops thicker and thicker like coral until they form a great reef that furrows to the west. They say the coal is a blessing, but she knows it's a curse as well, too close to ignore, the wage work too enticing, that it lures her father and brother half the week. Not like others in Lick Creek who stay away from the mines, who have not want of its dark, despite the extra cash. Her father can't help himself. That Val Jenkins, they say, never could stay out of a mine.

★   ★   ★

Delmar is learning to shoot coal from his father. He must learn about the cleat of the

15

coal, how to blast it so the seam breaks evenly and will be easy to work afterward. He must decide where to drill his holes for the blasting and how deep and at what angle. If he uses too little powder, the coal will break too big and he'll have to hammer it afterward by hand. If he pours too much, the seam will blow to slack and dust and will be worthless.

He curls a page of the *Beckley Herald* into a cone. There's an advertisement for a corset, a hairbrush, a bottle of cough syrup. He uncorks his tin and taps a forefinger so the black powder spills inside the cone. Val Jenkins watches, gestures to pour a little more. Delmar taps the tin again, corks it, hooks it to his belt. He carefully twists the cone and fits it in a drilled hole in the seam. Water is dripping somewhere in the tunnel. He looks back at his father, who points a finger at an iron rod leaning against the wall. The rod is about four feet long and has a needle at the end. Delmar takes the rod and pushes the needle end into the center of the cone, stuffing the newspaper and the powder deeper into the hole. He rests the rod on his shoulder, steps to the hole, packs dirt around the needle, spits on it, and fills it again. He can hear someone whistling far off, the sound echoed in the chambers. He steps back and slips the needle from the packing.

Behind him Val Jenkins's breath is labored, like that of a man twice his age, and the creases on his forehead are a script of fine soot. He nods approvingly at his son, and Delmar snakes a piece of waxed string into the hole and lets it hang by a few inches. A blast goes off in another section, a muffled pop, the pressure in their ears changing by the slightest percentage. Delmar looks at his dad again, who waits, sniffs the air, then gestures Delmar back to the fuse. They can hear the faint scratching of rats now out by their lunch buckets. Val Jenkins leans on his shovel, watching his son, then nods him to go ahead.

Delmar removes his helmet, cradles it in his hands, and touches the acetylene lantern to the fuse. A flame sputters and catches and sparkles white. Delmar scrambles out, trying to get his helmet back, yelling, tentatively because it is his first time: Fire in the hole! He joins his father, crouched against the wall, chins against chests, the two of them together, tucked under earth.

★　★　★

Emily's mother, Ada, had a way of knowing things before they happened. People said she had a gift. They'd go to her when they misplaced a pearl hatpin or a suitcase key. They'd make their way up Lick Creek Road and climb to the clapboard house with the Norway spruce spread in front and sit on the blistered porch swing and sip sassafras tea. Eventually they'd come around to the topic at hand. A lost photograph. A ten-dollar bill. A tuning fork. They'd consult her, and that night she'd dream the lost thing into finding. Wherever she saw it in her sleep was where it would be. She was rarely wrong.

It was June the day the mine blew. Emily and her mother were on the high pasture picking clover for tea, plucking the soft pink ends into burlap sacks, her mother humming some song. It was a clear day with clouds starched and high and the locust trees heavy with bloom. The cows were hanging their heads in the new clover, and suddenly her mother stopped humming and dropped her sack and looked stricken. She seized Emily's arm. Her hand was cold as a spoon.

Emily said, 'Mama, what — ' But Ada hushed her and waited, eyes unfocused, ears set to the breeze; and then, closing her grip tightly around Emily's arm, they heard it.

In the hills, sound carries far. You can hear a rooster or a man's voice or an engine idling a mile off as if it were a few feet away. Up on the pasture they could plainly hear the explosion. A muffled boom, something dreamy about it, as if the earth paused a second to sneeze. It sounded like a mattress falling in a meadow.

Emily thought it was the cows bolting and she looked back, but they hadn't moved, only their heads were lifted now, testing the air. Then she turned toward her mother who was already hurrying back to the house, running through the pasture, her sack on the hillside where she'd dropped it, the clover spilled on the pasture like seed.

By afternoon the whole county was at the mine. Ash drifted over the coal camp, a strange snow in summer. It covered fence posts and porches and fell on white sheets hung that morning to dry. The air smelled of smoldering leaves and coal ash.

All afternoon rescue teams arrived by train. The survivors shuffled about, stunned and collapsed, their clothes torn, faces black and bleeding. Guards with bayonets kept kin from entering the mines. By dusk the governor arrived.

★   ★   ★

Emily dreamed that night she was on the high pasture and could see all the way over the hills to the Gulf of Mexico. The water was copper, like a coin, flashing in the far distance, and she could see the rivers running blue as cobalt, and a harbor bristling with boats and people on the docks wearing dresses and bowlers, and she wondered why she'd never been there before. Then she turned, and Gianni and Delmar were climbing up from the pond, their shirts off, arms around each other. They were singing a song she faintly recognized, the *bandera rosa*, and she watched them stagger up the slope; but they didn't stop for her, and couldn't hear her cries, and she saw their cheeks were blue and lips loose and their mouths hung like marionettes, and their song wasn't a song at all, but the wind rustling in the reeds.

She woke in a cold sweat. The moon spilled on her sheets. She rose through the empty house out into the moonlight. Tree frogs were beating in the grass. The wind pushed scraps of cloud high above the hollow and blew inside her nightshirt and between her legs. It brought the smell of ash up from the mine, and she pictured the sacks of clover they'd left on the high pasture, how they'd be dusted now with soot.

★　★　★

20

By the next night the first bodies came out without arms, or legs, their faces grotesque with gas. They were carried on bare pine planks and tied with baling wire, some carbonized to husks. Others were already bloated and puffed with gas, their clothes popped where the flesh had risen.

They found Gianni that first night on a rock face with his father and a group of other Italians and two Russians and a Pole, in the southwest corner of the mine, where the fire had burned through the brattices. Delmar and his father were found on a north face, where the ventilation fans hadn't worked and the gas had choked them.

The following afternoon Uncle Garvin drove to camp to collect their remains in black cherry boxes. It was evening when he returned to Lick Creek. Swallows were taking their turns in the remaining light. The honeysuckle was in bloom, the air heavy with cut hay. People from the hollow had followed behind Garvin's buckboard and shambled into the drive, hats in hand, dressed in dark suits, the women in homemade cottons. They had little to say, and some helped Garvin, while the women stood on the porch. Emily sat in the porch swing in a daze. She'd been there since morning. She heard a low murmuring come up the road, and saw the procession of people climbing up the drive. They were foreigners from the coal camp. They carried candles of beeswax, and sang a hymn she'd never heard before, something Italian, and it made her think of all the songs Gianni played and how they seemed like brocade to her, like draperies of music, but now were nothing more than funeral cloth.

The procession swung into the drive, thirty of them, the men in long black coats and vests and the caps of their country, the women in silk head scarves, their candles guttered beneath faces. Gianni's mother stood in the middle of them, supported by two women, one at each side. They made their way to the front of the group and reached the flagging; the women left Gianni's mother alone, and she climbed the porch steps, where Ada nodded, and she walked past and sat beside Emily in the swing. She was wearing a lace veil, a piece of Venetian point lowered over her eyes, pinned in place with a hawthorn clasp. She held four gardenias in her hand.

They sat for a moment in silence, the swing shifting with the new weight. Emily stared up into the evening, where the clouds had blackened and the first stars were forming above. Gianni's mother said something in Italian, leaned over and kissed Emily's forehead and laid three gardenias in her lap. Emily looked down and saw the flowers for the first time, and it was then her shoulders began to shake.

★ ★ ★

She has touched Gianni's skin, and his flesh felt like the burnt husk of corn. His body smelled of creosote, his fingers charred and clawed like a chicken's. They left three streaks along the underside of her arm where she accidentally rubbed against them. She hasn't washed them off, and her skin has grown around the stains the way an oyster entombs a pearl, within its own mucus. And so it remains, this mark of coal, and even in the cooling rains of summer, under the curtains of water that fall from the eaves of the house, it does not wash away. As hard as she tries, it outlasts the flesh.

She carries him, through seasons.

2

She could hardly remember the weeks that followed, only that a brick seemed to have lodged inside her chest. That and the haunting certainty that they were all still alive; when she heard a sound in the kitchen or someone stumbling up the porch she was convinced it was Delmar or her father, or maybe even Gianni come to visit. No matter how many times she told herself otherwise, no matter how many times she repeated to herself, *Gianni is dead, Delmar is dead, Daddy is dead,* she couldn't quite grasp the fact that they weren't still living.

For days on end she cried. The tears stopped for an afternoon or a day, but they'd come back the next worse than before until her whole body felt scraped with a spoon, her insides completely scooped out, like a melon. In the long afternoons she sat in the parlor, staring out the window as the clouds turned copper and skirted low over the land and moved off like zeppelins in the last light of the day. If only she sat there long enough, she thought, they might come back. If only she concentrated and waited and believed with all her heart, then perhaps they'd reappear on the pasture road as they always had at that hour, with their dinner buckets swinging at their sides and their blackened faces, and the screen door would slam again and their life jerk back into motion like a film that had momentarily stopped. Some afternoons her mother joined her and they'd sit together in the parlor, side by side, not speaking, not daring to look at each other, both waiting at the window for a sign, the creak of a bucket, a footfall, a shout, a bird flying like an augur overhead.

Each day a neighbor arrived, Ruth Loudermilk or one of the McClung sisters or Rachel Toothman. They'd come bearing a corn pone or a crock of brown beans, a roast of venison, a casserole of squirrel and gravy. They were constantly preparing food or chopping kindling, trying to help whatever way they could. And Emily remembered their voices, hushed and cool in the kitchen, oddly unsettling, as she lay in her bed considering the brick inside her chest, how it was sharp and alien, undigestible, not like a stone, which would've been round and smooth like all the other organs she'd seen in the cutaway map at school. No, this was square and full of edges that cut each time she moved, each time she went to the kitchen, or walked outside, or tried to eat. And she wondered how, once inside her, the brick would ever work itself out.

Sometimes Ada sent the women away so she and Emily could be alone with their grief. By the middle of July the women began to come less frequently, and by August they stopped altogether. A great silence descended upon the house at the head of Lick Creek hollow. The curtains remained drawn, the hay fields grew untended. The garden erupted with strange weeds that had never appeared there before. And then one morning lying in bed, feeling the brick (it had moved into her belly) and watching the same square of light she'd seen each morning slide across the wall of her room, Emily heard something unusual outside, a soft groaning, an engine, a motor that grew louder and louder. She thought for a second it was Delmar or her father, that they were coming in an automobile after all. Then she sighed and pushed herself out of bed, tugged on a pair of Delmar's old trousers, a cotton shirt, and stepped into the parlor.

It was late August by then, and when she parted the curtains in the parlor, she saw a truck in the sunlight and dust swirling as it came to a halt. The truck was black and shiny, a gold lightning bolt painted on the cab door and the words *Appalachian Light and Power* printed in a circle around the bolt. The dog had run out and was barking at the tires, and Emily could see two men in the cab keeping the doors closed against the dog.

Emily tucked in her shirt, fingered hair out of her face, and stepped through the screen door. She shaded her eyes against the glare and called the dog away. Two men emerged from the cab, one fat and plump-faced, the other lean and tallish with a slight lantern jaw. The fat one wore a starched shirt and a straw hat, and the other a tan suede jacket, despite the heat, and a fedora slanted low over one eye. The fat one stopped at the bottom of the porch steps and fanned himself with his hat.

'Good morning, miss,' he said. 'Hot enough for you?'

Emily leaned against the porch rail and didn't say if it was or wasn't. The man carried a clipboard, and his collar was stained with sweat. He said he was from the power company and that they were putting in an electric line in the area. He pointed uphollow toward Keeny's Knob, and said the line was going to run about there, that it was heading all the way from the Ohio Valley down into Virginia, and that it would be one of the largest high-tension type lines ever built.

He removed a handkerchief from his back pocket and mopped his forehead. He began to talk about the right-of-way for the power line, but Emily stopped listening. She looked at the other man. He'd lit a cigarette and laid an elbow across the roof of the truck and he was surveying the pasture where it dipped down to the creek. The fat one was still chattering when the screen door banged and Ada stepped onto the porch. The man stopped talking; the other pushed his hat back. Ada stood in her blue quilted robe squinting in sunlight. She turned to Emily and nodded toward the men.

'What do they want?' she muttered.

Emily shrugged. 'Heck if I know,' she said. 'Something about an electric line.'

She turned back to the men. The fat one introduced himself and started the same speech once more when Ada interrupted.

'Hold on,' she turned to Emily. 'Go and fetch your uncle.'

Emily looked at the men. The fat one was waiting, the other watching, the cigarette clamped in his mouth.

'All right,' Emily said. 'I'll be back directly.'

She climbed down the porch steps. She was aware of both men watching. The tall one dropped his cigarette and crushed it with his boot. She walked straight into the pasture toward Garvin's place, and when she glanced back the tall one was still staring at her, grinding his cigarette in the grass.

Twenty minutes later the men were sitting in the shade of the front-yard spruce, hats off, glasses of water in hand. Emily walked past them and up the porch steps and told her mother Garvin was on his way.

His hounds arrived before he did, three of them circling Sheila and sniffing at the men's pants and boots, backing off and growling, before sprinting behind the house. Garvin was huffing up the hill behind. The fat man flattened the wrinkles of his trousers and held out a hand to Garvin, but Garvin ignored it.

'What can I do for you boys?' he said.

The fat one gave his name again and started the same speech as before. He said he was sent by the Appalachian Light and Power Company, that a power line was going to be built in the area and he was canvassing a right-of-way route. He began to talk about the utility commission and eminent domain when Garvin held up a hand, shut his eyes, and said, 'Hold on here a minute.'

The man stopped talking. Garvin swallowed. The sun angled in his face and he was still sweating from the climb. One of his hounds raced from the side of the house and stopped by his feet and stood panting.

'You-all talkin' about towers, right?' Garvin asked.

'Yes, sir.'

'And where you wantin' to put them towers?'

The man pointed to Keeny's Knob, then across the hollow to the other ridge.

'So you're talking about one up there.'

'Yes, sir.'

'And another yon side of the creek.'

'Yes, sir.'

'That makes her two towers.'

The man nodded his head.

Garvin removed his hat, smeared sweat from his forehead, and squinted up at Keeny's Knob.

'That electric goin' to stay in them towers?'

'Excuse me?'

'Is the electric a-staying in them towers,' he repeated, 'or is it goin' to come down here?'

'I don't follow you,' the man said.

Garvin pitched forward and spat and glared at the man. 'Are we gettin' to use any of that-all electric, or is it just passin' from one place to the next?'

The man smiled in comprehension and shook his head. 'Oh no, sir,' he said. 'It's not coming off those towers.'

'So we ain't gettin' any of that electric.'

'Well, not right away,' the man said. 'But

I'm certain in the future you will.'

Garvin shouldered sweat from his cheek. Emily approached with a glass of water, and he took it and thanked her and drank and handed it back.

'Well,' he said, pointing across the hollow to Keeny's Knob, 'that property belongs to me.' He swung his arm back and pointed to the nearby ridge. 'And that one belongs to Mrs. Jenkins settin' there on the porch.'

'We know that, sir,' the man said patiently. 'That's why we came here, because the utility commission has been invested with the powers to — '

'Hold on,' Garvin said. He held up a hand again and closed his eyes and waited until the man stopped talking.

'See that pad a yours?' he said.

The man looked at the clipboard under his arm.

'Now go and take that pen from you-all shirt and set down the letter *S*.'

The man didn't know what to do. He looked at his partner in the fedora.

'Go on,' Garvin said. 'We ain't got all day.'

The man took a silver fountain pen from his shirt pocket, bent on one knee, and wrote a large *S* on the page. Then he held up the pad from where he knelt.

'Good,' Garvin said, rubbing his chin, 'real

31

good. Now go and draw yourself two lines down the center of that *S* and tell me what it comes out as.'

The man looked at his partner again and wrote the two lines and stood back.

'Well?' Garvin asked.

The man conceded it was a dollar sign.

'Next time you come round,' Garvin said, 'you start talkin' 'bout some dollars and maybe we can kindly come to some agreement; otherwise you-all just a-wasting time.'

He tipped his hat and turned and whistled for his hounds. Then he walked up to the porch where Ada was sitting. Emily approached the men, took their glasses, gave a kind of curtsey, and told them to have a pleasant day. The tall man was smiling now, as if he were in on some secret, and he touched his cap to her in parting.

They returned the following week. This time the fat one didn't say much, and the other sat in the truck the entire time. Garvin and Ada signed a piece of paper, and the man handed them each a check for thirty dollars. After they'd left, Garvin stood on the porch, looking over the ridgetops, then down at the piece of orange bank paper.

'What you think, Emee?' he asked. He slapped the piece of paper with the back of his hand. 'You reckon they got the long end of the stick?'

Emily looked across the hollow, then down at the bank check, and shrugged.

'Yes, sir,' she said. 'I believe they have.'

3

The money from the electric line lasted only a few months, and though the company kept promising, the compensation from the mine never materialized. The days meanwhile turned chill in Lick Creek. Leaves drifted over the pasture, the last crickets creaked in the grass. In the frosted mornings Emily headed out of the house alone, hunting uphollow for mushrooms or ginseng roots or the tubers of black cohosh, anything she could sell to Laird's for a few pennies. Sometimes she sold fresh eggs or the velvet coat of a newborn kid. For it occurred to her, even if it hadn't yet to her mother, that they couldn't go on living off the charity of neighbors and whatever quarry Garvin occasionally brought in. If she were a man, she thought, she'd already be working a mine somewhere.

One morning she lay beneath quilts, listening to a turkey outside. She thought about Delmar and her father, how they'd be on the knob before daylight, behind a blind somewhere, and how the next night there'd be a roast on the table for supper. She closed her eyes and listened a minute more and heard the turkey again, a low haunting in the fog, like water gurgling in a drain. It was a tom turkey looking for a mate.

She rose and pulled on a pair of boots and laced them halfway. Outside, she hoofed through wet grass to the chicken coop. A cladding of frost covered the lawn, and when she opened the hatch the hens fled, a flurry of wings. Barred Rocks, Rosecombs, a Brahma. Only the rooster stayed behind, the fighter Garvin had given them.

'You heard him, too huh, Albert?' she muttered.

The rooster jerked his head sideways, rolled an eye back.

She slipped a wooden bucket from its nail and scooped a tinful of dried corn and sprinkled it over the trough. The rooster started pecking before she was done, and she poured a little on his head, yet he didn't notice. She rehung the bucket and searched the straw for eggs but found only guano.

When she closed the door she heard the turkey again. He was closer now, somewhere beside the creek, near the edge of the pasture. Emily waited, the hollow socked with fog. Another minute he called again. He was moving along the edge of the pasture, traveling east uphollow. Back inside, she toed her boots beside the door. Her mother had risen and was grinding coffee at the table, her hair a gray rope and rings around her eyes wide as washers. The dog lay at her feet.

'You're up early,' Emily said.

Ada shrugged and continued cranking the grinder. Emily walked to her mother's bedroom, where the sheets were unmade and the room smelled like a sour box. She swung open an oak armoire, and the odor of lavender greeted her. She remembered two years earlier how she'd picked the lavender and crushed the flowers in the dressers and drawers. Delmar had sneered and said it didn't matter what you smelled like in a mine, and Emily said it wasn't for the smell, idiot, but the moths.

The odor was still there a year later. Dried lavender, the leaves crisp, almost a powder. She found her father's woolen coat and buried her face in it, but there was no trace of his smell. She touched his two dress shirts, his thin black suit, the pairs of denim overalls all neatly pressed and hung as if any day he might return and invest them with his limbs. She'd tried once to rid the clothes from the house, packing them in a steamer trunk and hauling them out to the barn; but her mother stopped her halfway and dragged the trunk back indoors and folded the clothes again in their drawers. And there they stayed, the underwear and trousers, shirts and socks, all starched and crisp as if they were a kind of shrine. Her mother had even polished all their boots.

Emily groped behind clothes and felt the barrel of a rifle, and she brought out the .22 Smith & Wesson and stood it against the bed back. She knelt again and found a cigar box and fished it out as well. When she returned to the kitchen, a kettle sat on the stove and her mother had gone to the outhouse. She placed the gun on the table and removed from the cigar box an oiling tin, a felt rag, a brass brush, and a small screwdriver. She unscrewed the heads along the forearm and drifted out the barrel from the stock. She shoved the brush up the barrel, rotated it, and brought it out and rammed it up again. She checked the bore for dirt and ran the brush once more. By the time her mother returned, she was already oiling the gun.

'What you doing?' Ada asked.

'Cleaning it.'

Ada stared at her blankly, then went to the counter and spooned coffee into an enamel pot. Emily screwed back the walnut stock. Her mother held the spoon and watched her.

'You know what you're doing with that thing?'

'Uh-huh.'

She wiped the breechblock and the butt, squared the gun on her shoulder and sighted along the barrel. Then she swung it toward her mother and squinted.

'Emee, don't go pointing that at me,' Ada said.

She jumped out of the way, but Emily followed her with the gun.

'I'm gonna give you a hiding when you put that thing down.'

Emily was laughing, following her mother's feet around the kitchen.

'Watch out, Mama!' she yelled.

The water was boiling on the stove. The dog had risen and was barking furiously.

'Put that damn thing down.'

'Too late, Mama. Got you in my sights.'

'Emee . . . '

'Here comes a big fat bullet.'

'Put that damn gun down or — '

'Relax,' Emily said. She lowered the rifle and grinned at her mother and placed the gun on the table. 'It's not loaded anyhow.'

Her mother put a hand to her chest and exhaled. 'Don't you point that at me again. Devil.'

'Yes, ma'am.'

Her mother went back to the stove and picked off the kettle so it fell silent. The dog circled and sat once more.

'Just thought I'd try and wake you a little,' Emily said.

'I don't need no waking.'

'No,' Emily muttered. 'I reckon you'd rather be asleep.'

Ada didn't respond. She tilted the kettle over grounds. 'Only thing I need is this here coffee.'

'If you say so.' Emily shrugged.

'I'm saying it.'

Ada put the kettle down. Emily returned to the gun. She laid it on the table and began wiping the stock, one side and then the other. Her mother blew on her mug, and they sat a moment in silence as the stove crackled and wisps of fog feathered outside the window. Ada lowered her mug and nodded toward the gun.

'Since when you know how to clean that thing?' she asked.

'Since Delmar.'

'He learned you?'

'No,' Emily said. 'I watched.'

'You watch how to shoot it, too?'

'Uh-huh.'

Ada started to say something, but Emily held up a hand for silence. She'd heard the turkey again.

'Listen.'

'I don't hear a thing.'

'Hush,' Emily said. 'He's close.'

They waited. Wood snapped in the stove. Sheila lifted an ear. Then they heard it, this time distinctly, a long, low gobble. Emily thumbed a bullet in the chamber and took another from the box.

'C'mon, Emee,' her mother said. 'You never done fired that thing in your life.'

'Have so.'

'What at?'

Emily chambered another bullet and clicked the bolt closed. 'Cans,' she said.

Her mother rolled her eyes. 'Great,' she said. 'You gonna shoot some baked beans?'

Emily grinned and stood.

'Well, don't go shooting your hand off,' she said. 'I need 'em both.'

'That's right, Mama, I aim on keeping both.'

'And see if there's any eggs.'

'Yes, ma'am. I already did.'

'And?'

'Wasn't a one.'

★ ★ ★

That afternoon she crossed the creek and hiked into the woods, following an old logging trail that traced the fold of the mountain. Sheila led the way, looking back every few seconds to see she was heading in the right direction. They climbed a waterless draw, through wintergreen and dying culver root and down into a hollow where cicely still grew out of last year's leaves.

She heard a loud beating of wings and dropped to the ground, swung the gun, but lost whatever it was. A grouse, probably, she thought, and went on. The afternoon was growing warm; the fog burned off overhead. She found a place where three trees grew in a small triangle and for half an hour she snapped young branches from pignuts and shellbarks and Shumard oaks and built three walls of a blind, using each trunk as a brace and weaving brush between them. She tore the bark off a rotting hickory and leaned the moist planking against holes in the blind, then scattered handfuls of leaves over the entire thing. When she was done she climbed gingerly into the blind, crossed her legs, and sat.

Bores of sunlight fanned through the canopy now. The wind stirred and shredded leaves off branches. She watched as they drifted lazily, like pieces of crepe, twirling and eddying without a sound. She took an ash leaf and smoothed it on her knee and traced its veins with a finger. Gianni once told her that each falling leaf was a letter sent from overseas, a kind of airmail, and that they were written in a language no one could understand but trees. Once when they were walking on the Two Mile Road, he picked a leaf up and passed it to her.

'It's for you,' he said.

She turned it over and pretended to read it.

'What's it say?' he asked.

She slipped it in her pants pocket. 'I can't tell you,' she said. 'It's private.'

'Come on,' he said.

She shook her head and he reached for her pocket, and she spun aside, bent over in laughter. And she remembered how he'd grabbed her and kissed her, the smell of his mouth, the new hairs there; the rise in his pants where he pressed into her. Like a mouse, she thought. Something furred and alive underneath, not like Delmar's, which was white and grublike, or at least the color of a grub, and penciled straight sometimes when she saw him on the way to the outhouse in the mornings. Gianni's was fuller, or it felt that way that afternoon with him pressing into her and the leaf still clutched in her hand. She was scared someone would see them. That was two years ago. She was sixteen then, though it felt like a lifetime.

She turned the ash leaf over and sighed.

The dog raised an ear and looked to her. For the first time in months she wanted to but couldn't cry. She threw the leaf aside and grabbed the gun.

'Come on,' she said to the dog. 'It's time to get home.'

★ ★ ★

Early the next morning, when the stars were still bright and the hollow frosted in moonlight, she left the house with the gun. She made her way to the creek in the dark, heard the ponies blowing in the pasture, and felt for the fence line. She crossed into the woods and remembered what Delmar said about turkeys, how you had to be in a blind before they climbed off their roosts, otherwise they'd hear you and wouldn't come.

She followed the draw deeper into the woods, going by memory, stepping carefully over twigs. There was no light in the wood, and she went by the crease of the hill, walking as if she balanced water on her head. In ten minutes she found the blind and climbed inside. It was cold when she stopped moving, the earth damp through her pants. She dug into her breast pocket and removed a wooden lure she'd found in the cigar box. It fit neatly in her hand, a square of wood with a walnut lever set on a spring. Delmar had showed it to her once. When he squeezed the lever it rubbed against the wood and sounded exactly like a turkey hen in season.

Emily waited. Above the trees, the sky was softening to blue. When she could see the outline of her hand, she grasped the box and squeezed the lever. The sound was high-pitched, plaintive, like a rusty hinge. She yanked it back and forth, and it whimpered and clucked, and she waited again, silent, unmoving, the butt of the gun against her right breast.

She listened for the smallest sound but heard none. The tree trunks were beginning to define themselves against the dawn. For fifteen minutes she tried the lure, but no tom responded. Her legs grew stiff, her eyelids heavy. The forest was fully visible now, the dawn a uniform gray. She could hear her rooster across the hollow. She tried again, then put down the gun, leaned against the blind and closed her eyes.

When she woke later the sun skirted in a pale sheet through the forest. An insect buzzed beside her ear. She rubbed her eyes and stretched and was about to leave when she heard something below moving through underbrush. She lifted the gun and rested the barrel on the edge of the blind. The sound

44

was coming toward her, something large moving up the slope, perhaps a deer or a fox, too loud for a turkey. The thrashing stopped and began again. It came through the brush and flame azalea, and she felt the metal of the trigger and aimed. Then a man appeared, someone she didn't recognize. He wore a tan felt hat and a brown leather jacket. He carried a theodolite on a tripod under his arm and held a compass in one hand. Emily crouched low in the blind. The man paused, set up his tripod, and took a reading. He studied his compass, then closed the legs of the tripod, unbuckled a hatchet from his belt, and hammered a nearby tree trunk. He moved slowly, deliberately. He put the hatchet away, scanned the slope, walked a few more feet and took another reading.

Meanwhile a second man lumbered into view. Emily swung the gun toward him. This one was dressed in white paint-spattered coveralls and a brim hat, and he lugged a metal paint bucket. He stopped at the hatcheted trees, wiped his forehead, took a brush, and slopped a large red X across the trunk. Emily realized then that they were the electric men, and she thought for a moment the one with the tripod was the tall man who'd come months earlier, the one who'd stared at her and ground his cigarette in the grass and who'd touched his cap in parting.

She followed him above the gun's iron sight now, but he was obscured by bushes. The second man was brushing untidy X's on more trees. No wonder there hadn't been turkeys that morning, she figured. She felt the trigger beneath her finger.

'Baam,' she said aloud, and the man turned.

She hadn't meant to say it so loudly. She held herself still as the man with the paint scanned the woods.

'Hey,' he shouted to his partner, 'you hear something?'

Emily remained silent. The man searched the slope warily, his brush drolling red paint on the ground. Finally he shrugged and stuck the brush in the bucket. Emily lowered the gun. When they were gone she crawled from the blind and headed back toward the house.

★　★　★

In the afternoon she walked the Lick Creek Road into town. The day was swept with leaves, the sun full out, November in the air. She could hear the echo of axes downhollow. She passed the turn for the Two Mile Road, with the wooden barricade across it and the Bureau of Mines sign that read 'Closed by

46

Order of the State.' She hadn't been back since the explosion, and she avoided the road or even going near it. But that afternoon with the men in the woods and the trees changing color, it bothered her less than usual. For the first time in months she felt oddly light-hearted.

At the Crossroads the glass of automobiles glinted sky. A woman raking leaves waved and returned to her lawn. A boy was dragging a possum by a rope. The hardpack in front of Laird's lay studded with cola caps, hundreds shimmering in the heat. Two men sat on chairs, whittling sticks of wood. They stopped talking as Emily clopped up the steps, and they nodded hello and she to them as she pushed through the screen door.

It smelled of apples inside, the store dark and dust shafted in the light from the high windows. Mrs. Laird was behind the counter, standing on a foot ladder, stacking bars of soap.

'Afternoon, ma'am,' Emily said, and Mrs. Laird turned and regarded her through her glasses, then turned back to the soap.

'Afternoon, Emee. You got something for me today?'

'No, ma'am,' she said.

Mrs. Laird fixed the final bar of soap and climbed off the ladder and looked at Emily over the rims of her glasses.

'I need a can of paint and some turpentine.'

'What kind of paint you want?' she asked.

'The red kind.'

'The red kind,' she mused.

Emily smiled, and Mrs. Laird shuffled from behind the counter to a shelf across the store and peered at the labels of cans.

'What you cooking back there?' Emily asked.

'Puttin' up applesauce.'

'Smells nice.'

Mrs. Laird took down a can and blew dust off the top and looked at the label and put it back on the shelf. 'Vesper,' she yelled into the back, 'where's the red paint at?'

A voice came from the back room, but neither Emily nor Mrs. Laird could make it out.

'Can't hear you!' Mrs. Laird shouted.

Again a muffled voice came from the back, and Mrs. Laird looked at Emily and shook her head.

'That man's so lazy his voice don't even rise from the chair.' She shook her head again and trudged toward the back room.

Emily picked an apple from a crate, rubbed it on her shirt, and took a bite. On the counter stood a glass jar of pickled eggs, the liquid rose colored in the light. A wheel of yellow cheese sat inside a wire cage and loaves of salt-rising bread lay stacked in paper sleeves. Emily moved to a pile of magazines and flipped through pages with photographs of people in sunglasses, women with bobbed hair, women smoking cigarettes. She glanced at a pile of newspapers and saw a headline about Sacco and Vanzetti and felt something stab the back of her throat. She knew the names because of Gianni, but she'd confused them once with opera composers, and when she'd asked what opera Sacco and Vanzetti had composed, he'd flushed red and stammered, 'No . . . no opera . . . they are a shoemaker and a fishmonger; they are *anarchisti.*' And then he said they were 'like saints.'

She sighed and walked away from the papers. Mrs. Laird came back cradling two cans of Hubert paint and a small flask of turpentine. She plunked the cans on the counter and wiped their tops with a rag.

'One's enough,' Emily said, and bit into her apple.

'You can't do much with just one, 'lest you gonna thin it with milk.'

'One's fine, ma'am.'

'What you painting, Emee?' she asked. 'Henhouse?'

'Nope.'

'Outhouse?'

Emily shook her head and rummaged through her pockets for change. 'What do I owe you?' she asked. 'With a brush.' She held up the half-eaten apple. 'And this, too.'

Mrs. Laird waved a hand. 'Forget the apple. Got too many as it is. Take all you like.' She fixed her glasses again and penciled figures on a piece of butcher paper and looked back over her glass frames.

'Comes to thirty-four cents,' she said.

Emily counted the coins into Mrs. Laird's palm. She pocketed the turpentine and took another apple from the crate and grabbed the can by its bail.

'You wantin' anything wrapped?'

'No, ma'am.' Emily shook her head. 'Kindly for the apple.' She walked to the door, where the afternoon sun shafted on the boards and a few crisp leaves scraped in a circle as if animated by their own accord. Mrs. Laird was holding the change in her hand, still waiting.

'Hey,' she yelled. 'You never done told me what you're painting.'

Emily turned in the door and looked at Mrs. Laird.

'A masterpiece.'

★　★　★

By late afternoon she was back in the woods, beside the blind, studying the paint on the trees, seeing where the right-of-way would cut up from the pasture. She wiped the paint and discovered it was still damp. When she scouted up the hill and found the last marked trees, she was sure the men had quit for the day and she set to work. She splashed a rag with turpentine, scrubbed off the paint, then took clumps of earth and rubbed at the remaining paint until it blended with the bark. She worked her way down to the pasture, meticulously unmarking each tree with the turpentine and rag and handfuls of moist soil. When she reached the pasture again, the sun was riding low on the ridgetop and she could smell woodsmoke from the house. High above, crows were cawing across an indigo sky.

She climbed back into the woods, this time painting a new set of trees, making X's just as she'd seen the men do, only following a different course now, one that struck away from the house. When she finished, dusk had accomplished itself and the last streaks of pink horsetailed over the hills. Her breath fogged in the chill. She trudged back to the house. A screech owl called from the wood.

The ponies followed her through the pasture.

Inside, the house was flushed with heat. Potatoes boiling, turnips. Floured pork bones crackling in a skillet.

'I was starting to get worried about you,' her mother said. 'I thought you'd done shot yourself in the foot.'

Emily shucked her jacket and her sweater. She was wet behind her neck and under her arms. She stripped to her under-shirt and undid the tie in her hair.

'Where you been?' Ada asked. She was still in her blue quilted robe, holding a carving fork in the air.

'I was fixing the line,' Emily said.

'What line?'

'The electric one.'

'You did what?'

Emily walked to the sink and splashed water on her face, her neck, and under her armpits. Then she took a towel and wiped herself and looked up.

'I moved it,' she said. 'It was too close to the house.'

Her mother was still holding the fork.

'Emee,' she said. 'I don't know what in the thunder you're talking about.'

'That's okay, Mama,' she said. She walked to her mother and pecked her on the cheek. 'You don't have to know.'

Ada sighed and turned back to the stove and speared a potato. 'I suppose you found no turkeys, then,' she said.

'Well, there were two,' Emily said, toweling the back of her neck. 'But they both got away.'

4

She expected the men the next day, but they didn't come. Neither did they come the following day, or the week after. When the ground froze and December arrived, she realized the electric men would be gone all winter, and she looked over the ridges, dusted now with snow, and felt as if she were in a maze, closed in, with walls all around and no exit.

During the slow winter afternoons she retreated to the smokehouse with its odor of meat and blood and the deer carcass hung half-frozen from an iron hook. She'd sink into a bale of straw and think of Gianni, remembering him on the road or at the fair or in his house. The light would be slanting through the holes in the boards, and she'd push down the collar of her sweater and lick the freckles on her shoulder and smell the skin after. The odor reminded her of Gianni, and she'd touch herself then, clamping her eyes tight and rocking her head roughly against the boards, waiting for the slow wetness to come, the shudder; and afterward she'd sit with the bores of light fading and her breath clouds of pink and her shoulder still exposed to the cold. She felt empty and drained, like a broken bottle, like the creek in August all dried up, and though she wanted to she couldn't even cry anymore, not for them — not even for herself.

By the following spring she expected to see the electric men again. Her marks were still on the trees, the X's a maroon color, like dried grape juice. She foraged daily for fiddleheads, mushrooms, sassafras roots, shoveling ramps out of the earth, the oniony bulbs white as babies' teeth. She took them by the sack-load to Laird's, for the money had almost run out. They were still waiting for the compensation from the mine.

One April morning she entered the kitchen with a pail of goat milk and plunked it on the stove. When the milk began to steam she moved the pail to the table, uncorked a bottle of cider vinegar, and dribbled some in. The milk broke into myriad pieces, a kaleidoscope of curds, and she stirred them gently with a wood spoon and heard her mother behind.

'What you doing?' she asked.

'Making cheese,' Emily said.

'From the goats?'

Emily nodded. She stretched a piece of gauze over the enamel basin and clamped it with clothes-pins. The sun was streaming through the kitchen panes, her mother standing in the doorway, still in her bathrobe.

'What's Laird want with goat's cheese?'

'I'm not selling it to Laird's,' Emily said. She poured the liquid into the basin. The milk steamed and bubbled, and she set the pail down, wiped her forehead, and faced her mother. 'I'm bringing it to the hotel.'

'The Roncevert?'

Emily nodded.

'Who says the Roncevert wants to fool with that?'

'That's what they eat there,' Emily explained.

'Goat cheese?'

'Mrs. Laird says they do, and Gianni said they eat it all over Europe. His mother used to make it all the time.'

'Sounds right queer to me,' Ada said. She shook her head and lowered herself into a chair and sat watching her daughter.

Emily was checking the curds now. She remembered the afternoons at Gianni's when his mother made the cheese, how the windows fogged and the balls of curds hung from the rafters, three or four at a time, like a galaxy of pale planets, each orb dripping into buckets set beneath, so they plinked at different pitches, and the whole house smelled powerfully of goats.

Emily unclipped the clothes-pins, shook the cloth, and twisted it into a ball. Then she squeezed it gently, and hot whey streamed into the basin. She knotted the ends of the cloth and set it on the table.

'How you plan on gettin' to the hotel?' her mother finally asked.

'Train,' Emily said. She explained how she'd catch an early train at Talcat and get to White Sulfur by noon, how she'd find another train back in the afternoon and have enough time to climb home before dark.

She'd tied the ball of curds to the handle of the spoon and balanced it over the basin. She was waiting for her mother to say something. A puddle of whey had oozed onto the table.

'Ain't you goin' to even ask my permission?' Ada said.

'I was working 'round to it,' Emily said.

A piece of firewood popped in the stove. Emily wiped her hands on her apron, appraised the cheese, and glanced at her mother.

'What do you think?' Emily asked.

'I think your daddy wouldn't never have let you.'

'Not that,' she said. 'The cheese.'

Ada waved a hand dismissively at the ball of curds. 'I reckon it needs salt.'

Emily untied the strings of her apron and

pulled it over her head. The light was pewter now in the kitchen panes and the sun glowed in her mother's hair. Emily sighed and dropped the apron on a chair.

'He don't have much say in it, does he now?' she said, and folded her arms across her chest.

Her mother didn't answer. She was looking out the window as if expecting someone. The sun went in, and the room fell flat, and Ada regarded her daughter and shrugged.

'Hell, Emee, you do whatever you want. There ain't no point in askin' because you will anyhow.'

Emily sat and touched her mother's wrist. 'It's all right, Mama,' she said.

'Can't even control my own daughter,' she whispered.

'It's okay, Mama,' Emily said. 'You don't have to. I'll be fine.'

★   ★   ★

The next morning she dressed by lamplight, the clothes laid out the night before. An apple green dress. A white knit sweater, a pair of russet oxfords with wooden heels. In the beveled-glass she knotted her hair in two pigtails, went to the kitchen, and gathered the sack of mushrooms, the cheese, the ramps, the fiddleheads. There was a dollar bill on the table beneath a bowl of yellow morels. Her mother had left them there in the night.

By the time Emily reached the Crossroads, the soda pop signs at Laird's were just legible and the glass gas pumps glowed in the first light. She struck a path through a yard of old bleach bottles, rusted thunder pots, washtubs orange with oxidation. A rooster was crowing, another answering faintly in the hollow below. She climbed for an hour over Talcat Mountain, descended the other side, and in another fifty minutes she was out of the woods, across from the Talcat station. She wiped sweat from under her arms, fixed her dress, and clomped up the station house steps.

The place was empty inside, the ticket window abandoned, the glass in front of the schedule so filthy she couldn't read the times. She stepped to the iron grille and called if anyone was there, but no one answered. The sun angled through an upper window. Pigeons cooed somewhere. She waited and called again.

Finally a sound came from behind a door and a small man stepped through. He was struggling with a suspender strap, trying to untwist it, his cap askew. He fixed the strap, excused himself, and asked what he could do for her.

'When's the train to White Sulfur?' Emily asked.

'Nine-fifteen,' he said. 'It's the only morning train. Not much traffic since the mine closed. Coal cars only once a week now. The rest don't stop, just roll through. Nine-fifteen.' His right eye twitched. His hair was copper, his eyes eggshell blue. He studied her baskets, her face, then her baskets again. He was a full head shorter than she.

'I'd like one, please,' Emily said.

'One what?'

'Ticket.'

'Where you headed?'

'White Sulfur, sir.'

He was still staring at her, and then he nodded vigorously, unrolled a ticket from an iron spool, tore it off, hammered it twice, wrote in the date and time, and pushed the ticket across the counter.

'How much I owe?' she asked.

The man stuck a pinkie in his ear, rotated it, checked it for wax, and looked up at her. 'Excuse me?'

'How much I owe?' She rolled her eyes. 'For the ticket.'

'Fifteen cents.'

She placed a half-dollar on the marble

counter, and he opened a wooden drawer and dug change from the worn caverns. When she went to take the coins, he grabbed her finger and squeezed it. She pulled away, and he laughed in a high cackle and apologized. His eye twitched uncontrollably. He pushed the ticket across the marble, and she stuffed it in her basket.

'Waiting room's right here, miss,' he said.

'I'd rather wait in hell,' she said, and headed toward the door.

'What you got in those baskets, miss?' he asked.

Emily didn't answer.

'Hey, miss,' he shouted, 'what you got in those baskets?'

'Something like you,' she said, and opened the screen door and let it drop behind. She stared through the screening into the room and shouted: 'Fungus.'

★   ★   ★

The train was nearly empty, the seats oxblood, the leather cracked. She watched the empty fields out the window, the earth untilled, last year's corn still stubbled in the mud. Coal tipples dotted the hillside every few acres, and the river swung in and out of view like a shred of cellophane. They entered

61

a tunnel and the carriage fell dark, then thundered out again into sunshine. Emily leaned against the window and drifted asleep and woke again. She remembered years past, how she and her father and Delmar walked their cattle to White Sulfur each autumn, usually in October, driving the steers under the changing trees to the auction yard. She and Delmar took turns coursing the cattle, and the days were always cold and bright and dust covered them by noon as if they'd all been coated with cinnamon.

The last time she'd been to White Sulfur two years before, she'd taken the train with Delmar and Gianni to the state fair. Alone, she and Gianni walked hand in hand, emboldened by the crowds of strangers and no one seeming to notice them or care. In the late afternoon, before they met Delmar back at the station, they slipped under the bleachers and leaned against a stanchion where they could hear the crowds above, a voice over an electric bullhorn, and the stamping of feet on the boards. Gianni drew his mouth to hers, and they stayed there for a long time, his hand inside her camisole, then down her dress, and his smell of grass and sweat, in the dimness, against the lacing of bleachers, with the peanut shells and crushed popcorn and faint odor of urine, until he stopped and took his hand out, and squeezed her elbow, pointing to the people nearby. She became aware of them as if emerging from sleep, but she didn't want him to stop. She closed her mouth and fixed her underwear. She wanted to stay there. She could still feel where he'd touched her, something undone there, an itch; and when he put his finger to her nose and said, 'Smell,' the feeling started again. They left arm in arm, squinting into the fullness of the sun. They reached the station house and the train, and Delmar dropped into a seat. And for the next hour on the ride back, as the day was darkening outside and the telegraph posts pivoted past, she felt Gianni there, across the aisle, though she didn't dare look. Delmar had his chin in his hand. Every once in a while she glanced at the glass and saw Gianni's reflection, and she'd grin and he'd raise an eyebrow or hold his finger to his nose and smile, but never directly, and always when Delmar was turned the other way.

She woke in Elderson with the sun hot on her face. A few passengers had climbed on and were finding seats: two twins in matching pink pinafores and their overweight mother, an elderly man with a wooden ear horn. Emily moved into the shade of the nearby seat and dozed again. She dreamed of hillsides in June. Clover on the grass. Gianni kissing Delmar, taking down his pants. The two naked, the hairs under their arms like ink, Gianni's black, Delmar's honeyed. She woke with sweat above her lip, the train trundling slow, her dress sticking to the seat. They were coming into White Sulfur.

In another minute iron arches slid by and the train screeched to a halt. Liveried porters stood on the platform. Emily waited for the others to exit, then crossed the street to the hotel. A brick guard booth stood at the entrance. As she neared it a man rose from his chair and raised his hat.

'Afternoon,' he said. He wore an olive uniform with brass buttons and a leather holster with a pistol strapped inside. He was looking at Emily's shoes.

'Are you a guest, miss?'

Emily shook her head.

'Visiting?'

She held up the basket and the sack. 'I've got these to deliver.'

He looked at her sideways. 'To the kitchen?'

She nodded.

'Well, you're going the wrong way,' he explained. 'You got to use the service entrance.' He pointed up the road. 'Go about a quarter mile, the service entrance is on your right. Walk down beside some cabins and you'll see a path. Leads straight to the back of the kitchen.' He put his arm down. 'Is anyone expecting you?'

'Yes, sir, they will be, soon as I get there.'

He nodded, then looked at her once again. 'You sure?'

'Yes, sir,' she said, and thanked him, and headed up the road.

An old black man sat on a stool beside the service entrance, a cantilevered pole across the road. He nodded to Emily and she to him, and she passed small cabins, a laundry room, white sheets scrimmed under pines. She came at last to a double screened door with an exhaust fan humming above it, and she knocked on the wooden frame. A jaybird mewled in a tree. The sun lay on the screen. She knocked again, and this time a gaunt woman in a clean white uniform opened the door. The woman's cheeks looked sunken, as if they'd been popped by a pin. Emily held up her things and explained why she was there, and the woman nodded her inside.

They walked along a row of zinc tables. There was an odor of ammonia in the room. The woman motioned Emily to a table and uncovered her baskets and examined the mushrooms and cheese, the fiddleheads, the ramps. When she was done she wiped her hands on her apron and glanced at Emily for the first time.

'Wait here,' she said, and disappeared through a swing door.

Emily took in the room, the yellow-tiled walls, the vaulted ceiling, the row of brick ovens. There were shelves of china, soup bowls, ramekins, pots hung on racks, brushed-steel stoves. The woman returned, this time with a bearded man. She pointed at Emily across the room, but the bearded man hardly looked up. He was inspecting the fiddleheads and ramps. He picked up a morel, turned it, smelled it, put it back down. Then he unwrapped the cheese, pinched a piece between two fingers, and tasted it. He said a word to the woman and walked away.

When she came back she handed Emily the cheese and the baskets.

'He'll take the morels,' she said.

'Not the ramps?'

The woman made a face. 'He doesn't want hillbilly food.'

'I can get more muggins,' Emily said.

'He might like that.'

'And the cheese?'

The woman shook her head. 'Too lumpy,' she said.

'If I make it smoother, he'll want it?'

'No telling,' the woman said. 'Wait here, I need to pay you.'

She turned and came back with a black pouch and fished out a pad and wrote some figures, ripped off a receipt, and handed it to Emily along with a dollar bill.

'How about berries?' Emily asked.

'Excuse me?'

'Strawberries, huckleberries, raspberries. He need any of them?'

'If they're fresh and there's enough, he'll probably take them.'

Emily nodded. She folded the bill in half and in half again and slipped it in her dress pocket.

'Thank you, ma'am.' She nodded. 'I'll try the goat cheese smoother next time.'

'You do that,' the woman said, and headed back through the kitchen.

★ ★ ★

Emily went up the graveled path. It was nearly noon, and she had some time before her train. She wandered behind the hotel, past a stables and a croquet lawn where two women were leaning on mallets, laughing to each other. She came to the edge of a golf course; the grass was bright green and the mountains chalky blue behind. A lone golfer positioned his ball on a tee, and she watched as he swung and the ball took flight like a bird. She remembered what Gianni had said when they passed the hotel on the train, that after the revolution there'd be no golf courses, that the land would be given to the poor.

She came to an enclosed garden and stepped under a trellis. An indigo bunting was singing in a tree. There were boxwoods inside and rose bushes, a fountain, violets and Johnny-jump-ups overflowing marble urns. A statue of a girl stood in the fountain's center. She was cast in copper, naked above her hips, so her nipples pointed upward, and it seemed both fascinating and indecent to Emily. She walked to the marble rim and stared at the statue. There was no one in sight. She dunked a hand in the water and splashed her arms. The water smelled of sulfur. She leaned back and closed her eyes and let mist fall on her legs. When she opened her lids seconds later, a man was walking beside the rose bushes.

She pushed herself up and rubbed her eyes. The man looked somewhat familiar, though she couldn't place him. He was smoking a cigarette and wore khaki trousers. There was something big and clumsy about him, as if he didn't know what to do with his arms. He placed one leg on the rim of the fountain and rested an elbow awkwardly on his knee. He was gazing at the statue as if it were a sculpture in a museum somewhere. Emily glanced at it, too.

'Is she supposed to be someone?' Emily eventually asked.

The man looked over.

'Yes,' he said. He raised his cigarette and blew smoke. 'She's Hebe,' he said.

'Who?'

'Hebe. Goddess of youth. She's Greek.'

'Oh,' Emily said. She looked at the statue again. The legs had a patina like an old penny. She didn't look Greek to Emily.

'They say,' the man continued, 'that if you drink enough of the water here, you'll be like her, eternally young.'

'Who'd want that?' Emily said.

The man laughed and looked at her. 'You wouldn't?'

'No, sir, I aim on getting old.' She hung her head sideways and looked at the statue. 'And besides,' she said, 'who'd want to be a statue?'

The man smiled. His hair was sandy and thinning. He tilted back his hat. He had perfect teeth, she saw, like the keys of a piano. He stepped closer to Emily and stared at her a moment as if trying to figure something.

'Do you remember me?' he finally asked.

He was blocking the sun now, so his face

was in shadow, and Emily squinted up at him.

'Am I supposed to?'

He dropped his cigarette on the slate and ground it with the tip of his boot. He was grinning. His boots looked foreign. They were light brown, calfskin with pointy toes. And then she remembered that day in the hollow when the men from the power company came, and the lean one who'd stayed beside the truck, smoking, not talking, how he'd dropped his cigarette the same way and ground it with his boot and stared at her as she went to get Garvin.

'The electric company,' Emily said.

The man nodded. The corners of his eyes wrinkled with mirth.

'You went for your uncle.' He chuckled. 'He gave us quite a show. Are you visiting the hotel?' he asked.

'A friend,' Emily said. She held a hand up to her eyes. 'And you. Are you staying here?'

'The company keeps a field office here,' the man explained. 'While the line's being built.'

He put a foot on the rim of the fountain, laced his fingers together, and cracked his knuckles. The wind rose in the alders. A couple entered the garden, clutching tennis rackets. Emily watched as they walked through and exited the other side.

'So when they going to start building that electric line?' she asked.

He said they'd already begun, that two clearing crews were working east from Ohio and two others west from Virginia. He lowered himself on the marble rim and ran a hand through his hair. He stared at her again as if trying to remember something.

'Lick Creek, right?' he said, pointing with his hat. 'That's where you live, isn't it?'

She didn't answer; she didn't like that he knew where she lived.

'Tower 242,' he said almost to himself, and explained that the tower they were going to build there would be a transposition tower, that the clearing of the right-of-way would begin any day now. He was twirling his hat in his hands, then he placed it on his head.

'I'm sorry,' he said. 'My name's Robert. Robert Daniels.'

He held out a pink hand, and she pretended not to notice.

'You're not from around here,' she said.

'It's that obvious?'

She said it was. He told her he was from Philadelphia, that he was the assistant supervisor for the line construction.

'But you didn't tell me your name yet,' he said.

'No,' she said, and glanced at the

boxwoods, the violets, the Johnny-jump-ups. A mist was blowing from the fountain. Her spine felt tingly.

'Violet,' she said.

'Violet,' he repeated. 'That's a pretty name.'

The sun popped from behind a cloud and bathed them in orange light. She could see his eyes were green, jade in the sun, his jaw large like a horse's. When he didn't try so hard, she thought, he was handsome.

He pulled a cigarette pack from his pocket and lit one and thumbed his lighter shut.

'What's a transposition tower?' Emily finally asked.

'You really want to know?'

'If it's going to be near my house, I think I ought to.'

He pulled on his cigarette and explained it was where the three conductors on the line changed positions to keep equal tension and not interfere with radio transmissions.

'I see,' Emily said. 'But it's just a regular tower otherwise?'

'You wouldn't know the difference at all. Only the insulators are hung a little funny.'

She looked up at the sun. She could see some birds, high above and very small, like particles in a glass. It made her think of her mother, and she felt suddenly anxious about the train and the ride home. She picked up her basket and stood.

'I should be going,' she said.

He glanced at his wristwatch and said he ought to be going as well.

'So,' he asked, 'your friend stays here?'

'Friend?'

'The one you're visiting.'

'Yes,' Emily said. 'She works in the kitchen.'

He asked if she came to the hotel often, and she made a vague gesture with her hand like a bird fluttering upward. Then she turned to go.

'Hold on, Violet,' he said.

He took his wallet from his back pocket. The fountain was making a mist. He handed her a piece of cardboard between two fingers.

'It's my card,' he said. 'If there's any questions or trouble with the line or the crews, you let me know. I'm here most of the time. Suite 312. Just ask for Daniels.'

'Daniels?'

'That's what they call me.'

She took the card and stuffed it perfunctorily in her dress. He flicked his cigarette into the bushes and looked at her.

'You know, I think you were right about Hebe after all,' he said. 'You don't need to be like her at all. You're prettier the way you are.'

73

He winked at her and smiled, and she felt herself blush. She pulled a face and turned.

'Good-bye,' she said, and headed toward the trellis. The pebbles crunched under her shoes. She didn't look back, for she knew he'd be watching, just as he had that day in the hollow. She could feel his eyes behind her like tacks. But it wasn't altogether unpleasant. At least, she thought, someone was watching.

5

The next two days it rained in Lick Creek.
The windows streamed, spouts gushed, the
salt turned to rock in its shaker. When the sky
cracked open again and the sun poured
through, Emily pulled on boots and waded
into the pasture. It was May. Everything
seemed lacquered in the new light. The tin
roofs, the waxed trees, the green bottles
washed up along the creek banks. Mushrooms had erupted under the apple trees, in
the sand beside the creek. Everywhere she
looked, she found the spongy heads poking
out of soil. They called them muggins at
Laird's and morels at the hotel, the yellow
kind, *Morchella esculenta*. Delmar used to
call them cocks. She sliced them at the base
with a kitchen knife and collected them in a
sack.

In the afternoon she was back hunting
mushrooms when she heard a muffled sound
coming from Keeny's Knob. Sheila was
sniffing air, agitated, looking off into the
forest. Emily heard the sound again uphollow,
a kind of rasping, like a breath. She hiked
twenty minutes to the ridgeline, descended

the next hollow, and heard the rasping again, louder now. Her socks were drenched in her boots. On the next rise she shaded her eyes and saw a new trail cut down the side of the mountain as if a razor had been run down the hill. Trees lay here and there in great piles, and some oxen grazed high up among the tree stumps. Farther down she saw men working in the clearing, some shouldering cant hooks, others hunched over crosscut saws.

She squatted and observed them through the trees. She counted six in all. Their saws flashed in the lowering sun, and occasionally their voices echoed into the forest with an accent she couldn't identify. She stayed for a long time, watching, as her feet grew cold in her boots and the light thinned overhead. Thrushes began to flute in the wood. Then all at once, at some sign she wasn't aware of, the sawing stopped and the forest fell silent. The men loaded their oxen, led them by tether, and vanished up the clearing into dusk.

★ ★ ★

The next day she brought her mushrooms to the hotel and looked afterward for Daniels. His card was still folded in her dress pocket, but she didn't need it. He was at the fountain

76

again, in the garden, reading a book.

'They started cutting up the woods for your electric,' Emily said.

He closed the cover of his book and removed his sunglasses.

'I didn't know the path would be so wide,' she said.

He stuck the earpiece of his glasses between his lips. He seemed pleased to see her.

'The right-of-way,' he finally said.

Emily screwed up her face. 'What?'

'That's what they call the path.'

'Whatever it's called,' Emily said. 'I didn't know it'd be so wide.'

'Please,' he said. He gestured for her to sit, but she didn't. The day was windy, and she was wearing a thin cotton sweater, holding a piece of hair out of her eyes. He took the earpiece from his mouth and said the right-of-way had to be so wide because 130 kilovolts of electricity were going to run in the line above it and they needed the extra clearance on each side.

She asked how much electricity was 130 kilovolts, and he bit his lower lip.

'A streetcar runs on six hundred volts,' he explained. 'So the current will be like two hundred streetcars.'

'Two hundred streetcars.'

'Yes.' He nodded. 'All moving through the wires every second of the day.'

'And the night, too,' she said.

'Yes, the night, too.'

'That's a lot of noise,' she said.

'No, it won't actually — '

'I'm joking,' Emily said.

He laughed and leaned back on the bench. He was wearing a mustard-colored cardigan, a crisp cotton shirt, a lizard belt. The wind gusted again, and water misted from the fountain.

'What if someone decides to climb a tower and touch the wires?' she asked.

He let out a puff of air, a kind of laugh. 'They'd probably die,' he said.

'It sounds dangerous, that line of yours.'

'No.' He shook his head. 'It's perfectly safe.'

'But it can kill someone.'

He explained that the towers were difficult to climb, the conductors impossible to get to, that there were hundreds of similar lines all over the country. He began to talk about the various types of high-tension power lines, and she felt suddenly weary, as if a hundred streetcars were already clanging in her head. The wind rustled the alders; the flagstones were getting wet. She lowered herself to the bench and tried to pay attention. Yet there was something narcotic about his voice; she felt she could curl up on the bench and fall asleep. He talked about the different work crews, spanning three separate states, and how he was the assistant to the man supervising it all, in charge of accounts and payrolls and deadlines. The line, he said, would tap into the richest coal fields of West Virginia and bring lights to towns along the eastern seaboard and power to factories; he said that no other high-voltage line had been built through such hilly country, and that it was quite an engineering feat. To Emily it sounded as if he were practicing a speech, and she watched the smooth muscles of his jaw move back and forth, his legs stretched in front of him. He was wearing red argyle socks.

When he stopped talking he shook a cigarette from a pack and offered her one, but she shook her head. The wind had died, the sun was warm; it seemed a fan had been switched off. He pulled his sweater over his head, and she smelled something sweet and intoxicating, like oranges. His aftershave, she thought, or a deodorant, a familiar odor she couldn't identify. It entered her like a blade, so quickly that she could hardly catch her breath. He was talking again. She closed her eyes and realized it was the smell of Saturday afternoons, the way her father came home every other week from the barber. That was the odor. He smelled just like a haircut.

'Violet,' she finally heard, 'are you all right?'

He was on the edge of the bench, his face close. She'd almost forgotten her name.

'Yes.' She nodded. 'I'm fine.'

He sat back again and blew smoke. The fountain trickled. They could hear golfers knocking balls down the fairway. She stood and smoothed the fabric of her dress.

'I think it's time for my train,' she said.

He glanced at his wristwatch. 'Yup,' he said. 'Lunch hour's over.'

He gathered his book and his cardigan and stood. She'd forgotten again how tall he was. He seemed a plank of wood beside her, but the odor was still there, thin and velvety, like a scarf. They walked out of the garden and up the path. The big elms trembled. The sun fell on the lawn. Some pearl clouds inched high overhead.

'So when they going to finish cutting that right-of-way?' she asked.

'A few months,' he said. 'They're fast workers. Canadians. A first-rate crew. Before you know it, they'll be done.'

They walked past the stables, the croquet lawn, the white cottages. Emily rebraided one of her pigtails. They reached the service road and he stopped and drew something out of his pocket.

'Here,' he said. 'A gift.' He held in his palm a green cardboard box the size of a deck of cards, the letters *RH* embossed on its cover. 'Go on,' he said, and pressed it into her hand.

She opened it tentatively. There was no one on the path. A piece of waxed paper lay on top. Beneath were small candies, pastel colored, each the size of a jelly bean.

'Mints,' he said.

'Mints,' she repeated.

'They're from the hotel. I thought maybe . . . '

He stood a moment, grinning foolishly. She could smell his aftershave — or was it a deodorant — she couldn't tell. The mints looked like wren eggs. She thanked him, and he cracked his knuckles as if in response.

'Really, you shouldn't worry about the line. It'll be perfectly safe.'

'You'd be surprised at the things that can happen,' she said.

'Nothing will happen. I promise.'

'Good,' she said. 'I'll hold you to it.'

'All right.' He held out a hand. She didn't want to take it. His palm was damp, like cookie dough. He slid his sunglasses up the bridge of his nose.

'I'll see you next week, then?' he asked.

She didn't answer. She was already heading toward the service entrance, and she turned only once, to wave.

★ ★ ★

From that day on, she traveled to the Roncevert once a week. She'd arrive in the late mornings at the service entrance beside the white cabins and the pines. She'd wait at the kitchen for the double screen doors to open, the gaunt woman to let her in. Afterward she'd end up in the grove of boxwoods with the alder trees and the fountain trickling, the statue of Hebe and the patch of violets. And each time, as if they had an agreement or someone had told him beforehand, Daniels would be there, with his felt hat and khaki pants, his large shoes and lantern jaw. And each time he smelled the same, as if he carried a bottle of barber's tonic. He smelled, always, like a haircut.

She didn't travel to the hotel to see him, or to sell her things. She went instead to get away from home, away from the hollow, from Garvin, who never came around, from her mother's moping and sleeping, from Delmar's empty room with the blinds pulled down and the drawers still full and the dust thick as cotton on the dressers, because no one cleaned them. The second anniversary of the explosion came, and her mother stayed in her room, slept half the day, dragged her feet around with such lethargy that Emily said she'd need a new pair of slippers each week if she kept it up. Few of the neighbors came to visit anymore, asking Ada to dream their lost things the way she once could. For her mother had lost that talent, and when Ruth Loudermilk or the McClung sisters came, Ada would shake her head and barely invite them in. What was the use of finding things in dreams, she'd say, if she couldn't tell a mine was about to blow when fully awake?

The more her mother mooned about the house, the more she stayed in bed, the more industrious Emily became in response. She scoured the woods for mushrooms. She tried to perfect the goat cheese. She picked berries and made jam, anything to keep her away from the house. One day a week, as a bulwark against the other six, she'd ride to the hotel in the half-empty train, with the light bulbs jingling in their glass globes and the cigarette butts strewn on the floor, the dust balls, like cotton candy, almost incandescent under the seats. She'd close her eyes and feel the springs beneath the carriage and imagine she was being spirited away to some foreign city, that she was in Europe or England, New York or New Orleans. Anyplace with the word *New* next to it would suffice.

An hour later she'd arrive at the Roncevert with its white walls and Corinthian columns, its marble terraces and men in plus-fours and Harris tweed, and she'd almost convince herself she *was* in a different country. She'd find Robert Daniels beside the fountain or sometimes waiting behind the hotel, near the croquet lawn. He'd be finishing his lunch. Sometimes with papers in his lap, pamphlets from the National Electric Lighting Association, charts on the progress of the line, books about Henry Ford or positivist thinking, and one in particular, which he always carried, called *Some Features of Cost Keeping and Accountancy in Line Construction*. He'd rarely ask her questions. Once, though, he asked her about books she liked, and she told him Jack London and Robert Louis Stevenson and a book about insects written by a Frenchman whose name she'd forgotten. But her favorite, she said, was the *Encyclopedia Britannica*, because each month it used to come in the mail, one volume at a time. And yet it had stopped coming a few years earlier, so her set was incomplete.

'Where did it stop?' he asked.

'At the letter *R*,' she said. 'After 'Riparian.''

He didn't ask her why they stopped. He only said the eleventh edition was a masterpiece and left it at that. But it didn't matter to her. The less he knew of her life, the better. On the rare occasion he did inquire, she made up stories: Her father had died in a train crash. Her brother was a lieutenant in the army. An uncle was a famous stage actor who lived in London. He never pressed her for details. At first she wanted to tell him her real name, but soon it became too late to explain, and after a while she began to like the name Violet. It was like a funny hat, something with a feather or a tulle fan. When he called her Violet she felt a small thrill, as if she'd caught herself in a window wearing a chiffon dress, something she wouldn't have dreamed of. She began to like the way it looked.

Some days he talked about the line as if it were alive. He'd show her charts, diagrams with squiggles of colored pencil, pale pinks and milky blues, each growing on the side of the page, showing how much of the right-of-way had been cleared, how many tower foundations poured. He'd talk about deadlines and budgets. He'd talk about operating costs. And at these times the ironed creases of his khakis shivered, and he grew animated, flipping the brim of his hat back and forth, his wristwatch glittering. She'd sit half listening, breathing his clean, orangy odor. For even though she didn't really like the man, she loved the way he smelled, and afterward, on the train, she found herself sniffing the sleeve of her dress or a magazine he'd given her. She knew it had nothing to do with him, and when she thought about Robert Daniels the man a small weight, like a pharmacist's dram, would drop in her chest, and she'd think of Gianni again, the first day she went with her father to buy the kid, the white goat against his brown chest. And she realized then how Gianni would have hated Daniels, would've hated his charts and books, his pink hands and calfskin boots and argyle socks. Delmar would have hated him, too. That much they would have agreed on, if nothing else. In some way it made it easier for her to spend time with Daniels, in spite of them. It made her even like him, just a little.

★　★　★

Strawberry season arrived, then raspberry season, and she brought the berries to the hotel in wooden baskets, the splints stained crimson from their juice. The worst part of the season was over for Ada, and she emerged again from her room and began to work on what she called a commemorative quilt, a quilt that would memorialize the lives of her husband and son. The quilt had grown over the early summer so that it spread now across half the porch, the fabric tumbling across her knees, trailing in waves at her feet. She'd used up all of her husband's and Delmar's old and torn clothes and was now working her way through their newer shirts and trousers. She didn't cut the clothes into patches or make panels of them. Instead she incorporated the whole article into the quilt, sewing in an entire pair of boxer shorts or a singlet, a pair of trousers, or a whole drawer full of socks. In this way the quilt grew quickly, the clothes floating in a sea of fabric. Headless and footless, the disembodied clothes seemed oddly disturbing to Emily, but she said nothing. At least her mother was out of bed, engaged in some occupation. The quilt would continue to grow, Ada said, until she'd used up all their clothes and there was not a sock left to sew, and by then she'd have stitched her grief into a fabric to cover herself with it at night. So she quilted in her husband's Sunday suit against a field of white, appliquéd Delmar's overalls nearby, stitched in two wool mittens, waving ghostly against some old blue ticking. One afternoon the McClung sisters and Ruth Loudermilk hiked up the hollow to see Ada's handiwork, and they all fussed over the quilt. But afterward, on the road, as soon as they were out of earshot, they looked at each other in horror and shook their heads and said, Poor Ada Jenkins, she wasn't quite right in her mind anymore.

'Just like the daughter,' one of the McClungs mused.

'I believe,' Ruth Loudermilk added, 'that Ada's found a whole new meaning for the words *crazy quilt*.'

⋆ ⋆ ⋆

All that summer Emily woke to the sound of saws and axes, trees crashing, the voices of men uphollow. The clearing crew had come closer to the house, and by July they swung a half mile away, so she could see the cut coming off the mountain, down to the creek where the line would cross. Emily hiked out midmornings to meet Garvin, and they watched the woodcutters warily from the sides, making sure they didn't cut beyond the boundaries of the right-of-way. The men all sported beards, wore hobnailed boots, their hair sprinkled with sawdust. They spoke in a thick Quebecois accent that was hard to understand. Garvin sold them moonshine, pickle jars filled with the clear liquid: 120

proof. The meanest, they said, in Falls County. But aside from that, the men kept to themselves and slept in tents up in the woods, with their oxen and a pack of half-bred huskies. Emily stayed away, for the clearing crew had followed her diverted line, a strange dogleg near the house where she'd painted the trees. Yet for now, no one knew it. Not even Garvin.

One morning at the end of August she woke to the clock tapping quietly in the hall and the sound of sparrows outside, and she realized with sadness that the men were gone. It was high summer then, the grass parched, the creek low. The daylight seemed freighted with a terrible silence. Even though they'd been tearing up the woods, even though she had little contact with them, the presence of the clearing crews had been strangely soothing. She'd gotten used to the sound of their saws, the way one got used to rain or a voice in another room, or a radio left on, as if life existed elsewhere and there were possibilities, and she was not alone. The way the world seemed full in spring when the creek was loud like a constant applause, for that too was a way of hoping, a possibility. A movement. Yet that day, with no sound at all, the world seemed to shrivel. No wonder they called it a hollow, she thought. It was empty, like her life. If you shouted into it, your voice echoed back, like a dried-up well, and all that was left was the wishing.

That evening at twilight she climbed uphollow behind Garvin's, where the family graves buckled out of the earth. She stepped through the iron gate and sat among the stones. They were all tilted like teeth, the limestone filling in, losing names, dates, sentiments. She trailed a finger along their edges. The coarse sand a kind of Braille, her grandmother's unpolished, like the stories she told. Stories of her great-grandparents, how they'd come to Lick Creek the end of one August, up from the valleys of Virginia, from the docks at Norfolk before that, moving west the entire time, through the tidewater, over the Blue Ridge, up into the hills, into the hollow where the homeplace now stood. There was the story of the silver, still kept in the attic, which had been handed down so long that no one could remember exactly where it came from or on what boat it was brought, only that it had been carried inside a linen cloth on the back of a horse and used as barter for passage across the New River. There were only five teaspoons left in a set of six, and that was the evidence of their tenure there, the missing teaspoon. There were other stories, too, all of which seemed silly now to

Emily, like cheap fables or children's stories, all meant to keep them in their place, up in that hollow.

She felt the stones under her finger, flakes of dried lichen. Pale disks. The chisel strikes still spalled on the newer stone. Here Delmar. Here her father. The wind flew hot in the trees. A sickle moon was climbing into the evening. A single blade. A scimitar. *Lick Creek, Greenbrier, New River, Kanawha*, she whispered, and fished in her pocket for the card she knew was there. In the twilight she could make out the letters, the pebbled ink, the cardboard worn from where she'd worried it. 'Robert Daniels,' it read. Underneath was a streak of lightning and the words *Appalachian Light and Power*.

★ ★ ★

The next time she saw him, he handed her a package wrapped in butcher paper.

'Please,' he said, 'open it.'

The package was tied in a bow with blue string. She tore off the paper and exposed the encyclopedia. It was bound in emerald leather with gold-leaf lettering. She turned it on its spine and read 'S through T.' She didn't know what to say. It had been so long since anyone had given her a real gift. She laid the

91

book in her lap, and fingered the leather. And all that time, she thought, he *had* listened. The leather was stiff, virginal; when she opened the cover she could feel it crack. She opened to the random entry 'Siderolite' and read 'A meteorite consisting of iron phosphate.' She smelled the pages. The ink was new; the paper smelled of yeast.

Then he asked if she'd come to a hotel picnic the following week. He said they had one each year to coincide with the fair, that he was invited and wanted to bring an escort, a date.

She didn't really want to go. She'd have to wear some dress. But it didn't matter. He was cracking his knuckles, a cigarette clamped in his teeth. She stroked the book as if it were a lap-dog or a kid goat; she wasn't even conscious of it. Then she said she would go. The following week. A date. Why not. And she opened the book to where her finger still lay and looked at the next entry. 'Siderophile,' it read. 'Having an affinity for iron.'

6

The train was crowded the following Saturday with families, men in bleached boaters, women with paper fans. Boys and girls chased each other up the aisles. Vendors hawked peanuts and clinked together bottles of Nehi and Crush. Emily took her seat beside a window. It was the weekend of the state fair in White Sulfur, the one she'd been to with Gianni over two years ago. The day was hot, and she wore a powder blue cotton dress with white piping, a sunhat, and her hair pulled back in a simple plait. She'd borrowed a pair of heels from her mother, and she regretted it now, as they were too tight and pinched her toes. Her camisole strap kept slipping off her shoulder.

In White Sulfur the crowds got off and moved toward waiting horse carts to carry them to the fair. Emily searched the crowds for Daniels until he finally appeared.

'I couldn't find you,' he said. 'There were so many people.'

He was out of breath, his forehead glazed with perspiration. He held a derby in hand.

'They're going to the fairground,' Emily explained.

He looked off disinterestedly at the horse carts, then took her elbow and they crossed the street. Model T's lined the road, the windshields sparkling, the canvas roofs rolled down. Daniels wore a cream-colored linen suit and spats the color of beeswax. He seemed more fidgety than usual, mopping his forehead with a handkerchief and stealing glances at Emily's dress. There were people all over the grounds dressed in light pastels. Waiters carried trays across a lawn. A large white tent had been staked on the grass, and people were mingling beneath it. Daniels led the way toward the main lawn, nodding at people as they passed. Electric lights hung in the trees. A brass band tuned on a marble terrace, the players in Prussian blue suits with gold epaulets, their instruments glinting in the sun. Daniels squeezed her elbow.

'Could you wait here just a moment?' he asked. 'I must say hello to someone.'

Before she could answer, he strode across the lawn and she was left on the path, alone, in a pool of sunlight, shading her eyes, her shoes pinching, her dress sticking to the back of her neck. Some women in long crepe dresses were staring at her. They carried small beaded purses and wore fashionable hats. She had the urge to stick her tongue out, but wandered toward the shade instead and sat on a park bench. A catbird creaked in a shrub. She looked but couldn't find it. The women had turned away and were laughing at some joke. She remembered what Gianni had said about the hotel, that it was the perfect place for a bomb. At the time she'd thought he was joking, yet now she realized he wasn't. She scanned the crowd for Daniels and spotted him chatting with two men. They were looking over at Emily and one slapped Daniels on the back. She felt her armpits moisten. She had the sudden impulse to flee.

'Lemonade, ma'am?' a waiter asked. He was holding a tray of perspiring glasses filled with pink lemonade. Her throat was parched, but she didn't know how it worked, if she had to pay or not, so she drew her hand away.

'No thanks,' she said, and forced a smile.

'Yes, ma'am,' the waiter said, and the glasses clinked away.

'Sorry,' Daniels said when he returned. 'Business.'

He rolled his eyes, and his hand brushed against her wrist. They walked out onto the hot lawn, away from the bench, away from the women with hats. The grass was soft underfoot. People lounged under oaks or sat on folding chairs; some lay on blankets, and a few elderly women held parasols above their heads. In one corner people were knocking a badminton birdie back and forth, the men in tan knickers, the women in sailor shirts. Someone screamed, 'Telemachus!' and tore across the lawn.

They walked past tables set with silver trays, a barbecue pit where a suckling pig circled on a spit. They reached the garden, the familiar path, the arched trellis, but it was crowded inside, the benches filled, the whole place unfamiliar. Some boys in cardigans were strumming ukeleles. The place was unearthly hot, the sweat stinging her eyes. She felt her dress damp beneath her armpits, and she wanted to get away from the crowds.

'I'm dying of thirst,' she said.

'I know a place inside we can go.'

'Good,' she said, and slipped an arm in his. He looked down, surprised at her hand, and smiled. They climbed a cindered path. Stable boys ran this way and that, carrying saddles, leading horses, shoveling manure off the cinders. The sound of the band echoed across the lawn now, and Daniels put a finger to his ear and said it was Sousa.

They passed the croquet courts where wooden scorecards were set on a board, then followed marble steps to the back of the hotel.

'This way,' he said, and held open a door.

She'd never been inside the hotel before, except for the kitchen. It was instantly cooler, the hall quiet, sepulchral, as if they'd entered some cathedral or an underground cave. Daniels led her down the hall to a set of stairs. They turned into another broader hallway, which smelled of floor wax. The walls were papered with some kind of crimson Oriental print, and every few feet were white sofas and tables with porcelain vases painted with dragons or bonsai trees.

'Come,' he said. 'It's close.'

They descended a staircase and came at length to a large oak door with a wrought-iron handle where she could hear a piano on the other side. The room was dimly lit. A man in a tuxedo approached and nodded toward Daniels.

'Please,' he said. 'This way.'

She could see now small tables, lamps with paper shades, each one orange, so they looked like a sea of jack-o'-lanterns. She saw ashtrays, elbows, a lipstick case, the flash of a woman's bracelet in an island of light. The walls were decorated with wine casks. In one corner a couple was kissing in a booth.

The tuxedo man held a chair for Emily.

'What would you like?' Daniels asked.

She was staring at the names on the wine

crates. She hadn't heard what Daniels said.

'Violet?'

'Sorry?'

'What would you like?' he asked. 'To drink?'

'Oh, a cola, please.'

The man nodded, and Daniels said he'd take one too, then he gestured with a finger and whispered something in the man's ear.

When he left they sat in silence. Emily pried off her shoes. Daniels extracted a silver-plated cigarette case, popped it open, and extended it across the table. She looked at him with an arched eyebrow.

'Sorry,' he said impishly. 'I forgot.' He tapped a cigarette on the cover and stuck it in his mouth.

The piano began again. The tune was slow, a kind of rag she didn't recognize. The tuxedo man returned and placed a cardboard square in front of Emily and a glass on top and did the same for Daniels. The glasses were only partly filled. He handed Daniels a paper bag, and Daniels slipped him some bills.

'Let me fix your drink,' Daniels said.

He was grinning, the cigarette clamped between his teeth. He reached across and took Emily's glass under the table and handed it back full, then did the same with his.

'Taste it,' he said.

The piano had burst into a loud tune, so they had to shout above it.

'Go ahead.' He was already drinking his. She brought the glass to her lips and tested it.

'Well?'

She shrugged and sipped again.

'Strong,' she said. 'What is it?'

'Rum. From Cuba. Best you can buy.'

He winked and settled back in his chair. She was very thirsty, and the drink was cold, the ice in perfect cubes. The rum tasted of almonds and was much smoother than Garvin's moonshine. The ice kept clacking against her teeth; it made her lips numb.

When she'd finished the drink she pushed her empty glass toward him and asked for more. He took it under the table and filled it again. The music was slow now, a song she faintly recognized. A man and woman had gotten up to dance. There was something sad about the music. It reminded her of Sunday afternoons and the Victrola at Gianni's, and she closed her eyes a moment and seemed to feel each note in the small of her back, as if her vertebrae were being played, each bone a different ivory. A clavichord. The notes spiraled up, a cadenza of keys. She felt it rush up her spine to her head, and when she opened her eyes the room was spinning.

She caught her breath and fought her feet back into her shoes. The tuxedo man had brought two new glasses. Her camisole strap slipped again, and she fixed it in front of Daniels, not caring. She wanted another drink. The song ended and people clapped, and a new one began, this one fast and jerky. Daniels tapped his fingers on the table, a fresh cigarette between his lips. She finished another glass. The ice were tiny floes now. She crunched the cubes in her mouth, and Daniels asked if she wanted a tour of the hotel and she said, Yes, why not. The lights on the tables were beginning to blur.

In another ten minutes they left the room, Daniels gripping her elbow and Emily feeling as if she were floating on a sea of paper lanterns, past tables and wine crates and orange lamps like buoys by which they navigated. Her head felt like a balloon. She'd taken off her hat and was holding it, her hair coming out of its plait.

In the hallway the light from the windows blinded her. She put a hand to her face and squinted. She'd forgotten what time it was, that it was still light out; forgotten what day it was, what month, what season, and was surprised to see the afternoon still going on, the sunlight a square of gold on the wall. They were climbing steps, entering rooms.

Daniels was talking about furniture, pointing out things: Queen Anne gold and English mahogany and French cane chairs. The names and styles. She didn't know how he knew these things, but he did. They entered another room where men were reading newspapers, women drinking tea beneath a trellis. They looked up at Emily and whispered, and Emily glared back. She had the urge to raise her dress.

'Cows,' she muttered.

Daniels chuckled and steered her by the shoulder, and she didn't protest but let him. His mouth was near, yet she didn't notice the words, only that they felt good sitting aside her ear, along her neck. He smelled different now, musty, not like the haircut, but like cauliflower. They were walking over a parquet floor in a large ballroom, the panels creaking beneath them. She stepped on each square as if it were hopscotch, her shoes making wooden music.

Then they were climbing steps, her head creaking like the parquet. They passed old prints on the wall in gilded frames, and he said they were Hogarths, but they spun slightly each time she looked. They continued climbing around and around, one flight, then another, a landing, and another. She was short of breath. She leaned against him and he put an arm around her shoulder and she could smell the cauliflower again, coming from the inside of his jacket.

They reached the top floor. The hallway was dark and utterly abandoned. Daniels had gone ahead, and when she caught up with him he was holding open a door.

She didn't realize at first that it was his office. She had expected something more official, something with filing cabinets and rows of desks. The room was oak paneled with a chandelier in the center and French doors that led to another room. There were maps on the walls, papers stacked on a rosewood desk, a telephone running to a wall. The maps were topographic, and she stepped toward them, trying to find a name she recognized, a river or a mountain or a town, but all the contours kept twisting together like little strings, and it made her sick. She dropped into a black lacquered chair with a chintz cushion. She asked where they were going, and he said what, and she said the electric lines.

'All over,' he said. 'All over.'

He opened a panel in the wall, a hidden cabinet. She watched as he pulled a chain and a light flicked on over bottles, some brown or amber, others clear. He said all the suites had one, a secret bar, a wall safe, too. He was arranging glasses. She wanted another drink. She stood and made her way over. The safe was behind the bottles; she could see a brass knob, a small lever. She asked what they kept there, and he said the usual things. Valuables. Payrolls. He was pouring drinks. She asked where the key was, and he turned with the drink and said:

'That, my dear, is a secret.'

He put a glass in her hand, and she spilled some on the floor. He'd taken off his jacket, and there were dark stains beneath his arms, and she wanted to laugh.

They clinked, and the drink burned going down like Garvin's makings. She turned to a small desk and picked up a photograph framed in oyster shell. She could see Daniels inside the photo, his arm around a woman in a mink. She was pretty, her teeth perfect and white like his. Emily asked who it was, and he made a vague gesture and she thought she didn't hear right when he said the word. He was looking out the window, holding his drink. And she asked again, and he shrugged and said, 'Fiancée,' again as if she knew all along. Emily put down the frame. The word *fiancée* kept echoing in her head. It sounded like something they made in the kitchen. She sank into a leather chair. She thought she should be disappointed, but she wasn't. She was even slightly relieved — amused, really — and she started to laugh. She was glad he had his own secrets. She wanted to tell him hers. She wanted to tell him how she'd made up Violet, that it was not really her name, but a hat with a tulle fan or a feather, or the person in the opera, Violetta in *Traviata*, the one Gianni had tried to imitate. She wanted to tell him, too, about the mine and her brother and father and about the company. She started to tell him her real name was Emily, and he looked up from his glass.

'And I'm Herbert,' he laughed, 'Herbert Hoover.'

'No,' she said, and she started to explain again, but the words weren't coming out properly. They were all scrambled together, one on top of the other, and she had to concentrate to keep them in the correct order, for the room kept jerking to the right.

He pulled a chair across from her and sat and put a hand on her thigh. She wet her mouth and closed her eyes; her dress kept slipping on the crushed leather. His hand was moving up her leg. She felt dizzy. He pushed a piece of hair behind her ear, and his wrist brushed against her breast. She couldn't help her nipple rising through the cloth. He bent and kissed her, and she raised her lips to him and kissed him back. Something like wind swirled in her ears. He was touching her breasts now. She wasn't surprised. She tried to make him into Gianni, but his tongue was like a knife, jabbing in and out, and the smell of cauliflower came back in her nostrils. She opened her lids and saw sweat on his forehead, and she pulled herself away.

'Wait,' she stammered.

She was trying to stop the spinning. He took her by the arms and stood her up. He was leading her through the French doors, into another room where something purple swirled in her vision, a velvet curtain hung from the walls. Her legs felt like feathers. He was whispering things to her. He kept calling her Violet, and she wanted him to stop now, and she tried to explain, but he was kissing her neck, his jaw like a horse's. His hand was on her breast again, and she started to squirm away.

'Remember,' he said. 'You wanted to get old.'

She pushed him away, but he took her arm again and dragged her to the bed and laid her on her back. He kept telling her to relax. She wasn't sure she should. Something made her laugh, and she tried getting up, but he pushed her again. He was whispering now in her ear. She closed her eyes and felt something hot spread across her face. His fingers on the bones of her neck. She tried moving, tried punching her way out, but she was pinned beneath him. And then she felt it, a white flash like heat on her head, something cracking above her left ear, and she felt covered as if with red ants, all crawling over her, and she could no longer think in words, only in colors, a maroon presence from the curtains, something spreading. Lush, like the operas, like all the ones she heard each Sunday at Gianni's house on the Victrola, while his parents were out in the yard and the sun slanted on the sawn pine boards.

She feels saliva on her breasts. She is swimming in the curtains. If she could bury herself in their folds and fall asleep, the room would stop spinning and the ants go away. But the world is liquid around her, her dress pushed up to her waist. She is concentrating on the curtains. Trying to remember the color, a color she's seen before but can't quite place. She remembers the names Puccini, Rossini, Verdi, for if she can't remember colors, the names of composers might do, or flowers or vines. Digitalis, solidago, *Morchella esculenta*. She can feel her underwear slip along her ankles, her hair arrayed on the pillow, but she can't move. She can see only the color on the afternoon in the rain yet can't quite place what it's from. She tries once more to move out from under him, but his fingers tighten, and there is the whiteness again. Something squeezing. A heat in her head. A mountain above.

A kettle bottom is a petrified piece of wood that weighs five hundred pounds.

She is trying to remember the color. The blue skin of her brother after the gas burned through.

Do you know what it's like to be under a mountain? There are places only you know.

There is a raw rubbing now between her legs. Sweat rolling off his forehead. Each bead a diamond. She beneath bedrock.

Under the mountain, there are places only you know, the dark tunnelings where the water drips.

She feels him enter her fully like a rope, scraping. His lips are a rubber gasket. Outside, somewhere in the world of light, there is music. An orchestra is playing, the strains barely seeping through glass. The sound is very far away, a thousand miles or more, and the light there empties on the lawn, and the clouds are leaping over trees like horses, and the wind is stirring the first coolness of evening. And on the lawn there is the smell of grass, and the donkeys underground who smell it, who go mad in spring inside their tunnelings, deep down, where Delmar rescued fossils and brought them back, the small flutes of seashells, the whorls, the names he'd recite after, trilobites, diatoms, annelids. The dark bituminous bowls with all their deadened life.

She opens her eyes for the last time and catches a glimpse of curtains. They are streaming with the color of themselves, waving in their own dye. A bead of sweat drops from his chin, lands on her cheek, and she winces when it hits but doesn't look up.

They fall from the seams when undercut. The miners call them widow makers.

She can feel a blossom of something between her legs. A hot particle. A dull sickness, something spreading. Then it comes to her slowly, the color she's been trying to remember all along, like a memory of an afternoon in childhood, and she knows it now for blackberries on the high pasture in early August, the color of the berries when they're still hard and swelling, when they're bitter and taste of chalk, when the berries haven't yet ripened, aren't ready for reaping. And as soon as she remembers it, the world dissolves into red dots and she goes under.

★ ★ ★

She woke a little later. How much time had passed she couldn't tell, only that the light was leaving the windows and a blue stillness filled the room. She thought at first she was on a lake somewhere, rocking gently on a rowboat or floating on a raft. An automobile horn honked. A door closed somewhere. She heard voices, muffled, far off, like voices echoing underwater. She drifted and sank and dreamed she was on a boat at sea and her house was unaccountably on shore. And there was Delmar and Gianni in a porch swing, and her mother, too. Then she saw the house was on fire, the flames licking along the clapboards, ropes of creosote roiling into the air, and she saw herself tearing out of the front door with her dress afire.

She woke in a high sweat, panicked, her heart pounding. The walls were shaking in the room, the ceiling swerving. She tried to piece together where she was and how she'd gotten there, and then she saw Daniels standing across the room with his back to her, running a comb across his hair. She tried to push herself up, but the room pitched and she fell back and closed her eyes.

When she looked up once more, he was standing over her, his shirt buttoned, his hair neatly combed. He was fixing a gold cuff link in his sleeve, and he was saying something about food, about coming right back, but none of it made any sense and his head kept swerving to the right. He twisted the cuff link in place; it seemed so odd to her, a cuff link, and she wanted to say the word. Cuff link. He checked his sleeve, then leaned down and put his lips to her forehead. Then she heard a door shut, and she was alone in the blue stillness of the room.

She lay staring at the ceiling for some time. The clouds in the window were cinders, the ceiling shaded blue. A bird called from outside and fell silent. She heard a plane soaring in the twilight. Then the dream came back, her dress on fire, and she shot up in bed and knew she had to get out.

She fished around for her underwear. Her mouth tasted of cigarettes. The room reeled in circles. A wave of nausea broke over her, and she fumbled buttons into dress holes clumsily and realized some were missing, torn off, that the shoulder of her dress was torn, too. A hot, panicky feeling filled her chest; her head was throbbing. She found one shoe on the floor, another across the room, and stumbled toward the door.

Out in the hallway, the wallpaper kept weaving and the lights burned her eyes. She had a horrible feeling in her chest. She couldn't remember what had happened, how she'd gotten there in the first place. She thought any moment he'd return and drag her back to the room. She staggered over carpets, down steps, stumbling and righting herself, pausing every few seconds to stop the spinning. But what exactly had happened? She remembered only that morning picking out her blue dress and the train ride and the green lawn and the band playing in the sun, but it seemed so long ago, like another lifetime, and the rest was all unclear.

She staggered down a hallway, faintly aware of people staring, whispering, making way as she passed. She needed air; she needed water, an exit, a window, some place she could crawl through and enter her life again, as if it were a cave she could return to. She pushed through a door into darkness, and something erupted in her throat and a burning liquid gushed from her mouth. She vomited over and over in some bushes until nothing was left, and she fell to the ground and retched violently on her knees.

When she stood again her head felt twisted in a knot. The grass was already wet with night, her forehead drenched, but she knew now where she was.

She was lucky enough to catch the last train in time. The carriage was empty, the bulbs sallow in their cages. She slumped against a window and held her head in hands as the blackened fields fled past. Telegraph posts tilted against the night. A headlight burned up a road. She felt like crying, like sobbing. She still didn't know what had happened. The afternoon was so confused, like a jigsaw puzzle whose pieces didn't fit.

She shut her eyes and dreamed a short dream of the tobacco tin she had kept on her bureau as a girl. How in the early morning she'd capture some fog in front of the house and clap the cover down and wait until evening to show her father; and all day long she waited, watching the red tin on the bureau, thinking the fog was in there like a genie, and all she had to do was let it out and it would be there in the evening like a piece of the morning preserved through the day. But when she opened the tin at night, the fog had always escaped, and she never knew where it went. And maybe whatever had happened would be like the fog, not there when she opened her life again, like a dream or a mist or something wholly imagined.

She woke to the train idling at a station-house somewhere and the cold knowledge of knowing otherwise. The platform lay empty; the stars quaked above. She shivered and crossed her arms to keep warm. She realized now with a dull certainty that something awful had taken place, that Daniels was to blame, that she'd have to figure it out later because it was too much to countenance just then.

The train whistle shrilled. The pistons hammered. The carriage jerked forward with a squeal. Yes, she thought, she'd think of it tomorrow or the next day or the day after. She'd have all the time in the world then. All the time in the world to figure out what to do.

PART II

7

When the electric towers rose the following spring, they glimmered on the hilltops like heliographs in the April sun. The sections rose piece by piece, the galvanized steel floating up on pulleys, until whole sections ascended eighty feet in the air, with sharp elbows and the two peaks above they called the goathead. People came out to watch their construction. In the valleys, farmers tethered their teams and boys draped arms over fences and stared as the linemen pulleyed enormous X-pieces and floated them into position. Where the electric line cut close to a town, whole families drove out in Model T's, spread picnic blankets, and made an afternoon of it, eating and drinking while the towers rose before them like theater.

Some of the linemen grew entertaining. One in particular, a young man with curly black hair who locked his legs together and hung off beams upside down or juggled insulators out on a crossarm. His name was Joseph Gershon, and he had an accent that some said was Russian and others Polish, though no one knew exactly where he came from. At noon when the rest of the crew climbed off the tower for lunch, Joseph corkscrewed down the gin pole like an aerialist, and the crowd applauded, everyone except his fellow linemen, who rolled their eyes at his antics. But by the end of the day they joined in, too, handing out shiny rivets or broken insulators, the brown porcelain plates they called Roman helmets, the green glass Maydwells. The children carried them away like gems, excited but not sure what to do with them. The most coveted were the clear ones they called crystal balls. The linemen said you could read the future in them; and the future, they said, was electricity.

★ ★ ★

They lived that spring in canvas tents up in the mountains. Six linemen. Seven ground-men. A foreman, a welder, an ox handler, a cook. They wore blue denim overalls, sky blue chambray shirts, black leather boots with an extra inch of rubber as added insulation for when they worked the lines hot. In their matching outfits they looked like some army of electrification, hanging off beams, rigging ropes, their spud wrenches echoing into the valleys below. Saturday evenings the men spilled out of the mountains to the nearest town. Yet Joseph Gershon would stay in camp, along with his partner, a thin red-haired boy named Patrick Baird, who wore a checked motor cap and baggy pants. Sometimes two Italian brothers who worked as groundmen stayed behind as well. Joseph and Baird would set up a chess board cut from a wooden packing crate. They'd use three-penny nails for pawns and tower bolts for kings, and often the foreman joined for a game, with his Stetson and string tie, his pipe of Cavendish and crushed vanilla. And those Saturday nights were quieter than any Joseph remembered, with just a few of them in camp and no men coughing or arguing loudly. Only the sound of washers clicking on the wooden board and the foreman inhaling his pipe and the silence of the hills all around.

By late April they crossed out of the Blue Ridge Mountains into the Alleghenies. The hills turned hummocky and difficult to build on, the woods carpeted in white bloodroot. Salesmen often arrived in their camps, hauling suitcases filled with patent medicines or eyeglasses, bowie knives, or packs of thermal underwear. Other times the section boss and his assistant drove to the nearest road in a maroon Pierce-Arrow, smoothed blue-prints on the hood of the car, and studied the towers from a pair of brass-plated binoculars. But otherwise the crew was left alone on the ridgetops, and a whole week might pass before they saw a single other human.

One morning on a tower Joseph Gershon saw something flash in the woods. He was working alone on a crossbeam, and he shinnied onto the tower's arm for a better view. Two men stood in the woods sixty feet below, one squat in wool brogans and an animal pelt hat, the other lanky in oily coveralls and a beard that looked like a shred of steel wool hanging from his chin. The squat one shouldered an old shotgun, and the other held a flintlock rifle. Joseph waved to them from the tower, but they didn't wave back. They stared at him blank-eyed, unblinking, and there was a menace about their gaze that made the small hairs on Joseph's neck stand on end. He glanced behind at the rest of the crew: Baird was bolting a K-piece; a Kentucky boy named Ratliff worked the opposite arm. Joseph swung back and saw the men still staring. The squat one lifted one finger, pointed at Joseph, then drew his finger slowly across his neck. Then they both laughed so their teeth showed and slipped back into the woods.

When Joseph descended the tower at

lunch, he told the crew what he'd seen. The men were eating cold meat loaf sandwiches, metal lunch boxes open in their laps. Ratliff laid his sandwich down on a square of waxed paper.

'You know what you done seen?' he said, chewing.

Joseph shook his head. Ratliff picked at something between his teeth, wiped it on his trousers, and stared at Joseph under heavy lids.

'Ridge runners,' he said.

'What?'

'You seen ridge runners,' he repeated. 'Stump jumpers. Ridge runners. Hillbillies. They're all the same.' He circled a finger above his head. 'Reckon they're all around here,' he said. 'We just ain't seen 'em yet. And more than like they ain't too happy 'bout us being here, neither.'

Joseph glanced into the woods. The rest of the crew sat up, craned heads, scanned the horizon. Ratliff ripped a bite from his sandwich and sat, chewing. 'Why,' he observed, looking over his head, 'I bet they're watching us right this very minute.'

During the next few days Joseph Gershon began to imagine things in the woods: people slipping through trees, eyes in the branches, men glaring from the underbrush. One morning he crawled from his tent half-asleep before anyone else was awake. The dawn was a dark powder, the smallest shade of blue, and some birds were just waking in the trees. He parted the slit of his underwear and let an arc of piss steam into the ground. When he looked up a girl in pigtails was staring at him. He jerked himself into his pants and scribbled hot urine down his leg. But when he looked again the girl was gone, vanished into the forest like a ghost.

Shortly after, things began to disappear from the camp. Small things at first, so insignificant that no one seemed to notice them or, if they did, no one put them together in their collective absence. A few enamel mugs disappeared from the mess tent. A meat cleaver. Someone's Waltham wrist-watch. A nail clipper went missing from someone's shaving kit. A beaver-hair brush. Tentmates began to mistrust one another. Some thought an older lineman named Clement Veerd was responsible; others suspected the two Italian groundmen. But then larger things began to go missing. New beams that had been wrapped in tarps were removed from their tarps and dragged off into the wood. One night the legs of a tower were painted completely red. Another day the men found a half-rotten skunk tied by its neck to the first section of a tower. The skunk was bloated, a balloon of fur, two teeth sticking out like pencil stubs. The men mashed shirts to their faces, and Baird climbed up and cut down the carcass, so it burst apart at their feet, scattering bones and maggots. Hager took the handkerchief from his face and said it was probably some kids playing a practical joke, but Ratliff shook his head and said it was surely the work of some goddamn hillbilly. He said they never had more than two nickels to rub together but acted as if they owned the planet. He said the only reason they lived in such godforsaken hills was to thieve and feud without any law to stop them. He toed the remains of the skunk with his boot. 'Must have been a little too far gone,' he observed, 'otherwise the sons of bitches woulda eaten it.'

For the rest of the week the crew had to work elsewhere, and it soon became clear that Ratliff was probably right, that all the thieving and mischief making was the work of some local hill dwellers. And when a few days later a draft horse disappeared from its tether, the men understood with a sudden self-consciousness that they were being watched. That at night when they sat down to supper in the mess tent or lay on their canvas cots, someone was out there watching. And by day, when they worked the towers, someone was observing from the woods. Hager sent word to the sheriff in Talcat, but the sheriff never came. The section boss promised to send a new draft horse and armed guards, Pinkertons or Baldwin felts. But the crew decided to set up their own nightly watches instead. For a while the thieving stopped. The work went on as before. The men finished four new towers, dressed them with insulators, and moved a few miles farther in the hills. They loaded their ox teams and dray horses and staked a new camp in a clearing of old apple trees just coming into flower.

It was the beginning of May then. The dogwoods were in bloom, the trillium up in the forest. Black snakes emerged from their tunnels during the day and lay across the right-of-way like old bicycle tires. The men stripped to their waists at noon and squinted into the pale sun, the steel beams heating in their hands like electric coils. During lunch Joseph remained on the tower, hooked into a canvas bosun's swing, where he'd hang eighty feet in the air as if in his own hammock. He ate his lunch watching clouds or a kettle of hawks caught in a thermal. He'd slip a small notebook from the bib of his overalls and sketch the scene with a soft lead pencil, drawing clouds and the towers, the hawks, jotting notes about the weather or insects he'd seen. Then he'd rest the pad on his chest, close his lids, and drift briefly to sleep, waking moments later to the smell of warmed steel, the bosun's swing shifting, a wrench clanging against the tower to announce the end of lunch. The men would be rousing back to work below, a breeze faint in the crossbeams, and he'd yawn and look to either side where the land lay greening to the horizon.

One afternoon he watched the sky turn emerald, the color of ocean. He was on the third section with Ratliff and Baird. The tower was almost complete; only the goathead needed to be finished and the insulators hung. Joseph was spudding a bolt on a K-brace when a curtain of ominous clouds billowed toward them from the east. The wind hung unusually warm, almost tropical. Ratliff looked at the squall and dropped his wrench into the ring on his belt.

'That's it for the day, boys,' he shouted. 'It's clabberin' up for a storm.'

He swung down to the step bolts. Baird followed behind. Joseph stayed to finish the bolt on the K-brace. The sky was blackening by the second, the squall inching closer. Hager shouted from the ground for everyone to quit the tower and leave tools behind. The men were lashing beams, tying the gin pole, securing ropes. A flight of swallows hurtled past like leaves blown on a windblast, and the first drops seethed on the beams. As the men leapt off the tower, they piled tools under a tarp and sprinted toward a makeshift lean-to at the side of the right-of-way where they kept a fire burning. The first thunder cracked overhead.

Soon they were all huddled under the lean-to, wrapped in slickers, hunched against wind. The trees were pitching backward. The fire had gone out, and one of the groundmen was trying unsuccessfully to light it. Then the wind stopped quite suddenly, and the rain clinked softly against the beams. At the top of the unfinished tower, where all the beams angled together, a strange light began to glow, a blue illumination, a small reed of light. No one said anything at first, for no one believed what they were seeing. But then the glow turned paler and shot upward like a jet of green gas. Patrick Baird stood blinking. The Tarinis crossed themselves. Some of the groundmen took off their hats. The glow radiated outward and snapped back like a shirt caught on a limb. Finally Clement Veerd opened his mouth.

'Saint Elmo's fire,' he whispered.

Hager removed his pipe and nodded. 'The corposant,' he said, and sank the pipe into his mouth again.

The men watched as the glow thinned and brightened. The trees were spitting rain. The sky had turned a deep flagstone. A static sound was crackling now from the tower like a field radio, and the air felt charged around them. The older Tarini said he'd seen a corposant on a boat once in the Adriatic and that in his language it meant 'the body of a saint.' Clement Veerd said he'd seen St. Elmo's fire several times on power lines, and some thought it an omen of ill luck. He began talking rapidly about electrical phenomena he'd seen: the green glow from salt deposits on telephone poles in the Mississippi Delta, the ball lightning he'd watch bounce across the Mojave like phosphorescent bowling balls. He was about to say more when Baird stepped from under the tarp, pointed to the second section, and said, 'Look, it's Joseph!'

The men lowered their gaze and saw a man silhouetted against sky. He was forty feet up, legs apart, beams in hand, a black outline facing the illumination like a figure in an apocalyptic painting or a man in a crow's nest watching a squall at sea.

'What the hell's he doing?' Hager said.

'What he does best' — Ratliff nodded

— 'being a damn fool.'

Hager ran out of the lean-to and shouted for Joseph to get his ass down. The rest of the crew were muttering and shaking their heads. A vein of lightning stroked across the sky, and the tower turned briefly bone white before it sank into darkness. Baird ran toward it, sensing something was wrong.

★   ★   ★

Up on the tower, Joseph didn't hear the men yelling. He didn't feel the wind or the rain. He'd been trying to secure the bolt on the K-brace when the thunderheads rolled in. And as the glow appeared on the tower he stuck his wrench into the ring on his belt and felt all at once his body fill with warmth, as if liquid had been poured into him, as if he were a vessel, a filament. It entered him like heat, moving first through his wrists, then his arms, shoulders, and neck. He tried moving his legs, but they wouldn't budge. He tried slipping one foot off the beam, but it was weighted like a stone. And he remembered then, in a dreamy way, as if it had come to him in sleep, that his shirt was wet, his pants, too, that high voltage kicks you away and low draws you in; and he realized in the same sleepy way, as if it had come to him through molasses, something warm and sticky spilling over him, a kind of knowledge, that he was being sucked to the metal; and somewhere in that molasses were the figures for the 'let go,' the point at which muscles spasm and no longer have control, the point at which voltage takes hold of a human body and doesn't allow it to 'let go.' The figures came to him like an incantation, a prayer he once knew: 9 milliamps for men, 6 for women, 4 for children. And the numbers seemed to float around him like butterflies flitting in the rain.

A needle was jabbing in and out of his legs now, a hundred bees stinging. His right arm jerked uncontrollably like a shaft of a sewing machine. His body went warm all over; he felt gripped, embraced, as if he'd been picked up by something much larger than himself and placed in a warm bath, an ocean, where he was giggling and laughing. There were fish swimming around him, long silvery fish, rubbing against his stomach, making odd crackling sounds, like meat frying. They nosed against his crotch, nudged his thighs. They had sharp teeth. Then the glow disappeared and a large crash frightened them away, and he was left in an ocean of their absence, cold and blue, and he was going down.

For the briefest moment they could see him falling, a dark figure, dropping against sky. It reminded Patrick Baird of the time he'd seen a pigeon shot in flight, how the wings collapsed and it fell, with no resistance to air. For the other linemen it was what they'd envisioned hundreds of times before: their own fallings from towers, their own missteps on the beams, and they thought, *This is what it would be like. Not dramatic. Not planned. No yelling. No screaming. No warning beforehand. Just a piece of wood dropping out of the sky.*

The rain slashed against the lean-to. A fierce wind howled up from the valley and harried past the tower. Baird was the first to reach him, to find him splayed on a coil of rope, one arm twisted unnaturally behind his head and a bone splintered out of his pant leg like a blade of ivory. Blood oozed from his head in a dark gush and spilled into his face, and the rain splatted it to pink. Hager pushed Baird aside, knelt in the mud, and pressed an ear to Joseph's chest. The men followed behind and circled tight. Ratliff started to say something, but Hager shot up a hand for silence. The trees thrashed around them. Lightning lit the tower like fish bones. Hager raised his head and looked at the men.

'He's still breathing,' he yelled.

'We shouldn't move him,' Ratliff shouted. 'His back's probably broke.'

Lightning cracked again, and Joseph's face whitened in the flash; they could see a rill of blood pooled in the cup of his closed eye. The rain picked up harder than before. Hager glanced down the right-of-way, where the ground was fast becoming mired.

'We can't stay here,' he shouted over the downpour.

'But it's three miles to camp,' Ratliff yelled.

Clement Veerd pushed into the circle. 'There's a house,' he shouted. 'I've seen it from the tower.'

He pointed toward the valley, and Hager peered into the squall but could see only trees whipping back and forth.

'How far's the house?' he yelled.

'A mile,' Veerd said. 'Maybe more, but not much.'

Lightning ripped above. The air had turned icy. Hager glanced at the tower where a curtain of rain glistened off the beams.

'Hell, we can't stay here,' he shouted. He yelled to the groundmen to take the tarp from the lean-to, Ratliff to get two side braces and Veerd a coil of rope, and the Tarinis, who were good riggers, to tie a makeshift stretcher. Baird meanwhile unbuckled the toggles of his slicker, draped it over Joseph like a shroud, and began to wipe blood from his face with a handkerchief. The Tarinis set about tying lengths of rope to two steel braces, doubling them back, knotting them under, weaving a kind of rope bed with the braces as side stretchers. Hager, meanwhile, had torn up strips of tarp and was making a tourniquet for Joseph's head. A fork of lightning leapt overhead, closer now, and the Tarinis worked faster, the rain seething around them, sluicing hair into faces. When they finished, Hager threw the tarp on top as a cushion.

'Test it,' he shouted.

One of the Tarinis jumped inside, and two men raised him and put him down. Others had moved to Joseph's side. They rolled him off the coil and stuck the stretcher beneath and rolled him onto it. His leg fell and someone propped it back onto the ropes, and he didn't waken once. The Tarinis took one end, Hager and Baird the other. Veerd said he could lead the way. Hager yelled for everyone else to head back to camp, and with that the men lifted the stretcher and made for the woods.

They descended slowly, past briers and thornbushes. The rain slackened under the trees. The light was fading, the sky a dark indigo. They went in the direction of the valley, the ground leaping around them. They saw white flowers in the strobes of light, cinnamon ferns, Solomon seal, crystals dripping from leaves. Veerd scrambled ahead and came back, waving his hands wildly for them to follow. He'd found a path heading downslope, a faint trace like a game trail, and they picked their way down and came at length to a wire fence and passed the stretcher over it.

'Hang on,' Hager shouted.

They put the stretcher in the grass, regripped the beams, and raised it once more. They stood in a pasture of clover now, the rain a sheet of silver undulating in waves. A tang of woodsmoke hung in the air, and two ponies stood pressed against a tree, staring down at them on a hill. Veerd was already trudging up the slope. Through the rain they saw a frame house at the top of the rise with one window lit, a tin roof raked low over a porch. They scrambled in the grass up the incline. A dog was yelping from the house. They passed the remains of a rusted tractor, a hay rake, a buggy. A fence girded the extent of the yard, and some outbuildings came into view. Then the dog bore down on them, hair bristled, teeth bared, and Veerd scurried down the slope and hid behind the stretcher.

They all stopped as the dog circled and barked. Hager told Veerd to take his end, and Hager stepped to the dog and talked to it in soothing tones. The dog looked to the house, then at Hager, lowered its ears, and snarled.

'Keep walking,' Hager ordered.

The men inched up the slope behind him. Hager kept talking to the dog. Lightning split overhead, and the house flashed white against the hills. They reached the picket fence, the palings unpainted, an upturned coffee tin on a post. Hager unlatched a rusted gate and elbowed it open. The dog found a quicker route under and grew fiercer than before, lunging at Hager's legs. They could see the porch with its white filigree work and wooden swing, a rain barrel and enamel buckets and blue glass jars of various sizes left on the boards. There was a shovel and a watering can, a dead plant in a pot; and on a laundry line pink and blue sheets and flour sacks inked with names hung soaked in the rain. Then someone stepped out on the porch. It looked like a girl with her hair tied back, but it was hard to tell. She held a long stick and walked to the edge of the porch, then held up the stick and leveled it like a gun.

Before anyone could speak, they heard a crack like a branch breaking, saw smoke, and dropped to the grass. The shot sang over their heads. Veerd kept saying, 'Holy shit!' over and over again. They'd almost spilled Joseph in the mud. A gust of rain ripped against them, and the wind roared in the tin of the roof. Hager was the only one left standing, holding one hand in the air, shouting that they had an injured boy and needed help.

★　★　★

For Emily, it had been the perfect shot. She hadn't wanted to shoot into them, but just above their heads, near enough to run them off. And if she hit one, no one would question her. They were trespassing, already inside the yard, unasked, uninvited, and in this way it couldn't have worked better, for she'd planned something similar a hundred times in her head. Not with them, but with Robert Daniels, when he rode up in a company truck, as she thought he would, or when he walked up to the house, hat in hand, his heavy jaw smiling. She hadn't known precisely what she'd do, if she'd invite him in first or belt him, but after waiting for weeks, eager, nervous, he never came anyhow, not in a car or a truck or on foot; and after the months of waiting it no longer mattered. The only thing left was the shell of the thing, a small kernel, a pit of humiliation, like a coin buried deep inside a velvet sack. She recognized the taste of that coin now, for as long as she could remember, it was there. Ever since the mine blew, and before when people saw her with Gianni, it was there, or when she went into White Sulfur and the store owners looked at her as if she were some dumb hillbilly. But it was stronger now, a taste of copper, as if her whole life she'd been sucking on pennies.

The men had fallen to the ground. She reloaded slowly. The box of bullets balanced on the porch rail, the cardboard green, the words *REMINGTON 22-SHORTS* stamped across the lid. She chambered one bullet and held the bolt. Her fingers were trembling; her heart raced. The pieces were all falling into place. The men were shouting from the ground. They wore yellow slickers the color of summer squash. One wore a southwester. She cocked the bolt down, the ball worn to a dull metallic sheen. This is the gun that Delmar used on woodchucks, she thought. This is the gun her father used to kill copperheads from trees. This is the gun that sat cold in a closet behind clothes, the gun she never shot turkey with, the widow maker, kettle bottom, the limestone sink.

She sighted above the lead man's head and

tried to steady the barrel. She had to concentrate. The stock was trembling against her chest. She hadn't expected the shaking, nor had she expected her mother, hadn't even heard the screen door crash behind. She hooked her finger to the trigger and fired, but something crashed her side, a plank of wood or a chair, and the shot rang over the rail and sailed into open sky.

When she caught her breath, she lay on the wet boards and her mother stood above her, the gun already gripped in her hand.

'What's got into you, girl!' Ada shouted. 'You gone stupid?'

Emily put a hand to the throbbing in her shoulder and glowered at her mother. 'No,' she said. 'Smart.'

They stared at each other a moment. Rain gushed from the ruined drains. The wind cut across the porch. The bullets lay scattered over the boards like petals. Crab apple blossoms, she thought. She picked one up and dropped it, then parted the hairs from her face and peered at the men. They were lying on their stomachs still, flat in the mud, the stretcher on the ground. They hadn't moved since the first shot. Only one man was standing, the one in the Stetson with his hand held halfway in the air.

'We've got an injured boy,' he shouted.

Ada turned and looked through the rain. 'You working those towers?' she shouted.

'Yes, ma'am,' the man yelled.

'Your boy's hurt?'

'Yes, ma'am.'

Ada yelled for the dog and stood the gun on the porch.

'Well, what you waitin' for?' she shouted.

She waved them on, but they hesitated. Then one stood and another, and one by one they scrambled to their knees, regripped the stretcher, and started toward the house.

Emily eyed them between the balusters of the porch rail. There were five in all, a sixth in the stretcher. The fronts of their slickers were coated with mud. She peered at the gun in her mother's hand, but it was too late now.

As they approached the porch they watched Emily, too. She was sitting up now, in a green-and-white-checkered dress wet on one side where she'd fallen. Her legs were folded beneath her, her feet bare, long reddish hair strewn about her shoulders. She was staring at them oddly, almost sneering, studying their every movement.

They reached the steps, and the woman held the door open. She wore a blue robe, and her skin was leathery, her eyes dove gray. She gripped the collie by its collar, and it growled and she smacked its head. It sank down and growled again and looked across at the girl.

They maneuvered the braces between the doorjamb. Blood had dribbled from the stretcher, and the dog leaned and lapped at the spots, looked back at the woman, and licked some more. A lace panel hung in the transom pane. They passed a hall tree with a beveled mirror, a bowl filled with sticks of old lavender, walls papered with a faded print. They followed the woman into a darkened room.

'Wait a sec,' she said, and disappeared. She returned with a taper, lit a hanging lamp, and replaced the glass flue. The room brightened, and they could see a long wood table beneath the milk-glass lamp, a cook stove, a kitchen cabinet, a pie safe with punched-tin doors. Bunches of herbs hung on a wall, a drugstore calendar, and some roots were drying on a screened rack. Ada was clearing the table of dishes. The walls were painted milk green. She finished and motioned to the men.

'Okay,' she said. 'Set him down.'

They shuffled to the sides of the table and gently lowered the stretcher. Ada picked the wet slicker off the lineman and removed the loose tourniquet. Blood had spidered down his face in thin striations, and she parted the sticky hairs and exposed the gash on his scalp, a crescent of pink, the skin severed in a flap like a piece of loose fabric.

'Emily!' Ada shouted, and turned back to the man. She pressed a kitchen towel to his wound with one hand and took his pulse with the other. Then she turned to the doorway and saw Emily leaning against the jamb.

'Don't just stand there!' she yelled. 'Get some towels and put the kettle on!'

She returned to the injured man. She wiped blood from his head, and inspected his leg, his shoulder, his hands. When she looked up again Emily was still hovering in the doorway.

'Emee! What on earth's gotten into you?' she shouted.

Emily moved slowly from the doorway and disappeared to another room. Ada glanced at Hager and nodded to the injured man's side.

'His shoulder's out,' she said.

Hager leaned in and the others crowded close.

'If anyone knows how to set it, be my guest.' She glanced at the men, but they all stared back expressionless. 'I see,' she said. 'Give me some room.'

She moved to the side of the table, and the men shuffled back. She swung the lineman's arm gently away from his body and held it outward as if she were teaching him to fly.

The lamp sputtered above, their shadows shivering on the wall. Ada swept her robe aside, lifted one foot, placed it under the lineman's armpit, and balanced on her other leg. She nodded back to Hager.

'Get behind and catch me if I fall.'

She gripped the lineman's wrist and jerked it suddenly toward her. The shoulder snapped and dropped into its socket. Ada placed the arm back on the table, smeared a sleeve across her forehead.

'If he was goin' to wake, he'da done it then,' she observed.

The lamp flicked and guttered. Veerd slipped out of the room. Hager fished his wet pipe from his slicker and propped it in his mouth. Emily came in, placed a pile of fresh towels on a chair, and left again.

Ada handed a towel to the older Tarini and told him to keep pressure on the head wound. She went to the lineman's leg next and untied his bootlaces. She gently pried off the boot, and a flow of fresh blood spilled on the table. Baird stepped forward with a handkerchief, but Ada waved him away. With a scissors she cut the dungaree up the length of the leg, folded back the fabric, and revealed the exposed bone that had severed his skin. The flesh around it had turned purple and bits of shattered bone were caught in the black hairs like flakes of meal. Some of the men had to look away. Ada moved to the end of the table, gripped his foot in hand, and carefully pulled his heel straight so the bone slipped back under flesh. She handed the scissors to Baird.

'Get him shed of that wet stuff,' she said. 'And try and not move him any.' She wiped her hands on her robe. 'Better cut off that shirt, too. I've got to go fetch some things from out of doors. I'll be back directly.' She glanced at the lineman again and pointed to Hager. 'You start cleaning that blood off his leg, careful of the bone.' She hurried toward the back door and grabbed a jacket from a nail and the back door slammed behind.

The men stared at each other uncertainly. The flame twisted and righted in the glass. They looked down at the torn leg, the alabaster face. Baird began unhooking the brass catches of the overalls. Hager took a towel from the pile and held it in two hands. A gust of rain pelted the house, and the porch swing shot against a wall. Then the wind moaned in the eaves and strummed into the woods beyond.

Emily stood in the doorjamb outside the throw of lamplight. She was curious now about her mother, how she'd sprung to life from her torpor as if she'd been hibernating the last few years, and the presence of men in her house had shocked her back to life. She was curious too about the men. One was dabbing the injured man's leg with a towel, another untying his bootlaces. A third snipped at his shirt with a scissors. They looked unusual under the spray of light, tall and crouched, hair pasted to their skulls, like some strange surgeons who didn't know what to do. The one in charge bumped his head against the hanging lamp, steadied it with a hand, and went back to dabbing the leg. He was doing an awful job at stanching the blood. Finally Emily moved from the doorway and stepped into the circle.

'You're doing it all wrong.' She elbowed Hager aside, dumped the towel in the basin, and wrung it out with both hands. The men stopped and watched as she pressed the towel firmly to the injured man's leg.

'What happened to him, anyhow?' she asked.

'He fell,' one of them offered. 'From a tower.'

She dunked the towel again and fisted it dry.

'He shoulda been more careful,' she said. 'People ought to keep their feet on the ground instead of messing around on towers.' She gripped the lineman's calf with one hand

143

and pressed the towel with the other. The wind rose outside. The porch swing shot against the house again. The men eyed each other, then slowly moved back to the table and began snipping and mopping again. Emily freshened the towel and studied the injured man's face. His hair was thick and curly, his lips parted, his teeth small and yellow, like a string of antique pearls.

The back door slammed and Ada tunneled through the men, carrying clumps of wet yarrow, catchweed, sweet woodruff. She set the plants on the table, portioned them in two piles, and handed one to Emily to set in boiling water for a poultice. The others she began tearing into a glass bowl.

By now the injured man lay nearly naked on the table. His overalls had been completely cut off except for a small section pushed around his hips, and the waistband of his underwear was visible. Small curls of hair boiled up from his crotch and spread across his naked chest. His skin looked pale and papery, his hipbone stained with blood. In the cold his nipples had puckered into points.

Ada threw Baird a towel.

'Dry him off,' she said, and turned to Emily, who was staring down at the lineman. 'Go fetch him a blanket and some of Delmar's clothes.'

'You used them all for your quilt,' Emily said.

'There's some still in the closet.'

Emily looked down at the lineman again. 'Do we have to use Delmar's for *him*?'

Ada stopped shredding plants and glared across the table. 'I'd smack you for that if I had the time.'

Emily shrugged. 'You already smacked me once today, why not try another?'

'If it'll knock some sense into you, I just might,' she threatened.

Emily looked at the man on the table. She pulled her hair back, twisted it in a bun, and leveled her eyes at her mother.

'Okay, Mama,' she said, 'but I hope you know what you're getting into.' She shook her head and disappeared from the room.

The kettle was whistling now. Ada went to the stove and poured steaming water into the bowl of plants. At the table she began cleaning the lineman's wounds, washing away dried blood, placing clumps of catchweed and woodruff on his head to stanch the bleeding. She worked her way to the bruises by his ribs and then down to the splintered bone.

Emily returned with clothes, dropped them on a chair, and left the room again. Ada handed Baird a quilt and told him to cover the man. She went to the cabinet next and

145

mixed a fistful of oatmeal with the boiled yarrow, and when it was cool enough she fingered the poultice onto the lineman's head gash, patted some on his ribs, and applied some to his leg, then covered each with strips of sackcloth. Finally she took a long wooden spoon and tied it to his leg as a temporary splint. When she was done she dropped into a chair and sighed.

'Well, that'll have to do for now,' she said, and wiped her hands on a towel. Her elbow was flecked with dried oatmeal. 'May as well fetch yourselves something to set on,' she said. 'Looks like it might be some time 'fore he comes to.' She gestured toward the room opposite. 'There's plenty of chairs in the parlor.'

The men thanked her and shuffled out of the room and returned with small split-bottomed chairs. Evening had come early. The rain was still falling out the windows, but the lightning had moved off and the sky was malachite and turning dark. The men removed their slickers and sat. The front door opened and Veerd returned from the porch. Ada asked if he wanted a seat, but he shook his head and said he'd rather stand.

Ada shrugged. Veerd went back to his pacing. The collie came in, looked at the men, lowered its head, and slunk out again. Baird held his cap in both hands and flipped the brim up and down. He leaned in his seat toward Ada.

'Ma'am,' he asked, 'you think he'll be all right?'

'I reckon so.' She nodded. 'I just thought he'd come to by now.'

'Is he going to?' Baird asked.

'Goin' to what?'

'Come to.'

She shrugged and looked at the lineman. The men returned to silence. Rain ticked against the glass and the sound of peepers belled from the pasture. Emily came in carrying a lamp with a scalloped reflector and set it on a sconce in the corner, and the room brightened. The ceiling fell in relief, the beams kerfed and blackened, some old initials carved in the wood. Baird rose from his chair and walked to the table.

'What is it?' Ada asked.

'His eyelids,' he said. 'I think they're moving.'

The men stood and Ada walked over. The lineman's eyelashes were twitching, then his mouth closed and opened as if he were trying to wet his lips. Ada stepped to the sink and returned with a glass of water. Baird leaned down to the table. The lineman was whispering something barely audible. Then a rictus of pain seized his face, and his fingers clawed the table. The tendons of his neck tightened. Ada put down the glass and held his head.

'It's okay,' she said soothingly. 'Okay.' She smoothed his forehead with a hand. The muscles in his neck relaxed, and his hands unclenched the table. His mouth hung slack again and his eyes stopped twitching. He exhaled heavily and fell back to sleep.

Ada laid his head back down. Baird let out a long breath.

'Did you catch what he said?' Hager asked.

Baird shook his head. 'Sounded like German.'

'Sounded like gibberish to me,' Ada said. She felt the lineman's wrist and tucked the quilt under his chin. 'He's sleeping now,' she said. 'We should let the boy rest.'

Hager stuck his pipe in his mouth, and the rest of the men wandered back and hovered beside their chairs. They watched the injured man, his face peaceful now. Hager turned to Ada.

'Pardon me, ma'am,' he asked, 'but is there a telephone anywhere nearby? We ought to send for a doctor.'

Ada shook her head. 'Laird's store's the closest,' she said, 'but it's near three miles down the holler. It'll be right muddy on a dark road, and the lines might be down tonight. You're best to spend the night and see to it directly in the morning.'

Hager pulled a watch from his pocket and flipped the lid. He thanked her but said they all should be getting back to their camp.

'Not that one' — she gestured toward the table — 'he ain't goin' nowhere.'

'No.' Hager nodded. 'I expect he isn't.'

'He'll just have to stay put,' she said.

'If that's all right with you, ma'am, it's much appreciated.'

Ada nodded silently. Hagar thanked her and said she'd done them a great service, and probably saved the man's life. He said they'd send for a doctor first thing in the morning, and if it was all right with her, he'd like to leave one of his men behind to help with the injured man. The rest of them would head back to camp.

'Of course.' Ada nodded.

'I'll stay,' Baird volunteered.

Ada touched his arm and told him the bed was already made. Hager started to say something but stopped. He looked around the kitchen as if searching for something, then turned with a troubled expression toward Ada.

'What's wrong?' she asked.

He took the pipe from his mouth. 'Will it be okay,' he said, 'with . . . your husband, him finding a man laid out on his table when he comes home?'

Ada laughed and put a hand to her neck. 'I allow, sir, as he won't be coming home.'

'No?'

'Not tonight.' She shook her head. 'Unless he does from the grave, and he hasn't in near three years, so I don't expect he'll be starting no time soon.'

Hager stuffed the pipe back in his mouth. There was a slight grin on Ada's face.

'I'm sorry, ma'am,' he muttered.

She waved it away. 'We'll take care of your boy just fine.'

Emily stepped to the table and scratched the back of her ankle with her foot. 'He got a name?' she asked.

'Joseph,' Baird said. 'Joseph Gershon.'

Emily stopped scratching. 'Funny name,' she said.

'I'm sorry,' Ada broke in, 'I never got round to introductions.' She held out a hand and introduced herself and Emily. Bo Hager told them his name and those of the rest of his men, and they stepped forward, one by one, nodding. Afterward they all stood around like strangers at a party, shuffling from foot to foot, not knowing what to say. There was mud on the floorboards, damp squares and triangles from the bottoms of their boots, and the younger Tarini began picking them up, piece by piece, until Ada stopped him. Hager addressed her again.

'The company will repay your kindness, ma'am,' he said.

'They certainly will,' Emily huffed.

Ada scowled at her daughter. 'They'll do no such thing,' she said. 'Hospitality don't call for no reward.'

The older Tarini stepped forward and took Ada's hand in his and said it was a blessing the lineman fell near her house and he was honored to make her acquaintance. The rest shuffled forward and uttered similar sentiments, then wandered away from the table. Hager pushed his arms through the sleeves of his slicker, and they all turned and looked once more at the injured man before heading down the hall.

Outside, the night was pitch. A wind was roaring in the trees. Ada accompanied them to the porch and handed a miner's lamp to Hager by its wire bail.

'We'll get the doctor sent first thing in the morning,' he said, and thanked her again and tipped his hat.

And then they were off, into the night. The lamp swung shadows against the house. The wind howled ahead of them, and the light bounced up the pasture like a golden ball growing dimmer and dimmer until it diminished altogether as if extinguished by the wind.

8

The storm died later that night. The temperature dropped by the hour. Emily lay awake in her bedroom, unable to sleep with the men in the house, one in Delmar's old room, the other in the kitchen, unconscious where they'd left him. The air in the house seemed thin and electric, the windows filled with moonlight. The clouds, blue and white, billowed like spinnakers above the hollow.

After midnight, she threw her covers aside and crept from her room. The planks felt cold underfoot, and the door of Delmar's room was shut. She put an ear to the wood and heard a faint snoring within and walked on.

In the kitchen the lineman lay on the table with a quilt still covering him. A Lincoln Log pattern. It had been Delmar's once; she recognized the frayed edges, the odor of mothballs. The lineman's face lay above it, bathed in moonlight, his skin pale as parchment, his nose knifed above, his eyes sunk in cavernous shadows. He smelled faintly of urine.

She bunched her hair into the back of her robe and went to the chair where his tattered overalls hung. The cloth was still damp, the fabric torn. She found his wallet in a pocket and brought it to the kitchen window and emptied bills on the casement, a wet five, some ones, a twenty. There were damp pieces of paper in the billfold, cards from hotels and roadhouses: the Holdemeyer Hotel in Zanesville, Ohio ('Your home in the Buckeye State!'); the Coffee Drop in Roanoke, Virginia; Clingman's Boarding House in Bowling Green. A door closed in the hall, and she froze by the window, expecting the other lineman or her mother. A branch tapped the windowpane; the clouds raced high above the hollow. She waited, but no one came.

She emptied the rest of his wallet on the windowsill. There was a borrower's pass from the Brooklyn Circulating Library, a card from the International Brotherhood of Electrical Workers. She unfolded a frayed piece of paper stamped across the top with the words *United States Department of Labor Immigrant Identification*. She read 'Josefsky' over Surname, 'Gershon' over Given. She scanned the rest: black hair; brown eyes; 5′6″. Port of arrival: New York City. For place of birth it read: 'Russia.'

She searched the wallet for more. The leather smelled of glue. There was a tiny waxed paper sleeve with a photograph inside, a small square of a woman in a high white collar, her black hair pulled in a bun. Her eyes burned out of the cracked emulsion like two dots of India ink.

Back at the chair, Emily returned the wallet and searched the overalls again. She found a pocket knife in the bib pocket and a notebook the size of her palm with a pencil stub shoved into the spiral. She flipped open the damp cover and made out small scribblings, drawings of insects, birds, a tower, a landscape; here and there pages of nothing but words.

She studied the lineman again. His lips were parted. His curls formed a thick frame around his face. He was breathing evenly now, his nostrils flared. She pulled open the knife and held it above his head, a small shiv of steel, shiny in the moonlight. She touched the blade to his neck, then closed it, and hurried back with the notebook to her room.

9

In the morning the lineman lay in the same position, with his mouth hung open and his arms splayed at his sides. Ada stood over him in the dark. She'd woken at four-thirty to check him, holding a lamp above his head. In the yellow light she could see blood had leaked through the plasters and dried in ruddy splotches so it seemed as if lichen had appeared overnight on his wounds.

She checked his pulse, his leg, his ribs. He smelled slightly of yeast, and there was another odor in the house she couldn't identify, one she'd smelled from the moment of waking, so familiar, though she couldn't put her finger on it. When she stood and saw the damp overalls in the lamplight and the wet boots beside the stove, she realized it was the smell of men in her home, an odor she hadn't breathed in years.

She sighed and turned to the stove. She built a fire in the grate, pulled down the flour bin, the sifter, and dusted the dough board for biscuits. She hadn't been awake so early in years, let alone made breakfast, but the motions came back instantly, with the light not yet up and the house as quiet as she remembered on mornings before Delmar and her husband went to work. She crushed coffee in the grinder, stuck biscuits in the oven, and set the kettle on. When the first light appeared over Keeny's Knob, she felt good, almost giddy, as if she'd remembered the lines of a song she'd once sung as a girl.

By the time Baird came in, the day was brightening in the windows and the panes were steamed from the stove. Coffee was brewing, the smell of biscuits filled the house. Ada and Baird maneuvered the kitchen table with the lineman on it into the parlor, where they wouldn't disturb him. They set the table down gently beside the couch, and Ada checked the lineman's breathing again before returning to the kitchen.

Sometime later, the sun full in the window now, Emily marched into the kitchen and stood staring at Ada, who was forking bacon from a skillet. Ada turned to her and smiled.

'Good morning,' she said.

Emily didn't answer. She nodded toward the parlor. 'What happened to your patient? He wake yet?'

Ada shook her head. 'He's still sleeping.'

'What's he doing in the parlor?' Emily asked.

Ada didn't respond. She forked a strip of

bacon from the pan and laid it on a folded newspaper. Emily grabbed a biscuit from the warmer, took a bite, and studied Baird, who sat nursing a mug of coffee, his motor cap on his knees, his hair combed neatly to one side. He was staring into his mug.

'Is your boss coming today?' Emily asked.

Baird looked up and reddened. 'Yes, ma'am. I expect so.'

'And his boss, is he coming?'

'I wouldn't know, ma'am,' he said. 'But I wouldn't think so.'

'You wouldn't think so?' she repeated, and grabbed a piece of bacon from the newsprint. Ada turned to her with the fork.

'Can't you hold a minute!'

Emily ignored her and continued staring at Baird.

'You know his name?' she asked. 'Your boss's boss?'

'Pardon me?'

'The name of your — '

'Emee!' Ada interrupted. 'Stop fussing at the man and leave that food alone, I'm making breakfast for all of us.'

Emily pushed off the counter, mumbled something to herself, and stalked out of the room. A minute later she returned, this time dressed in a plaid wool shirt and black rubber boots, carrying the rifle as if it were a suitcase. Baird slunk in his chair. Ada stuck a hand on her hip.

'Where you think you're going now with that, miss?'

'To shoot something,' Emily said, and headed to the stove and shoved another biscuit in her shirt pocket.

'But I made breakfast!' Ada protested.

'Congratulations, Mama. I knew you could.' She winked at her mother, toed open the back door, then let it drop behind.

Ada strode to the kitchen window, wiped condensation from the glass, and saw Emily stomping through the grass, heading down the pasture, the dog loping ahead.

'I just don't understand what's got into that girl,' Ada said with frustration. She glanced back at Baird and shook her head. 'Reckon as it's all this excitement.' She looked out the window again, though Emily was already gone from sight.

★   ★   ★

After breakfast Ada straightened the house. She hadn't realized how filthy the place had become. The floors themselves hadn't been washed in months, and the boards had taken on the permanent color of calf liver. Now, with two strangers in her home and the

159

doctor coming from White Sulfur, she felt a sudden panic to clean. First she moved Delmar's old bed into the parlor, and with Baird's help, maneuvered the injured man onto it. Then she took out a bucket and brush and scrubbed the floors, mopped them, dusted the shelves in the parlor, broomed cobwebs, gave the stove a quick cleaning, and wiped the lampblack from the glass flues.

By one o'clock she changed into a housedress and arranged lilacs throughout the house. The afternoon had turned hot and muggy, a small breeze stirring the cotton-woods. The doctor arrived soon after, panting up the road, bald-headed, in a black vest and a white shirt arrowed with sweat. When he reached the porch he dropped his pebbled leather bag on the boards, fell into the swing, and sat mopping his forehead, catching his breath, his hat in his lap, explaining to Ada that the Lick Creek Road had been washed out by the rains and he'd had to make the last two miles on foot. Ada went inside and returned with a pitcher. The doctor drank an entire glass and handed it back for more.

'Some climb,' he finally said.

'Keeps most folks away.' She filled his glass again. The doctor smeared a handkerchief across his forehead.

'How's the boy?' he asked.

'Well, his leg's done broke and a few ribs are broke, too. He got some kind of burns on his hands and a big gash on his head, and he don't seem to know rightly where he is.'

The doctor refolded his handkerchief and wiped the back of his neck. 'Has he said anything yet?'

'No, sir. He groans at times, but otherwise he's been sleeping. I reckon he's got some concussion of sorts.'

The doctor shook his head and worked the handkerchief behind his collar and brought it back for inspection. A kingfisher rattled over the house, and the doctor watched it flash into the trees across the hollow.

'Pretty view,' he said.

Ada looked up from the porch and shrugged. 'You kindly get used to it,' she mused.

'Well . . . ' The doctor lifted himself off the swing. 'Let's go and have a look at him.'

★ ★ ★

In the parlor the lineman lay still unconscious, his head turned to the side, his lips cracked and bloodless. The room was bathed in afternoon light now, and the plasters Ada had set were turning papery and gray. Baird stood when the doctor came in, and Ada

161

made the introductions. The doctor fitted a pair of gold-plated glasses around his temples. He removed a stethoscope from his bag and hung it from his neck. He checked the lineman's head, his leg, his ribs. He checked his breathing, stretched open one eyelid and the other. The lineman groaned and his lips moved and the doctor patted his arm.

'It's okay, son,' he said. 'Relax. I'm going to check your wounds now.'

He waited for the lineman to stop moving, then began removing the plasters, gently peeling away dried oatmeal so it came off in flaky sections, purplish where the blood had dried, yellow from the pus, the hair underneath matted and greasy with blood. With a surgical scissors he snipped hair away from the gash. The wound had turned slightly blue and orange, crusted with dried blood, like the lip of a closed clam. When the doctor was done he removed his glasses and turned to Ada and Baird.

'Left tibia's broke,' he said. 'Three ribs broken, too. The sixth and seventh. He's got some first-degree burns on his hand, nothing serious, but his head doesn't look so good.' He turned to Ada and smiled. 'Just as you said. And I'll need to fix a splint for that leg.'

Ada rose and went to the kitchen and

returned with two flat pieces of wood. 'Will these do?' she asked. 'They're hickory.'

The doctor turned one over and peered at Ada. 'I'm beginning to suspect you didn't need me here at all.'

Ada grinned so her gums showed. 'I'll go boil up some water,' she said, and headed toward the kitchen.

For the next hour the doctor cleansed and dressed the lineman's wounds. Baird assisted and Ada brought bowls of boiled water and fresh linen. The lineman woke occasionally and groaned or moved his lips. The doctor stitched the head wound with a sewing needle, painted the stitches with iodine, and rolled gauze. Then he attended to the ribs and the leg and raised the lineman's foot in a canvas sling so it hung in traction from the footboard of the bed.

When he finished Ada brought in a pot of sassafras tea and a plate of shortbread. The doctor washed and dried his hands, unhooked his glasses, and folded them in their case. He took a cup and some cookies and lowered himself in a chair, and they all sat with the sun in the west window, sipping tea and eating cookies off pink glass plates, looking at the lineman stretched on the bed.

'You say he fell from a tower?' the doctor asked Baird. 'How high up was he?'

'Forty, fifty feet,' Baird said.

The doctor blew on his tea. 'He's one lucky son of a bitch,' he said, and glanced at Ada. 'Pardon me, ma'am.'

Ada waved a hand.

'Well,' the doctor said, 'he's lucky that's all what's wrong with him.'

'What about his head?' Baird asked.

The doctor placed his cup in his saucer. He said the lineman had some kind of concussion, but it was too soon to tell how bad. He said they should try to wake him every few hours to see if he'd gained consciousness, but that there was nothing else they could do but wait and hope he'd come out of it soon.

'And if he doesn't?' Baird asked.

The doctor bit into a piece of shortbread. 'Doesn't what?'

'Come out of it.'

'We'll cross that bridge when it comes.'

'Shouldn't we take him to a hospital?' Baird asked.

'I don't recommend he be moved just now.'

'But he can't stay here,' Baird said.

'Why can't he?' Ada asked.

The doctor turned to Baird, and Ada turned to him as well and waited for an answer. Baird looked back and forth, from one to the other, and suggested it might be inconvenient for the ladies. Ada said not to

164

worry. The doctor brushed crumbs from his vest and took another piece of shortbread from the plate. He said what the injured man needed now more than anything was a quiet place to recuperate and that moving him would not be ideal, and staying in a hospital was not necessarily better than where he was right now.

'Besides,' the doctor added, 'that road's all washed to hell. He couldn't go anywhere even if he tried.' He raised an eyebrow and bit into the cookie and sat chewing. The afternoon was growing old, the light lengthening through the windows so it glowed on the brass finials of the bed and on the white bars. They could hear house finches chattering beside the porch.

'This doesn't seem like such a bad place to recuperate, does it now, Mr. Baird?' the doctor asked. 'Why, I wouldn't mind resting here myself a piece if it wasn't for having to get back to town.'

He winked at Ada, and she tried not to smile. The doctor said in the end it was the electric company's decision, but he would make his recommendation to the foreman, and the foreman, no doubt, would take it up with his superior, but he was satisfied they were following the right course of action.

He blew on his tea and took a last sip. A

cow bellowed from the pasture. The doctor positioned his cup and saucer on the table and stood.

'Well, I ought to be going,' he said. 'It's a long slog back through the mud.'

He began packing his bag, the surgical saw, the scissors, the various flasks and bottles, setting aside a fresh roll of gauze and bottle of iodine for Ada. He told her she should change the dressing every day and see that nothing was infected. He snapped his bag and took his hat from the table when the lineman moaned on the bed.

'He's awake,' Baird said, and leapt from his chair.

The doctor stepped to the bed. The lineman was looking around the room with a confused expression. Ada poured a glass of water, and the doctor knelt and brought the glass to the lineman's mouth.

'Drink,' he said.

The lineman drank slowly, with great effort, watching the doctor the whole time. His Adam's apple bobbed up and down, and water dribbled down his chin and pooled in the hollow of his neck, and when he was done he closed his lids and lay back, exhausted.

'Do you know where you are, son?' the doctor asked.

The lineman shook his head. The doctor

asked if he knew what year it was. The lineman concentrated, then shook his head again. A fly landed on his gauze head wrap, and the doctor waved it away.

'*Krahvyets*,' the lineman whispered.

'What is it?'

'*Krahvyets*,' the lineman said, a little louder this time, his eyes still closed. Then he said some other words they couldn't understand and the doctor turned to Baird.

'What the heck's he saying?'

Baird shook his head and said he didn't know. The doctor patted the lineman's arm again.

'You rest now, okay?'

The lineman nodded, his eyes still clamped, and he seemed to fall back asleep.

The doctor picked up his bag from the table, and went to the front door while Baird and Ada followed behind.

Outside, shadows fell in the clumps of burdock, and mayflies were bobbing like a thousand flecks of dust all down the lawn. The doctor turned to Baird.

'Where'd you say that boy's from?'

'Brooklyn.'

'And what's that language he's talking?'

Baird shrugged. 'He's from somewhere in Russia,' he explained. 'But I think he speaks Polish or German, I don't know, maybe both.'

'Can't say I know either one of 'em. We may need us a translator before long.'

'You think he's lost his memory?' Baird asked.

'Hard to say,' the doctor mused. 'He's got himself a bad concussion, and a man can lose his memory from one, sometimes for a few days or hours and other times for longer. I once heard of a man who'd been shot in the head and could remember everything up until the age of ten clear as day, but couldn't recall a thing after. Sad.' He shook his head. 'No, I wouldn't rule it out, but it's too early to tell.'

He regripped his bag and turned to Ada. He told her he'd be back in two days' time and to send for him through Mr. Hager if anything seemed wrong or if the wounds became infected. He looked back inside through the wire screening, and Ada looked as well. They could see the lineman in bed, a figure lit in orange, with his head swaddled in gauze and his leg lifted and wrapped like a ball of cotton batting.

'He's just lucky to be alive, I'd say,' the doctor reflected. 'All he needs now is rest.' He squared his hat on his head and raised a smile to Ada and shook Baird's hand. Then he walked down the pasture, backlit, moving through the mayflies, a black figure with the mountains shadowed behind. They watched as he waved once, then disappeared into the decline of the hill, and they couldn't see him any longer, only the mayflies dipping and rising in the remaining sunlight.

A damp chill rose from the earth now, and a cold coppery light seared the hills across the hollow. Ada could smell the musk of apple blossoms. Baird tapped his knuckles on the railing and said he should be heading back to camp.

'You're welcome to stay for supper,' Ada said.

'Thank you, ma'am, but I should be getting back. They'll be expecting me at camp.' He held his motor cap in hand, delicately, as if it were an injured bird. 'I'm sorry,' he said, 'about your daughter.'

'What about her?'

'Her not being happy' — he waved the cap toward the screen door — 'about this.'

Ada made a face. 'Never mind that,' she said. 'She's just contrary, that's all what's wrong with her.'

She picked up an empty canning jar from the porch and flung its contents over the rail, and some black leafy muck caught on the balusters. She looked up at Baird again. His eyelashes were gold in the sunlight. He was about Delmar's age, perhaps a little older, no more than three or four years, and she had a sudden urge to throw her arms around him and beg him to stay, to sit with her, to sleep over in the house, to have supper, anything, just so she wouldn't be alone again. She pursed her lips and looked down the pasture.

'You know how to get where you're going?' she asked.

'Ma'am?'

'You know how to get back to your camp?'

'Up behind the house,' he said, pointing. 'The shortcut's up there, right?'

'Just keep straight on her and turn left by a big oak. Unless,' she said, 'you'd rather stay.'

Baird thanked her again and said he couldn't. Then he bowed awkwardly and hurried down the steps and shot up a hand in parting. Ada watched as he crossed through the vernal grass, reached the edge of the wood, and was gone.

Afterward, she stood alone on the porch, holding the empty glass jar. A pair of barn swallows banked over the pasture, their breasts fired each time they turned toward the setting sun. She watched them awhile, flashing back and forth like semaphores, until she tired of them and turned toward the creek. The goats were nowhere in sight, and the ponies were gone, too. She scanned the small valley for Emily, but there was no sign of her either. A gray cat slunk up the steps, stopped at a chipped saucer, and cried.

'Oh hush,' Ada wispered, and entered the house. She went to the kitchen to start the embers again. The light was nearly drained in the windows. She lit the hanging lamp and heard the lineman in the other room mumbling in the foreign language. She brought him a teacup filled with water and sat on the edge of the bed.

'Hey,' she said.

His eyes were red slits, and he was saying something she couldn't understand.

'You gotta drink more and talk less,' she whispered. She cradled his head in the crook of her elbow and brought the cup to his cracked lips. 'Go on,' she urged.

He took a sip and glanced at her. Then he looked toward the door, and she heard footsteps on the front porch and Emily came crashing inside. She stood in the threshold a moment, and Ada saw a dead pheasant clutched in her hand, its head a brilliant velvet green, its wing shattered and blood-stained, and its neck hung limp like a hose. Emily stood staring into the room, first at her mother, then at Joseph, and back at her mother; and it seemed to Ada just then that her daughter appeared half-wild, hunched in the doorway, mud on her arms, her hair loose and matted with leaves, and the bird held in her hand like some ancient offering. Emily made a harrumphing sound and stomped into the kitchen, came back through the parlor without the bird, just the gun in her hand and her hair hanging over the bed rails.

'So he ain't gone yet,' she said accusingly, and stared at the man's head in her mother's lap.

Ada didn't answer. She was still holding the cup beneath the lineman's mouth.

'Why don't you go and get washed up,' Ada suggested.

'Why don't you not tell me what to do!' Emily snapped. 'Did anyone else stop by but that doctor?'

Ada shook her head. Emily jerked her head toward the door.

'Well, I sure hope they're paying,' she said. 'Room, board, and nursing fees.'

She turned and stormed down the hall. Ada heard the door of her bedroom slam. The lineman looked up, bewildered, staring at the space where Emily had been.

'Well, that would be my daughter.' Ada sighed.

The lineman searched the room again.

'Never you mind,' she said. She laid his head back on the pillow and set the teacup on the table. 'You rest now, I'll be back directly.' She left the parlor and walked to her daughter's room. Emily was staring out the window, the gun still gripped in her hand.

'Okay, Emee,' Ada said. 'What in the world's eatin' you?'

Emily turned and gazed at her mother. 'That man is,' she said.

'What about him?'

'They put up those damn towers and think they own the place.'

'Emily?'

'Well, what do we get out of it?' she asked. 'What good does it do us?'

Ada didn't answer. Some bells were banging in the pasture.

'Emily,' Ada finally said, 'put the gun down.'

Emily looked at the gun almost in surprise and leaned the barrel against the window sash.

'You won't tell me what's goin' on?' Ada asked.

Emily inspected her fingers as if there were something stuck under a nail. 'Ever since Delmar and Papa died,' she started, 'you been laying about in bed as if the world had come to an end, and now you jump up and start dressing strangers in their clothes.'

Ada put a hand on her hip and stared at her daughter. 'I don't see what that's got to do with that man out there.'

'It's got everything to do with it,' she said. 'You don't know these men, Mama.'

'I know one's hurt bad and comes from some other place and don't even know where he is right now.'

'So?'

'And I know when Delmar and your daddy died there wasn't a thing in the world I could do but sit and wait for them to come out of that hole all burnt to hell, and now here's a man in trouble, and I can do something this time. Don't you think I'm thinking about them? Don't you think I'm thinking of them every minute?'

She'd raised her voice and was glaring across the room.

'It's not the same,' Emily muttered.

'And thank God for that!' she said.

'You just don't know these men,' Emily said again.

'And you do?'

'Yes,' she uttered. 'They ain't no good.'

'Since when you become such a judge of men?' Ada snorted.

Emily turned her back and stared out the window. She felt something collapse inside her like a wave. She wanted to cry just then; she wanted to punch the wall. She picked at some paint on the sill. The sun had gone behind the hills, and the last fans of pinkish light glowed overhead. She exhaled once more, heard Sheila bark, and saw out the window, in the penumbra beneath the fence line, a figure coming down toward the house. She jerked a thumb toward the window.

'Here comes another one,' Emily said.

'Another what?'

'Another man.'

Ada stepped to the panes and looked outside and saw the foreman walking down from the woods, his white Stetson floating above the pasture as if suspended from an invisible string.

'I reckon that's Mr. Hager,' Ada said.

'Great,' Emily muttered, and dropped on the bed so the springs twanged. Ada walked to the door and stood in the threshold.

'We ain't done with this, Emee,' she said, and looked at her daughter a moment before she left the room.

Emily lay back on the mattress with her boots still on, a strand of hair wisped over her cheekbone. She was exhausted and hungry. She hadn't really slept the night before. The room was darkening, a paper wasp bouncing off the ceiling. She heard steps on the porch, then the man's voice, deep and alien, like an engine in another room. She could feel herself grow hot in her clothes, the wool shirt prick her skin. She blew hair from her face and said out loud, 'No, we're not done with this. We're not done with this at all.'

10

That night the lineman woke to the whisper of the creek outside and thought he was back in his childhood bed, the Prut River falling beyond the cobbled road.

The wind woke him a second time, the panes batting lightly. He could hear the creek sound again, purling and rushed in the dark, like someone sighing or speaking his name over and over in the night. He tried to rise, but something hot ripped his side, as if a burning coal had branded him. The blood hammered in his head; his eyes hurt. The creek was going again, a gentle soughing now, soothing almost. With his good hand he explored his face — his cheek and nostril, his mouth and eyelids. He found the bandage on his forehead, a strange bowl, a hot turban, and he followed the thick gauze around the perimeter of his forehead, then worked his way down over his face again, to his throat, his Adam's apple, his clavicle, down to his rib cage, where he felt more bandages about his midsection.

He lay back and let the pain pass. With great effort he angled himself up so he could see his leg hitched to the bed rail, swaddled in plaster, so large and white it seemed a thing apart from him, like a paper wasp nest or a great ball of yarn. He lay back, exhausted, breathing hard. The moon loomed starkly in the glass. Bits of moonlight splintered into the room and seemed to auger into his brain like metal filings. Each time he breathed, the blood pounded. His temples hurt. He had to close his eyes.

A minute later, or maybe an hour (he couldn't quite tell the time), he opened his eyes and everything seemed basted in a milky blue light. He saw a couch and a night table. Two ladder-backed chairs. Small objects on a sill: a medicine bottle, a lantern flue, a glass cup, all cast in blue outline. A white pitcher stood on a table, an oil lamp hung from the ceiling. The curtains lay flat and diaphanous against a window, and he could see beyond the thin sheer the shapes of mountains in the night.

An owl hooted. The panes ticked in their mullions. He tried to piece together where he was or how he'd gotten there. He remembered only faces hung over him like balloons. A circle of light. A dull silvery place where men appeared and disappeared, their faces like those in old photographs. And they came back disjointed, floating and shimmery as if seen on a shred of celluloid or a tin plate. He saw a glass bulb glimmer. He saw his father's face long and glazed in the light; he saw his mother, too, wrapped in black, with a white chalk mark X'ed on her coat. Then there was the foreman, Hager, and the thin redhead, the two Italians, and the steel towers rising like masts; and he saw sailors hailing him, waving wrenches from the rigging, and then it wasn't a ship at all but the electrical tower, and they were screaming at him to get down.

He closed his eyes again and concentrated. The wind had died, and he heard a clock tapping faintly in another room. There were pieces he was trying to put together. A bald man leaning over him. A bottle of iodine. A girl in the doorway with a dead bird. The creek soughed in the night. The moon sliced into his head. He saw something flash at the side of the room and strained to look. It was the girl, he was convinced of it, her face a wedge between dark hair. He didn't know if she was real or imagined, and he tried his throat, but it didn't work. He swallowed and made a soft croaking sound, yet she was already gone from the room.

★   ★   ★

The next morning, a woman stood over him. She wore a quilted blue robe, and her hair was auburn and graying and pulled tight across her skull. It seemed they'd met before. She brought her face close to his.

'Good morning,' she said. 'How do you feel?'

He blinked and pressed the bridge of his nose between two fingers. He had a sudden need to urinate.

'Hurts, don't it?' she said.

Her skin was the pallor of a paper bag, her eyes flannel gray. He squeezed the inside of his sockets, then whispered, 'Yes, it hurts.'

The woman clasped her hands.

'You speak!' she exclaimed, and her cheekbones rose like two shelves.

'I think so,' he whispered.

'Well, thank the Lord,' she said. 'They all thought you weren't going to pull through, but I knowed better.' She stood and said she'd get something for his head, but he stopped her before she left the room.

'Can you . . . ' He faltered, and couldn't remember the English word. 'I need . . . '

'What is it?' the woman asked.

He finally pointed to his groin, and the woman covered her mouth and tried not to laugh.

'I'm sorry,' she said. 'I'll go and fetch you something.'

She left the room and returned a moment later with an enameled pitcher and left him alone. He fought his penis from his underwear and tried to angle it right, but he missed and felt heat along his hips. He found the correct angle and closed his eyes and emptied himself. Afterward, he fished out the container and set it on a table and closed his eyes again. The beating came back in his head. The silver place where the water eddied and the faces passed, and he tried to remember where he last was but could recall only the tower in the rain and the bolt that needed tightening. When he opened his eyes again, the woman was standing over him.

'Whyn't you call?' she asked.

She took the pitcher and held it as if testing its weight.

'I didn't know your name,' he muttered.

'Ada,' she said.

'Ada,' he repeated.

He went to hold out his arm, but it hurt too much. And then she explained that he'd fallen from a tower and his crew had brought him back unconscious and he'd been in her house for two days. She explained about his leg and ribs and head, but she was talking fast now in a thin, scratchy voice like a claw on a record, and he couldn't follow what she was saying. The pain came back in his temples.

180

He closed his eyes and felt the wet sheet beneath him. He heard bells banging somewhere far off and the tapping he'd heard the night before. She said something about him speaking a foreign language and something else about a doctor, and when she stopped talking he opened his eyes again, worked saliva into his mouth, and made a circular motion with one finger.

'Please,' he said. 'Could you tell me where is this place?'

'Lick Creek,' the woman said.

'Lick Creek,' he mouthed.

'Yes, sir. Lick Creek hollow, Falls County, West Virginia.'

'West Virginia,' Joseph nodded. He pinched the bridge of his nose. Then he remembered his canvas tent, the socks strung on a string like paper dolls, his clothes in a footlocker. His head was pounding once more. His ribs cut when he breathed. The woman took the pitcher by its handle.

'I done forgot,' she said. 'I'll get something for that head.'

She left the room and Joseph lay alone, taking in a split-bottom chair, a blue sofa, the oval rag rug. There was a small bookcase filled with green encyclopedias. The wallpaper behind his head was buckled and printed with purple roses and anchors.

The woman returned and helped him with a glass of water and two tablets of aspirin. Then she went to the windows and opened the casements wider and the sound of the creek came back. He could smell lilacs. The sky looked overcast. She said the doctor and his boss wanted him to stay in her house until he felt better. She said he had a concussion and she talked of his injuries, but by then he wasn't listening anymore. He was looking out the window at the soft humps of mountains, blurred and distant behind the wire screens, and he felt lost in a place he'd never known, this view so strange and new. His shoulder flamed again. The woman's voice was a thin needle, going in and out of his ear.

'I told him,' she continued, 'that I wouldn't take a penny off a hurt man, but he said I had no choice. So if it makes you feel any better, you're a paid guest in this house, so there ain't no point in being shy.'

She pressed the back of her hand to his forehead, and he could feel the bones of her fingers, long and twig-like against his head. He heard bells banging through the windows. The woman smelled of eucalyptus.

'You built up an appetite yet?' she asked.

He shook his head.

'Hmm. Reckon you would've by now.'

She removed her hand and fixed the quilt

around him and raised a smile. 'Well, I'm glad you're back with us,' she said. 'You rest now, you'll be needing to.'

He nodded and closed his eyes and thanked her. The woman said something else, but he was already halfway asleep.

★　★　★

For the rest of the day he drowsed in the parlor, waking occasionally to voices or the creek sound or someone arguing in another room. He slept into the afternoon and the evening, and then it was dark again, and he slept without dreams, seamlessly, as if sunk in a deep blue twilight, waking once in the morning to the woman standing over him, and another time to the girl, and the hours passed this way, in blocks of day and night.

On the fourth day he woke to coolness, a damp along his arm, and he felt rested, the pain gone from his head. It seemed he'd been on a very long journey and had come back after months to a familiar shore. The room smelled of roasted meat. He stretched and glanced out the window. The evening was coming on. Clouds hung over a hill, pale and cream-colored. A blue sheet flapped on a laundry line. For the first time in as long as he could remember, he was overwhelmingly hungry.

A dog trotted into the parlor, looked at him, tilted its head, and turned back the way it came. Then Ada came in, holding a candle and an oven mitt.

'You sleep well?' she asked.

'Yes, madam,' he said. 'Thank you.'

'Well, you done look a whole lot better.'

She put the candle on the night table and pressed a hand to his head. Water had begun to plink on the roof. He could smell onions on her apron.

'Fever's gone,' she said. 'You ready to eat something now?'

'I think I can eat the horse.'

'I ain't serving horse,' she said, 'but I'll try and fix something halfway edible.'

She grinned and walked to the lamp stand and touched the flame to the wick, and the room filled with an orange glow.

'Your friend Baird was suppose to stop by this evening,' she said, 'but I expect the weather'll keep him.' She brought the candle to her face — he could see the crevices around her lips — and she blew it out and stood staring at him with the candle smoke breaking about her.

'I want to ask you a favor,' she said. 'And I know it may sound right silly, but I was wanting us all to eat together, being Sunday evening and all.' She was about to say something else but hesitated and looked at him again.

'Is it Sunday?' he asked.

'Yessir.' She nodded. 'Now, I don't want to push you, seeing as you're just awake and all, but I was wondering . . . ' She paused and picked at some candle wax, then lifted her eyes to him. 'Well, I was wanting to bring the table in here so we could all share a proper Sunday supper.'

Joseph nodded. He didn't know what to say.

'Yes,' he ventured. 'As you wish.'

Ada's mouth creased into a smile. 'You'll make an old widow happy,' she said, and hurried from the room.

A moment later she came carrying the kitchen table into the parlor, Emily on one side with a slightly amused expression. She hardly glanced at Joseph. She helped shuffle the table into the room, and Ada instructed where to set it so it sat shoulder level with Joseph. Afterward Emily folded her arms and shook her head.

'You're out of your mind, Mama,' she said.

Ada told her to hush, and Emily rolled her eyes and left the room.

When the plates were laid and the

glassware set and a lamp placed on the table, Ada brought in the meal, one dish at a time, a roasted pheasant, caramelized carrots and onions, a bowl of whipped potatoes, turnip greens, biscuits, a jar of canned peaches, and a pitcher of brown gravy. Emily carved the pheasant while Ada helped Joseph upright in bed and secured a napkin around his neck. She placed a dough board on his lap and fixed him a plate, cutting the meat and carrots into manageable pieces. Emily looked on with a supercilious expression and was about to start eating, when her mother laid a hand on her wrist.

'Emee,' she said. 'Please.'

'What is it?'

Ada laced her fingers together and bowed her head.

'Jesus,' Emily said. 'You're kidding.'

'No,' she said. 'Please.'

'Since when — '

'Hush,' Ada urged.

Emily shook her head and put her fork down, and they sat a moment in silence.

'God bless us this food,' Ada began. 'And God bless us the delivery of this injured man.' She lifted her head and looked at the others. They could hear rain drumming faintly on the roof. 'Would you care to add something?' she asked Emily.

'No, ma'am.'

Ada looked at Joseph, but his head was still down. Exasperated, Emily picked up her fork, stabbed a piece of meat, and shoved it in her mouth.

They ate in silence, Joseph with difficulty, Ada helping him now and again with his napkin or his fork. Emily stared across the table, watching the lineman as he chewed and rested and chewed again. Every once in a while he lay back against his pillow and paused before he could eat again. Emily almost felt sorry for him. After a while she set down her glass and addressed him.

'So where you from, anyhow?' she asked.

He was eating a forkful of potatoes, and he covered his mouth and swallowed.

'Brooklyn, miss,' he said softly.

Emily stabbed a carrot. 'Where's that?'

'It is near New York City,' he explained.

'I mean before that.'

'Before?'

'Your accent.'

'Emily, can't you see the man's trying to eat his supper?'

'It is okay,' Joseph said. He put down his fork and looked across the table. 'I come from Europe before that.'

'Europe?'

'Russia, actually . . . from near the Black Sea.'

'So you're Russian?'

Joseph took his napkin and touched the side of his mouth. 'I'm from Russia,' he explained. 'But I am not Russian.'

'So what are you, then?'

He laughed and put the napkin to his side. 'What am I? A little bit of everything. Some Russian, some Polish, some German.'

'Like a mutt,' Emily said.

He smiled uneasily. 'Yes, a little. Like a mutt.'

'You have kin there in Russia?' she asked.

'Excuse me?'

'Family, you got family there?'

He shrugged and moved a piece of gristle from one side of his plate to the other. 'Not actually,' he said.

'What's that mean?'

'Emee!' Ada interrupted. 'Stop interrogating the man and let him eat.'

'I'm just asking, Mama.'

'It's okay,' Joseph said, and waved his good hand. 'She should ask.'

They both turned and regarded him now. He lay back on his pillow and put his arm on the table. A muscle twitched in his neck. His face looked small and dark beneath the white bandage.

'What I mean to say,' he began, 'is I have family there, but they may not be alive.' He lifted his glass and sipped. 'My father,' he continued. 'He came to America when I was young. Then my mother and I came to meet him. But my mother, she was sent back to Russia.'

'And you don't know if she's alive?' Emily asked.

'No.' He shook his head. 'She died many years ago, but her sister, my aunt . . . well . . . '

'You don't know about her.'

'This is correct.'

Ada shook her head. 'I'm sorry,' she said, and took the empty pitcher from the table and retreated to the kitchen. Joseph was staring into the lamp, Emily at her plate. Her pheasant lay half-eaten in a pool of brown gravy, and the grease gave off a smooth, reflective sheen. They sat a moment without talking, the rain steady on the roof, and the sound of peepers belling from the bottom-land. Small hairs of soot floated to the ceiling from the table lamp; Emily turned the knob of the wick, and the shadows shrank on their plates.

'We lost our own a few years ago,' she said.

'I am sorry, miss.'

''Least we know where they are,' she said.

'What happened?' Joseph asked.

'Coal,' she said. 'They worked in a mine and it blew up. Twenty people died.'

'I'm sorry,' he said. 'That is a terrible thing.'

Ada returned with the water pitcher and set it on the table.

'Please,' she said. 'Can't you talk about something else?' She poured Joseph a fresh glass of water and asked how long he'd been working on electric lines.

'Six years,' he said, and told her he'd been up and down the East Coast and all over the Midwest.

'You like building them towers?' Ada asked.

'The towers?' He shrugged. 'Actually, I prefer working on them when the power is running.'

'You do that?' Ada asked.

'Yes.' He smiled shyly for the first time. 'They call it working the lines hot. They have special clothing and tools for it.'

'Sounds right dangerous,' Ada said, lifting her fork.

'There's really no danger to it. People are afraid of electricity because they cannot see it, but actually it is very predictable. Like that flame.' He nodded to the lamp on the table. 'You're not afraid of that fire because you have been around it. It is the same with the electricity.'

Ada put down her fork and looked at Emily. 'Ain't that fascinating, Emee?'

Emily didn't answer. She tipped her chair up on two legs and sat studying the lineman. 'You know,' she said, 'we're not getting to use any of that electric in those towers. It's all just passing through, right on top of us.'

'One day it will come,' he nodded.

'I'm not gonna hold my breath,' she said.

He shrugged and put down his glass. 'No, this is wise. It may take some time.'

'I don't rightly understand what the rush is to get that electric,' Ada said. 'Seems to me it just makes a body all nervous with all them lights and wires and such. I just as soon not fool with it.'

Joseph shook his head. Emily sat in silence. They could hear the dog's claws clicking on the front porch.

'I have heard that said,' Joseph commented, then closed his eyes and pressed his fingers against his temple.

'You feel all right?' Ada asked.

'Yes,' he whispered. 'It hurts just a little.'

'I'm sorry,' she said. 'We shouldn't keep you with all this talk. It's too soon.'

She stood and stacked some plates and utensils and turned to the kitchen. Emily studied the lineman again. He was rubbing the side of his head below the gauze, then he lifted his face suddenly and gazed across at her. His eyes looked obsidian in the lamplight.

'Do you mind, miss,' he said, 'if I ask who you lost in the coal mine?'

Emily tipped her chair to the ground. 'My father and brother,' she said, and gestured toward the bed Joseph was lying on. 'That was his bed, my brother's.'

Joseph looked down at the mattress. 'I am sorry, miss,' he said.

She stood and gathered her fork and knife and balanced her glass on her plate.

'So am I,' she said. 'So am I.'

11

The next morning Ada left the house early for groceries. Emily crept into the parlor with a bowl of steaming water and set it on the night table. She went to the windows and skirted back the curtains to rouse him. The sun streamed in and Joseph woke, shading his eyes against the glare.

'Good morning,' she said brightly. She stepped to the bed and removed from her apron a shaving brush, a straight-edge razor, a porcelain shaving mug.

'What time is it?' he mumbled.

'Time for a shave.' She pulled a towel from her shoulder and dropped it on his chest. 'Can't have you looking like a stiff if you're staying here.'

She dipped the brush into the steaming water and began whipping lather in the mug. Joseph was still covering his eyes. He tried to raise himself on the mattress but couldn't, and he lay back helpless and watched the steam swirl around Emily. She wore a lemon dress with a V-neck collar beneath her apron, her hair tied on top. Some hairs had fallen loose as she whipped the brush, and she glanced up and caught him staring.

'It's the polite thing to say 'good morning,'' she said.

'Good morning, miss,' he muttered.

'That's better,' she said.

She dunked a washcloth in the bowl and wrung it out. Joseph was about to say something when she draped the hot cloth over his face, lifted it, and began brushing cream on his cheeks. She lathered his chin and neck and stood the brush on the table. Then she unhinged a razor with a horn handle and held it to the light.

'Hold still,' she said. She pressed one finger to his cheekbone and brought the blade to his chin. Joseph winced, and a rose of blood bloomed in the white cream.

'I told you to keep still,' she said.

'I'm sorry,' he mumbled.

She leaned into him and shaved slowly down the length of his cheek. At his jawbone she picked up the razor and wiped the blade on a towel.

'That man Hager,' she said. 'Is he your boss?'

Joseph nodded groggily under foam. She brought the blade back to his face and scraped gently down his cheek.

'And does that Hager have a boss?'

Joseph nodded again.

'Who's that?'

'The section boss, miss,' he muttered.

She swished the blade in the bowl and leaned over him.

'So the section boss,' she went on. 'What's his name?'

'Daniels,' Joseph said. 'His name is Mr. Daniels.'

Emily held the blade upright like an ice-cream cone. A breeze was skipping through the room, the sun in her hair. A reddish strand was dangling along her neck.

'You ever meet that Mr. Daniels?' she asked.

'Me? No, not actually. Sometimes he comes in a car and watches. He looks through a glass.' He made the gesture with one hand of looking through field glasses.

'Binoculars,' she said.

'Yes, these binoculars.'

'Hold still,' she said. 'I don't want to cut you.' She pulled the skin tight around his jaw, shaved between the cleft of his chin. His eyes were closed again, and she studied his full mouth, the black curls sticking out from under the gauze, the small, irregular teeth, pebblelike between his parted lips. She lowered herself again in the chair and wiped the blade clean.

'What do you know about this Mr.

Daniels?' she asked. She was trying to sound casual.

Joseph opened his eyes and looked perplexed. 'What is there to say?' He shrugged. 'He is a boss. He comes on payday in the car. He is like any boss.'

'Does he know you're in this house?'

Joseph shrugged again. 'How should I know?' He flicked foam from the corner of his mouth, then thrust his lower lip forward. 'Maybe he knows. Maybe he doesn't. Perhaps if Mr. Hager told him. I am sorry, I do not know, miss.'

'If he knows you're here,' Emily persisted, 'will he come visit?'

Joseph raised his hand again and wiped the rest of the lather from his lips and inspected his hand. Then he looked at Emily in her seat, waiting for an answer, the razor poised upright. The sun was on her arms, and he could see her freckles and the fleece along the inside of her elbow.

'No.' He shook his head. 'I don't think this man will visit. For me? Why should he?'

Emily stared a moment, then splashed the razor in the basin.

'I don't know,' she said, and fingered the piece of hair behind her ear. 'Hold still now.' She touched the razor to his face again, scraped beneath his jaw and down the small bones of his Adam's apple. He closed his eyes again. A cow bellowed somewhere down the pasture. The sun went in and the room fell flat. She rinsed the blade and shaved one side of his neck and the other, and he lay with his eyes closed and his lips shut tight and his black curls motionless against the cotton pillowcase.

'What's it like,' Emily finally asked, 'up on those towers?'

'You can see far,' Joseph said without opening his eyes. 'Sometimes it seems you can see the end of the earth.'

'You don't say.'

'Some days when the wind is blowing bad,' he continued, 'you get the mal de mer.'

'The what?'

'Seasick,' he said. 'All the tree branches go around you and the towers move a little this way and that. It makes the motion like the sea.'

She pinched the side of his face and shaved under his nose, down the filtrum.

'And you get ill?'

'Yes, a little.'

'Hmm,' she said, and took the towel and pressed at the nicks of blood on his neck. He opened his eyes once more, and she threw the towel on the table.

'Are you finished?' he asked.

'For the moment,' she said.

He felt his cheeks and wiped lather from his sideburns, then studied Emily. The light was coming sidelong through her dress, and he could see the small hairs beneath her armpits.

'May I inquire about something, miss?'

'Depends on the question.'

'Why do you want to know about this Mr. Daniels?'

'Curiosity,' she said.

'Curiosity,' he repeated, and shook his head. 'Do you know him?'

'No.' She started cleaning the brush, squeezing out bristles, and folding the razor. Then she stood and picked up the bowl and leaned it against her hip.

'Anything else?' she asked.

'Actually,' he said, 'there is one thing.'

She curled the corner of her mouth. 'What's it now?'

'Thank you,' he said, 'for the shave.'

'Don't thank me, thank my mother. She's the only reason you're here.'

'Okay, miss.' He bowed his head slightly. 'Then I thank your mother.'

'And stop calling me 'miss,' my name's Emily.'

'Yes. Miss Emily.'

'Not Miss Emily. Just Emily.'

'Okay.' He tried not to smile. 'Emily.'

'That's better,' she said. 'And don't forget it.' She glared at him a moment, shifted the bowl to her other hip, then turned and left the room.

★ ★ ★

By noon she'd changed into a pair of old trousers patched at the knees, and sat on the porch, shelling peas. Her mother hadn't returned yet from town, and Joseph was sleeping in the parlor. From time to time she crept to the door and checked inside, saw him dozing, and returned to the peas. She could still smell the shaving cream on her hands.

She was almost done with the basket when the dog stood and barked, and she saw Garvin's hounds racing up the pasture. Garvin walked behind them, hatted and hunch shouldered, with the same slouch she remembered from her father. When he reached the yard he removed his hat, elbowed sweat from his face, and stood catching his breath. A round tobacco tin heaved in his breast pocket. Emily waited, vaguely annoyed by his presence.

'Heard you got one of them electric boys inside,' he said, and put a hand on the porch rail.

'News gets around,' she observed.

'The whole damn county knows, but I got to go to Laird's to find out.'

'You should come by more often, Uncle.' She snapped a pod and let the peas plink in the bowl.

Garvin turned and spat. A fly landed on his neck and he smacked it. He shuffled up the porch steps, lowered himself into the swing beside her, and pinched her knee.

'How you keeping?' he asked.

'All right.'

'You staying outta trouble?'

'Are you?'

'Trying my damnedest,' he said, and laid his hat on his knees. The felt brim was frayed and greasy. He smelled of unwashed clothes and alcohol, and he took the tobacco tin from his shirt pocket, pinched a nut, and worked it into his gums.

'I was wanting,' he said, 'to have a word with that electric boy.'

Emily nodded toward the house. 'He's sleeping,' she said. 'You best not to bother him.' She unzipped a pod and dropped peas in the bowl.

'How long you reckon he's gonna be staying?' Garvin asked.

'I wouldn't know,' she said.

'You wouldn't?'

'No, sir, you gotta ask my mother. She's in charge of the ward.'

Garvin closed the tobacco tin and wiped his fingers across his trousers. 'Well, soon as he's fixed to crawl, you send him out. Too many damn people up here, next thing the law will pay us a look-'round.'

Emily glanced up from her bowl. 'You worried about your business?' she asked.

'I just don't want no trouble,' he said, and pushed himself off his knees. He stepped to the porch rail and spat a glassy brown stream into the grass. 'You send that feller out, you hear? The sooner the better. Now I'm goin' to take me a look. You want to show me in, or do I got to do it myself?'

He centered his hat on his head and waited. Emily put down her bowl and sighed.

'All right, Garvin,' she said. 'Take it easy. I'll show you in.'

★ ★ ★

The curtains were drawn now in the parlor, and there was an odor of iodine in the room. Emily stood in the threshold, adjusting her eyes, while Garvin stepped past her, and peered at the figure on the bed. Joseph lay sleeping, a white sheet rising and falling on his chest, his head still bulbed with gauze. He looked younger now with his chin and cheeks shaved. Garvin removed his hat.

'He don't look so good,' he said.

'Shhh. He's sleeping.'

'Why, I can see that.' He took a step nearer and inspected him closely, then stepped back to where Emily stood.

'You say he fell from a tower?' he whispered.

Emily nodded.

'Looks more like the ground flew up and smacked him in the head. What's all them cuts on his face?'

'He got those shaving,' she said.

'Shaving?'

'Yes, sir.'

He glanced at her a moment uncertainly, then shook his head and shuffled toward the door.

Outside, she returned to her seat and placed the bowl in her lap. Garvin spat over the porch rail.

'I don't expect that boy'll be putting up any towers no time soon,' he said.

'No, sir, I wouldn't expect so.'

'Don't he have no kinfolk?'

'Not around here,' she said. 'He's a foreigner.'

'Well, he sure does look strange,' Garvin mused. 'But he ain't a bad-looking fellow, now, is he, Emee?'

'I wouldn't know, Uncle,' she said.

'You wouldn't?'

She saw Garvin grinning so his front teeth showed, and she dropped peas in a bowl and shrugged.

'No, sir,' she said, 'but it's sure nice having a man around. Even one down off his legs is better than some standing straight up.'

She raised an eyebrow at Garvin. He wagged his head and balled his tongue at the side of his cheek. Then he spat again off the porch and crushed his hat on his head.

'You just be careful, Emee, that's all. I don't trust them electric boys as far as I can throw one.'

'Is that so?'

'They're all coming from one place and going to another. Shifty up one side and down the other. Soon as that boy's fixed to crawl, you send him packing, you hear?'

'Whatever you say, Uncle,' she said.

Garvin smeared a sleeve across his mouth. A hen clucked and fled through the yard. Then he walked to the porch steps, stuck two fingers in his mouth, and let loose a whistle for his hounds.

12

Everyone in Lick Creek soon learned about the lineman at the Jenkins house, and over the course of the following week the women came to visit, not so much out of sympathy as curiosity.

They didn't wait for an invitation, as Ada wouldn't have invited them, but came anyhow with a corn pone or a huckleberry cobbler, a can of pears or a buttermilk pie, or a bouquet of tea roses or delphiniums. The McClung sisters came one day, and Ruth Loudermilk the next. Rachel Toothman arrived one morning, and even Betty Laird took a rare afternoon off from the store. They hiked up the hollow to the wooden gate and crossed up the dirt road to the house at the top of the hill. Ada had no choice but to let them in, and though they were coy at first, sitting out on the porch and talking politely of the weather or their gardens or of this man or that child, and who was not getting on with whom, it was clear they had come for one thing and wouldn't leave until they got it. So after they sat on the porch for a spell, talking and sighing and resting their feet, Ada would stand and ask them in, and they'd pretend surprise at first or refuse outright, saying they'd rather just sit where they were, knowing the whole time that Ada would have to ask again. The second time they didn't hesitate, but pushed off their knees and said all right and came shuffling in the door and ducking into the parlor, where they hovered by the threshold, gawking and clucking like hens.

Ada introduced them to the lineman, one by one, and they made little waves with their hands and then shambled out again. And that's what they wanted all along, to just see him, for some had heard he was covered head to toe in electrical burns, and others that he'd lost his memory entirely, and still others had heard that he was a Greek.

On the weekend a few crew members came to visit, the thin redhead with the motor cap, the two Italian brothers, the foreman with his Stetson hat and pipe smelling of vanilla. Not since the mine exploded had so many people hiked to the Jenkins house, and for Ada the arrival of the lineman seemed a kind of deliverance and a blessing. It was as if her own had come back from the mine this time only injured, and she could attend to him in a way she never could with Delmar or her husband. There were times in the early morning, passing through the parlor, when she stopped and stared at the bed, looking at Joseph's feet or the bulk of him beneath the quilt, and she'd convince herself that he was Delmar, that he'd come back from the dead, that he was there this time to stay, and she wanted to get down on her knees and weep for all that had passed.

Each morning she brought him enormous breakfasts of eggs fried in bacon fat, coffee, bowls of grits with butter melted in the middle, hot biscuits, jam, maybe a slice of country ham if she had any. In the early afternoon she came with his dinner of meat loaf and mashed potatoes or canned tomatoes and venison, or squirrel and white gravy and dinner rolls on the side. She baked crumblers and chiffons. She forced on him glasses of fresh milk with the fat floating on top. She changed his dressings and washed his wounds. She nursed him with a passion bordering on penance. She even began to attend church on Sundays, even though she hadn't been to the Lick Creek Methodist in years. For in her heart she began to believe, in some mysterious way, that Joseph had been sent there, to their house, to the hollow, like a gift or a piece of grace, and it was her job to keep watch of him.

Emily observed all this with cool detachment. She watched her mother baking pies and going off Sunday mornings with her white gloves and straw hat. She watched her rising early in the mornings as she hadn't in years. She watched her arrange red peonies in glass vases and place them in each window throughout the house — as she had when her father and brother were alive. At first she was amused by her mother's solicitations, but then it angered her, and then she became indifferent to it all, as if her mother were some kind of weather system she could no longer predict. Emily just sat back and waited. She waited for Robert Daniels to show up, as she still thought he might. She waited for an opening, a gap, something she wasn't sure of, a way of getting back at the company, of enlisting Joseph in her plans. She thought of Gianni and his talk of bombs. In the barn was a hidden tin filled with the black powder Delmar had used in the mines, and some nights, lying awake in bed, she fantasized about blowing up one of the towers once the electric was in them, and how she'd get Joseph to help her accomplish this end.

In this way, she waited. She observed her mother. She observed the lineman. She had his pocket knife and his notebook still hidden in a drawer in her room, and in the evenings after supper she'd take out the notebook and scrutinize the crinkled pages, trying to decipher the scrawl, trying to find something that might link him up with Daniels or disclose a clue about his past or personal life. But she searched the pages in vain, for the words were all in an alien script, impossible to read, and the few English words she could find, 'OPAL, AMALGAMATE, FIRTH, STENTORIOUS,' had dictionary definitions scribbled after them, once in English and again in the alien alphabet. She found herself flipping through the pages with increasing frustration, for they were like the lineman himself, a mystery, a cipher, something impossible to read.

★ ★ ★

One night when June bugs were banging against the screens, she stood in the threshold of the parlor, staring in at the lineman. He was lying in a pool of lamplight, his head wrap removed now and a smaller bandage taped like a beret over one side of his head. He turned as if sensing she was there and raised a smile as she entered.

'Hello,' he said.

She stepped toward the bed and scratched

her ankle with her toe. He had a book spread open on his chest.

'What are you reading?'

He turned the book so she could see the spine. It was one of the encyclopedias, volume O through P.

'I am learning all about the ocean currents,' he said.

'Interesting?'

Joseph shrugged. 'Not actually. Please, you will sit?'

Emily brought over a chair and set it in the circle of lamplight. Joseph closed the book and stared at her.

'I have something for you,' she said, and took the notebook from behind her back. 'I found it out on the pasture. It was laying in the grass. I didn't know what it was at first, so I . . . ' She shrugged and handed it to him. 'Well, I believe it's yours, anyhow.'

Joseph took the book and ran a finger over its cover. He opened the first page and glanced at her. He seemed about to say something but turned back to the book.

'I was wondering,' she said. 'I couldn't help but see that language in there. Is that what you were speaking the night you first came here?'

'I wouldn't know,' he said. He opened the cover and thumbed through pages.

'Is that Russian in there?' she persisted.

He didn't answer. He was still fingering pages as if searching for something. He closed the notebook, studied its cover, and looked at Emily again.

'No.' He shook his head. 'It is not Russian.'

'Then what is it?'

'Another language.'

'What other language?'

He sighed and lifted the encyclopedia off his stomach and set it on the night table. She was still waiting for an answer.

'Why are you so curious about this language?' he asked.

'Why shouldn't I be?'

'Why shouldn't you . . . ' He pursed his lips. 'Well, this other language, if you must know . . . it is in fact Yiddish.'

'Yiddish?'

'Yes,' he said, 'Yiddish.'

'What kind of language is that?'

'Jews speak it,' he explained.

She looked at him with confusion. 'Then why do you know it?'

He laughed, then fell silent and peered at her to see if she was serious.

'Because,' he said, raising his eyebrows, 'I am one.'

'A Jew?'

'Yes,' he nodded, and looked down at his hands.

'You ain't got horns, have you?' she asked.

'Only two,' he said.

She grinned. A tiger moth flew in from the night and circled the lamp several times, trying to land on the hot flue; Joseph watched it a moment as it rose and fluttered away.

'My father,' Emily said. 'He knew a fellow who worked the mines who was a Jewish man. The only ones I ever knew were those in the Bible, and they were just stories.'

Joseph nodded again. The moth was crawling up the lamp base, and he put a finger out to it. Emily set her chin in her palm and studied him.

'You still speak that language?' she asked. 'That Yid . . . '

'Yiddish,' he said, and shook his head. 'No, not especially.'

'Why not?'

'Why should I? I am in this country now. With whom would I speak it?'

He lowered his eyes to the notebook. She waited for him to say something, but he didn't. She wanted to ask him more, yet talking to him just then seemed like prying open a clenched fist, pulling back fingers to see what he hid in his hand. She looked at the glazed darkness in the windows and sighed.

'Well,' she stood, 'I won't keep you any longer.' He put a hand out to stop her.

211

'Please,' he said. 'I'm . . . ' He paused and dropped his hand. 'I don't tell many people.'

'You don't tell them what?'

'Where I come from, for example. What I am.'

She pressed her hip against the chair back and looked at him quizzically. 'Why not?'

'Because . . . ' He took the notebook from the bed and set it gently on the table, then looked down at his leg and shrugged. 'Most people don't want to know about Jews.'

Emily went around the chair, hooked her feet under the spreader, and sat with a perplexed expression. The moth fluttered on the bedstand. The flame shook its shadow against the wall. Then it stopped moving, and its legs twitched and stiffened.

'What exactly is it you want to know?' Joseph finally asked.

'Hell, I don't know. Anything.'

'Anything?'

'Like where you come from, how you got here. What the hell you do up on those damn towers.'

Joseph studied her a moment. 'You couldn't find anything in my notebook?' he queried.

She shook her head in disgust and started out of the chair.

'Please,' he said, 'I'm sorry.' He gestured

for her to sit again, and she slipped warily back in the chair.

Joseph swallowed. His eyes were dark and leveled at the near distance. He shifted on the mattress uneasily, reached for his water glass, and cupped it against his chest. And then he began, slowly and by degrees, to tell her his story.

13

I grew up in Russia,' he explained, 'in a village in Bessarabia along the Prut River. Have you heard of Bessarabia?'

Emily shook her head.

'Well,' he said. 'It is in southern Russia. Not far from the Black Sea. The houses there are made of stone.' He lifted the glass and drank, then put it down and closed his eyes. He thought about the village along the Prut River, and he thought about his father, Berl Gershon, how he'd hitch a sewing machine to the back of a donkey each month and head off into the mountains to ply his trade. He could see the black Singer sewing machine with the gold lettering and the thin gray donkey with its backbones exposed like a worn sofa. And he began to tell her about the Carpathian Mountains and the sewing machine and his father, Berl Gershon.

He was a tailor by trade, Joseph said. But he had higher aspirations and thought of himself as an inventor. Each month when he returned from his travels, he'd bring back a pannier filled with odd items Joseph could only guess at: an engine cog or a calipers, a battery cell or a vacuum tube. Standing in the stone yard of their house, Berl Gershon pulled from his bags wires and cathodes the way a magician might produce a pigeon or a rabbit from a top hat. And to Joseph it was magic, but his mother didn't think so. She'd watch from under the lintel of the doorway, a hand on her hip, face downcast, with a slight air of disapproval. Only once did she say something outright, when his father returned with a Delco bulb, the glass thick and handblown, slightly bluish, like a large soap bubble. His mother tore off her apron and threw her hands in the air. Where had he been for two weeks? she shouted. And what were they going to do with that glass bulb? There was nowhere to plug it in, nowhere in the entire village. She marched inside and slammed the door, and Berl Gershon still held the bulb in the air until he shrugged guiltily and wrapped the bulb gently back in its newsprint.

One night two months later when snow covered the village, his father stood over Joseph's bed, holding a jacket.

'Come, get up,' he said.

Joseph rose from the bed. He crawled into the twin arms of the coat, pulled on boots, and followed his father's figure through the kitchen, under the low lintel, and out into the yard. The stars were icy above, the moon a piece of parchment in the north. The snow cracked underfoot.

A brazier was lit in the shed and a spirit lamp whose flame doubled in the frosted panes. His father shut the door and took Joseph by the shoulders and steered him to the corner and picked up a wire insulated with gutta-percha.

'I want you to hold this,' he said.

His father's face was more distracted than usual, the black eyes like stones in their sockets. Sweat stood on his forehead, and his cheeks were shaded with stubble. The shed smelled of cedar and engine oil and the thin alcohol odor of the spirit lamp. Joseph grasped the wire, and his father followed the other end back to the bench and hovered above a crude armature he'd built out of pie pans and magnets and courses of copper, the whole thing set on a gimbal so that the pans could be rotated by an old cider press crank.

His father checked the contraption and returned to Joseph, this time with the Delco bulb. Joseph hadn't seen it since that day his father had first brought it back, and standing in the shed, his father instructed him to hold the wire in one hand and the bulb in the other and to touch the wire to the bulb's metallic base but not to touch the base

216

himself. He left Joseph and walked back to the armature.

'You ready?'

Joseph nodded. His teeth were chattering. He wasn't sleepy anymore. Outside, the moon appeared in the panes. His father rolled up a sleeve and began rotating the cider crank. The pie pans squeaked and strained, turning in opposite directions from each other.

'Anything?' his father asked.

Joseph shook his head. He was holding the wire to the bulb.

'Now?'

'No,' Joseph said.

Berl Gershon cranked harder, looking back and forth from the armature to Joseph.

'Anything?'

Joseph said nothing.

'Are you holding it right?'

Joseph was about to answer when he felt a sharp sting, something biting through the cracked gutta-percha like a bee or a hornet, only sharper and quicker so his hand went numb. The tiny filament inside the glass began to fill with red as if some substance had been poured into it, and then the bulb brightened and filled with light, and the room glowed yellow around him, and he could see his father back at the bench, laughing and cranking and shouting with his head flung back, bathed in the yellow glare; and even though his fingers were on fire, Joseph couldn't help but laugh, too, for he'd never seen his father so animated or happy or proud.

When he came to, he was on the floor. He couldn't remember what happened, only that everything had suddenly gone dark. There was something sticky on his face. He was lying in a circle of glass, his father kneeling before him.

'Are you all right?' he asked.

Joseph touched the blood on his chin. He felt slightly dizzy, and he picked a piece of thin glass off his stomach. His father helped him up, removed the rest of the glass, and brushed him off. Then his father went back to the bench and started tinkering again with the armature. After a few minutes he looked back at Joseph, surprised to see him still there, and told him to get back to bed.

★ ★ ★

From then on Joseph became fascinated with electricity, with this thing that had no shape or color, this thing he couldn't see but was alive nonetheless like a nest of hornets. He learned the names it went by: galvanic,

218

faradic, Franklinic, animal. When he first saw a wall socket on a trip to Chernovtsky, he stared into it as if it were a face, the holes like two round eyes and the indentation below like a mouth. He thought it was the face of electricity or God or both.

His father taught him the little he knew and continued on his monthly trips to the mountains. But one week he returned without the donkey or the sewing machine, his coat torn and his face badly bruised. Joseph gleaned only the barest of details: He'd been attacked by a group of men on the mountain road because he was, apparently, a Jew. His sewing machine had been smashed and the donkey stolen. Aside from that, it wasn't clear what else had happened, only that he'd come back with a black eye and mud in his hair. He retreated into his shed and refused to talk about it after.

That was just the beginning of a series of harrowing incidents in the village. One night a militia came through the streets, smashing the windows of the Jews and setting some houses on fire. A neighbor knocked on the door and urged Berl Gershon to come to her house for protection. At first his father refused. He never overtly considered himself Jewish. He wasn't religious and hadn't brought Joseph up to be, either, and they lived separate from the other Jews in the village. Yet Joseph's mother pleaded, and after a while they followed the woman across the lane to her house. It was a dark night, and Joseph could see torches burning across the river and hear dogs howling. The neighbor rushed them through a gate into her yard, and she opened a stall door and said, 'Here, this is the safest place.' Joseph didn't know what it was at first, but the stall smelled thin and acidic, and out of the corner of his eye he could see the shapes of animals and hear them grunting. The men were coming closer now on the road; he could hear them singing, drunk, boisterous, and he heard glass smashing and laughter and guns going off. His mother was trembling in the dark, his father grim and silent. Sometime early in the morning, after the noise had died down and the air turned chill, the woman returned from her house with a lamp and said it was safe to come out. It was then that his father saw the pigs emerge from the corners of the stall, thinking it was time to be fed, only then that he realized they'd passed the night in a pigsty.

After that night something happened to Berl Gershon. He became withdrawn and quiet and spent all his time alone or on mysterious trips to Odessa. Then one day, quite suddenly, he announced that he was leaving for America. He said there was no future for them in Russia and that if they weren't killed by their neighbors, they would no doubt die of hunger, and he promised to send passage for Joseph and Joseph's mother once he'd established himself in New York.

Within the month he was gone. Six months later an envelope arrived with six crisp American bills — four tens, two fives, a one — and a scribbled note: 'Will send more.' His mother stuffed the cash in a sock and told Joseph to hide it above the rafters in the shed. The note she crumpled and threw in the fire.

Then a whole year passed and neither Joseph nor his mother mentioned the letter or the money or America. The pogroms had ceased, and his mother found work in a knitting mill in town. During the long afternoons while she was at the mill, Joseph retreated to the shed, where his father's engineering manuals still lay in dusty piles. He'd examine the wooden spools, the sewing machine parts, the magnets and coils and watch parts his father had found in his travels. He'd open a tattered English-Russian dictionary and spend hours scribbling down words, writing definitions, studying by himself. Last, he'd take the sock from the rafters and remove the American bills and stare at the men in the green ovals, Lincoln,

Washington, and Hamilton, hoping to construe something in their faces about the place where his father had gone.

A year later, in August, the tickets finally arrived sealed in waxed paper. The following month when the buckwheat was ripening and the fields shimmered like old brass, Joseph and his mother left the stone village along the Prut River, traveling by train overland to Trieste. Joseph had just turned eight years old.

★   ★   ★

There were Montenegrins on the ship, Serbs, Romanians, Italians. The steerage smelled of vomit. Joseph stayed on deck at night beside braziers of burning coal while the frost hove up from the ocean and the steel boat shuddered beneath him, and his mother stayed below, growing sicker and sicker in steerage.

By the time they reached New York Harbor her eyes were pink, and the rings under them had a bluish tint. On Ellis Island a nurse picked her out of line and led her away, while Joseph followed up a series of stairs, past guards, into a white-painted infirmary with rows of iron beds and caged windows. The room smelled of cabbage. A man talked to

Joseph in Yiddish and led him to another room with bunk beds where he could stay until his mother recovered. And there he waited several days, sleeping on an upper bunk, waking to people hacking and muttering in a stew of languages. He'd visit his mother in the mornings in the hushed hospital room with only the sound of nurses slipping back and forth. Some days he walked along a rooftop and watched ferries going back and forth in the bay and seagulls hurtle this way and that and the buildings of lower Manhattan turn gold in the autumn afternoons.

Days passed. Word came from his father that he was waiting. His mother's eyes improved, then worsened again. One morning Joseph went to the infirmary and found her propped in bed, her head shaven, her eyes sunk in their sockets, and he couldn't hide his horror, though he tried, he couldn't help but stare.

A few days later they let her out, still weak, her eyes only a little better. Joseph waited beside her in line to be inspected. A doctor in a clean white coat stood at the head of the line. Next to him was an interpreter wearing wire-rimmed glasses and behind him a policeman in a blue uniform. The doctor was tall with a long nose, and he checked people's mouths and eyes and waved them on. Sometimes he picked up a piece of chalk and marked someone's coat with the letter *E* or *S* or *I*, and the policeman stepped forward and took the person away. An old woman on line said they were looking for criminals and that they could see it in people's eyes. A man turned and said, Nonsense, the *S* means syphilis, the *I* insanity, and the *E*, he said, meant the eye disease conjunctivitis.

The nearer they came to the doctor, the more agitated Joseph's mother became. She began shaking, lightly at first, then harder, and then she started muttering something beneath her breath. Joseph didn't know what was wrong. The others on line were watching with distress. He tried to silence her, but she shook him off. They were approaching the doctor. She was saying some kind of prayer now. The interpreter leaned forward and asked what was the matter. The doctor looked on, cold and impatient. Joseph said she was just happy to be in America. The doctor stepped forward and tried to look at her eyes, but they were filled with tears. He said something sharply to the interpreter, and the interpreter asked them to step aside until she'd stopped crying.

They waited at the side of the line. The doctor kept looking over at them. A bell was gonging somewhere down the hall. The doctor removed a heavy pocket watch on a silver chain from under his medical frock and put it away. More people came and went. A clock gonged again, and the doctor waved over Joseph and his mother. He was impatient now. He grabbed Joseph's mother's jaw and forced open her eyelids with two fingers. Then he let go, picked up the piece of chalk, and drew a large *E* on the lapel of her coat. The policeman stepped forward and asked them to come with him. Joseph tried to argue, but the policeman held out his arm and waited.

Then they were stepping down a corridor with brown and yellow tiles and a faint odor of ammonia. His mother was no longer crying. Joseph tried to wipe the *E* off her coat, but the policeman turned and warned him. The rest of the day was a blur. Officials came and went. Papers arrived from his father. Joseph didn't know exactly what was going on, but he knew his mother was being sent back. He told her he'd go with her, that he'd return, too. She said she was like an old tree that couldn't be transplanted, and she shouldn't have been moved in the first place. Joseph didn't know what to do. He wanted to save her. He wanted her to stay. She told him she'd try to come again when she was better.

She said that he couldn't go with her, because he'd regret it later on, and that his father was waiting on the other side. He tried to argue with her, but she wouldn't hear it. Then some time later he watched her being led down a hall, thin and skeletal, with a coat wrapped around her and her head so white and naked it looked like an egg balanced on a plinth, until she turned and he saw her face was stained with tears as she waved good-bye. He felt something tear inside him, like a piece of cloth that couldn't be sewn back together, and everything around him went fuzzy, as if he were looking at the world through a piece of waxed paper. He felt numb and alone. He began to cry. He tried to convince himself that he'd see her again, but he knew otherwise.

Later that afternoon he crossed the harbor to Manhattan. He stood in the corner of the boat, confused, sad, the gulls keening and diving overhead; and he realized then that the prayer his mother had been saying was the prayer for the dead, the Kaddish, the mourner's prayer. He wasn't sure then whom she was saying it for, if she was saying it in order to cry so she could hide her eyes from the doctor or if she was saying it for herself. But he tried not to think about it just then, for his father would be waiting on the other side.

Berl Gershon seemed much older than Joseph remembered, and it shocked him at first. His hair had gone completely gray, and he seemed somehow shrunken, as if his insides had been drawn together by a string. His father seemed neither happy nor excited to see him. They didn't talk at first. His father merely picked up the suitcase and the bags, put a hand on Joseph's shoulder, and steered him through the crowds; and when they were outside in the street, he took his hand and led him through honking automobiles and horse carts.

They walked for a long time. The air was filled with voices, people speaking English, heels tapping, hundreds of pedestrians moving and rubbing against each other. The buildings went all the way up into the sky and made him dizzy. It was rush hour. Suited men were marching toward the water, pouring into subway stations, black men in soiled overalls toting lunch buckets, secretaries in flannel skirts, with their hair pinned into hats, small boys hawking evening editions. Streetcars clanged. An autobus screeched. The office windows flashed in the afternoon sun.

They climbed down steps under the earth and entered a dark tunnel with a string of dim lights. His father paid a coin and they went through a turnstile and waited. A blind man was singing. Men were reading newspapers. The train came and they crushed into it and started into the darkness, and then they clattered onto a bridge, his father looking out the window at billboards, advertisements for hair tonics and shirt collars. Bridge girders whirred by. The water flashed brown. They floated above apartment buildings, the red bricks burgundy in the afternoon and the sun streaming brilliantly through the windows like bright blocks of orange, but no one seemed to notice. His father looked dull-eyed out the window, and Joseph wanted to scream at all the newness around and scream at what had just happened to his mother.

They sank underground again. Ten minutes later they stepped off. His father led the way, a few paces in front, not bothering to hold his hand anymore. They climbed to a tree-lined street. The evening had washed in, and the air was chilled. Some children were shouting nearby, the street lamps already burning, the bulbs pale in the cold decrease of the day. Some leaves scraped on the concrete. They came to a small bridge and crossed a highway and entered a neighborhood of warehouses and factories and smokestacks silhouetted against the departing dusk. A dog barked behind a fence. A tobacco shop was shuttering its gates for the night. His father turned into a small lane where laundry hung in backyards and light wires ran from building to building in blackened webs. His father unhooked an iron gate and said, Here, we are home.

The building was brick, the number in the glass faded, the gold paint flecked, so it could have been a 28 or a 23, he couldn't tell. The last light of the day gloomed in the transom. They climbed a narrow case to the third story. There was an odor of garlic and mice in the hall. His father opened a door with a key and pulled a string, and a bare bulb revealed the small rented room, with a threadbare armchair and a curtainless window letting off into some back alley. In one corner a cot was pushed against the wall, and in the opposite corner was a mattress set on two seltzer crates. Between them stood a low coffee table with a newspaper on it, and behind a wall was a stove and a double-basin sink.

His father set down the luggage and pointed to the mattress and told him to rest. The place smelled strongly of pickles. A man's voice was coming through the wall, speaking English without stopping. Berl Gershon disappeared into the kitchen and some time later returned with two bowls of soup and a loaf of rye bread.

They ate on a folding table under the bare lightbulb, sipping lentils off spoons that tasted of tin, bowing their heads like worshipers while night filled the windows and he could hear traffic churning on some nearby street. They talked then about his mother, about trying to get her back and what they would do. They talked about the years his father had been away and the jobs he'd had and the jobs he didn't have. His father talked in a clipped tone, his eyes dull and black, explaining how he was a steam presser now and worked in a warehouse in Manhattan, and Joseph asked about the inventions and the engineering, but his father only smiled wearily and shook his head and said that was the past and there was no time for such foolishness now.

His father fell silent and finished his meal. Joseph watched him, the heavy lids, the sunken cheeks, the spoon going up and down. And he saw, with the eyes of an eight-year-old, how his father had failed, how he was broken in spirit; how the moments of animation when he'd come home from the mountains with the engine parts and the calipers and the spools of wire were gone forever. It didn't occur to him then, but years later, thinking back, Joseph knew that on the same day that autumn, he'd lost both his mother and father, his mother to the immigration service and his father to something much more insidious and incomprehensible, something he would never be able to name or even describe in any language he knew.

Berl Gershon finished his soup, stacked the plates, and went into the other room and turned on the water tap. Joseph was tired. He was thinking about his mother. He felt something cold and ironlike go in and out of him. He wanted to close his eyes and open them again and find things different. Outside, a horse cart passed. Someone shouted in a foreign language. The English voice was still going in the other room, low and measured; then there was a break and he could hear music through the thin walls, and he realized it was not a man at all, but a radio. The thought somehow cheered him.

His father came in with a clean, folded bedsheet and a pillow and dropped them on the cot and said, Try to sleep now. Then his father undressed to his underwear and his socks, pulled the chain from the ceiling, and the room fell dark. He could hear the cot twang as his father climbed into it. Minutes later he could hear his father snoring, soft at first and then louder, as if nothing remarkable had happened that day, neither the arrival of his son, nor the deportation of his wife. Joseph lay awake in that strange apartment with its odor of pickles and mice, listening to the snores of his father and looking at his dark bulk in the corner he wouldn't even know was a person, let alone his own father. After a while he got up and went to the window at the side of the room. There were streetlights burning outside, some near and some far, like jewels strung from standard to standard. And farther out, he imagined he could see the water wrapped around Manhattan. He wasn't sure of it, until he saw lights move erratically and blink off and on like navigational lights, as they made their way out to the ocean or inland in some direction he didn't yet know. He stayed awake watching the lights as they winked on and off, and the sound ceased from the streets. He thought of his mother heading back on one of those lights, and he thought about the chalked *E* on her coat and what she would do, returning to Russia. And how she'd have to make the journey again, this time alone or with her sister. He felt sad for her and wished she were there. And he thought of his father, too, in the cot next to him, how he seemed taciturn and beaten, like a stranger on the berth of a train, both of them hurtling to some destination neither of them could know.

His father was still snoring. The radio had been turned off in the other room. He watched the lights late into the night. Finally he saw the moon go down over the tenements and the sky begin to brighten behind the smokestacks, and he fell asleep thinking over and over that this was his first night in America.

★   ★   ★

Three days later he found work scaling fish at a chowder house in downtown Brooklyn. Two months after he was painting bridge girders, hanging in a rope sling over the East River. The following year he was apprenticed to an electrician, a quiet German Jew with big ears and a harelip and a habit for cheap cigars. His name was Mack, and he taught Joseph by silence, letting him learn by his mistakes. Allowing him to cross wires and shock himself, letting wires burn in his fists, fuses blow on contact.

Mack told him a few things straight out: Never work on electricity with your left hand. It is the closest hand to your heart, and the electric will run up it like a mouse and seek out the heart as it works its way toward the ground. Always touch a live wire with two fingers splayed in a V. The current looks for the quickest way out of the body and will go in one finger and arc harmlessly out the other. He told him amps were like veins and volts like the blood that flowed through the veins. He told him about the 'let go,' the amount of amps a body could withstand before it couldn't let go of the current. But aside from this he said little, and Joseph was left alone to experiment with the electric. He licked his finger and touched live wires. He placed the sharp copper hairs on his tongue and felt fire roll down his mouth. He tested himself against a voltmeter, seeing how many volts he could take, training himself to know the current, to keep his finger longer on a wire and withstand the ringing pain, for if he knew the electric, if he could feel its edges and corners, he wouldn't be afraid of anything.

★ ★ ★

Sometimes he'd get carried away, like a deep-sea diver who'd gone down too far, and he'd find himself unable to surface, his limbs having reached the 'let go'; and like the diver, he'd start to hallucinate in that static state and see eels floating around him or the stone house in the village in Bessarabia or even his mother waving to him, with the shaved head and the tears. And each time, Mack would slam a chair into him to break the current, and Joseph would come to, rising out of a haze like an opium addict with his hand pulsating and his head ringing. But after the third time Mack had had enough. He took the cigar from his mouth and jabbed it in Joseph's face and said if he did it again, he wouldn't bother to knock him free, and if he lived, he could find a job elsewhere. Joseph was still on the ground, his head reeling, his fingers the color of pink coral.

'I've got one piece of advice for you,' Mack said, still jabbing the cigar in his face. 'Stay off the goddamn juice.'

But he didn't. He began outdoor work. He wired street lamps over roads, along highways, draping ribbons of rubber-cladded copper from lamp post to post. He wasn't afraid of the heights. He'd balance on the tops of ladders, volunteer for bridge jobs. He liked the view up there, the acres of sky, the wind that seemed clean and redemptive. At eighteen he joined the International Brotherhood of Electrical Workers and was handed their baked-enamel button and a pair of steel climbers. He set out on his first line job with a duffel bag, a *Webster's* dictionary, a pair of lineman's '109' buffed-hide gloves. Electricity was erupting across the country,

235

power lines spidering from city to city. Linemen were in demand.

On the crews they called him Brooklyn or sometimes, simply, Joe. He learned rigs and knots, writing the names in a notebook. The keg and clove. The crowfoot. The sheepshank for shortening a rope. He loved the travel, the smell of clean sheets in the boardinghouses, coffee in thick porcelain mugs, roadhouse dinners of turkey and mashed potatoes; and pulling into the motor camps at night with the truck lights blooming on the clapboard huts. In small towns they tipped up forty-foot poles, staked lines to houses, ran them right through Main Street; and afterward they stayed for the inaugural night, when the lights *whooshed* on and a band played 'Jeannie with the Light Brown Hair' and the blue ribbons were cut. But by next morning he was already on the road to another job.

In this way he worked his way west, on railcars, in automobiles or line trucks, sending letters always to his mother, postcards, small packages with American bills tucked inside to the village in Bessarabia along the Prut River. And the years passed; the lines grew larger, the voltages higher. The single poles became H-frames, then steel towers. He changed jobs often, as did all the linemen, moving south in winter, north in summer. An army of migrants following the latest power lines. The names of the companies blended into each other: Indiana Electric, Cleveland Power, Illinois, Otter Trail, Piedmont Light and Power.

What he liked best was working the lines hot, crawling into the insulated suits, the black rubber pants and rubber coat, the overshoes and gloves (always a few sizes too big), so he felt like some surgeon in an open-air theater. The other crewmen plucked the electrified lines away from the crossarms with ten-foot insulated sticks and guyed the hot wires against the poles, like a bridge on a violin; and when the wires were safely pulled away, Joseph went in alone, changing a broken insulator or splicing two hot wires together, working close by the current, aware of the invisible electrons seething and spinning around him, the free radicals and split molecules alive and flying through the air. It is like stepping into a room where a fight has just occurred and the air is jumped and unsettled. He is aware too that at any moment the sticks might slip and the wires snap at him like plucked strings and brand him from behind or sandwich him between crossarm and conductor in a shower of white voltage. With the hot wire in his hand, he is aware too of the current beneath the thin rubber sleeve of his insulated glove, the current thrumming in its casement. He can feel it in his arms, as if his bones are singing, a constant *ohm*, an incantation in the teeth, like a continual prayer, sixty cycles per second. He knows the electric is alive, like a thinking thing, prescient and moving, ambulatory almost; it has its favorite objects, those it likes to pass through and those it does not. His fellow linemen talk about the electric all the time. They dream of it at night. It surrounds their waking hours, this thing they cannot see and has no weight and occupies no space but can move mountains and fly at the speed of light and is everywhere, in clouds, stingrays, fish, the human body and brain, and packed into the earth in buried bands called leylines or dragonlines. He knows too that electricity flows over the face of the earth but is landless, that it sojourns endlessly like a Gypsy, and that what it seeks, above all else, is to burrow back into earth, to be grounded; and that secretly he seeks the same, like his father and father's father and so on for generations back. For he, too, has wandered the face of the earth and wishes to end his journey, to be grounded, to find some earth, some home, some acre or quarter of land, wherever that may be. And this is what he tries to tell her, late into the night,

238

excitedly, his mouth dry, how all things are electric, and opposites attract, positive and negative, how the world is one big magnet and the ohm that measures resistance in a wire is also the sound of the planet as it rotates and grinds on its axis.

★   ★   ★

The room was dark, the oil lamp guttered. The curtains hung flat against the windows. It was morning now, and a chill had slipped down from the mountains and crept into the room like a third party sitting between them in the parlor. Emily sat shivering, clutching her elbows, glued to her chair. Joseph lay with the empty glass still nestled against his chest. He hadn't talked so much in as long as he could remember, and his throat was dry. For a moment he lay embarrassed by the silence, thinking he'd spoken too openly and too long. Why would she care, anyhow? He couldn't see her face in the dark, but could smell her across the room. They sat a moment quietly, in the absence of his voice, as if a piece of furniture had been taken away.

Emily finally broke the silence.

'So,' she ventured. 'Whatever happened to your mother?'

Joseph lifted the glass and tried to drink again, and Emily heard him sigh and the bed shift with his weight.

'She went back to Russia,' he explained. 'I wrote her for many years. For a while I didn't hear from her. It was hard to get letters from there, and hard to get them on the road. And then I learned from my aunt that she died. This was six years ago.'

'I'm sorry,' Emily said. She leaned back and shuddered against the cold spindles of the chair, then rested her chin in her palm. An owl hooted outside. The moon was icy in the windows.

'And your father?' she asked.

'What about him?'

'Is he still in New York City?'

Joseph shrugged in the dark. 'Yes,' he said. 'At least, I believe so, but I am not sure. Who knows? We haven't spoken in many years. You see, they have a phrase in the Yiddish language for men like him. They come to this country and leave their family and sometimes, poof! they disappear. Sometimes it is not only physical. In the newspapers there are advertisements looking for them. Missing husbands, missing fathers. They call them *farshvunderer mannen*.'

Emily tried to repeat the words and gave

up and then asked what they meant. Joseph set the glass on the night table and turned to her in the dark.

'The men that disappear,' he said. 'The disappeared men.'

14

They slept until ten the next morning, Emily in her bedroom, Joseph in the parlor. Ada busied herself about the house until she grew impatient and roused Joseph to change his bedsheets. By the time Emily walked in, Ada was making hospital corners and Joseph lay propped against a pillow, a cup of coffee on his chest. Ada regarded her daughter a moment and went back to making the bed.

'What happened to you?' she asked. 'Decided to sleep in?'

Emily yawned and stretched. 'No,' she said, 'I couldn't sleep.'

'Somethin' keep you awake?'

She shook her head. Ada glanced at Joseph, who was staring into his coffee.

'Funny,' Ada said. 'Same thing happened to Joe.' She took the old sheet and cradled it in her arm. 'I reckon there must be something goin' around.'

★ ★ ★

Later that morning Ada was drying dishes at the sink when Emily walked in humming, holding a handful of purple phlox. She watched as Emily set the flowers on the table, opened the cupboard, took down an empty pint jar, and tried the flowers in it. The jar was too small, and she tried a quart jar next, but that didn't work, either.

'What you got there, Emee?' Ada asked.

'Flowers.'

'I can see that,' she said. 'Since when you taken to arranging flowers?'

'Since the notion came to me.'

Ada put down the dishrag and studied her daughter as she grabbed a half-gallon Atlas jar and stuffed the flowers in that.

'You be careful,' Ada said.

Emily looked up in surprise. 'Careful of what?'

'You know what,' she said. 'You just watch yourself, girl, that's all.'

Ada stood staring across the room, and Emily stared back with a perplexed expression. A breeze was furling through the kitchen. Sunlight pooled on the drying dishes. Ada wiped her hands on her apron and marched across the room.

'Here, let me help you with that.' She took the jar from Emily, pulled out the phlox, found a white hobnailed vase on top of the cupboard, and stuck the flowers in it. Then she held the vase arm's length in front.

'There,' she said, 'don't that look a whole lot better?'

Emily glared at the vase. 'What was wrong with mine?'

Ada chuckled. 'Canning jar's for beans, honey.'

Emily rolled her eyes. 'What do you know,' she said, and turned for the hall.

Ada stuck a hand on her hip. 'I know one thing,' she snorted. 'I know what's keeping you up at night.'

⋆　⋆　⋆

That evening, despite her mother, she returned to the parlor, and the night after she did the same. Nothing was said beforehand; they had no pre-arrangement. But each night of the following week, after the dinner table had been cleared and the dishes done and the lamps blown out, after Ada had gone to bed and the whole hollow lay in repose, Emily slipped out of her room and entered the parlor, where his lamp was burning and a book lay spread on his lap. He pretended the first two nights not to expect her, but by the third all pretense was gone. And each night she was full of questions. She wanted to know about Russia and New York and the places he'd been. She wanted to rummage through

244

the chest of keepsakes she thought all foreigners kept, to find the odd coins and bits of cloth, the keys, the words they knew, like the insects under rocks that scurried away when the light hit them. And each night he gave her something, a different word, like a digit. One by one, a new finger opening up.

'*Baum*,' he said one night. 'A tree.'

'Galicia, the name of a region in Poland.

'*Malochim*. It means 'angels.' '

His fist was opening, his hand slowly revealed.

He told her the puns they had when he first came, how they called America 'Ama Reeka,' which meant in Yiddish 'the hollow people,' and he told her that the word *electricity* came from the word *amber*. He told her all living things had electricity, and certain fish, like the torpedo fish and the gynmotus fish of South America, had enough to knock a man out, and that all people had one microvolt of electricity inside their bodies, but others, like the luminous woman of Pirano, were known to have considerably more.

And each night she returned to hear more, and he would be waiting with the lamp haloed around him as if his bed were an island on whose shores he'd beached. A man at sea too long, he in this unlikely harbor. As for Joseph, the days were merely periods of preparation for night, for that moment when she came to him like an apparition, her nightshirt ghostly, her bare feet whispering against wood, a kind of music he waited to hear. So long he'd been in the company of men, so long unconfessed, that he waited each night now to pour himself out, like a bottle long corked. And afterward, after they'd talked and she'd gone to bed and he lay alone, listening to the creek sliding off the mountains, he'd wonder by what design he'd gotten there, to that parlor with the peeling wallpaper with its purple pattern of anchors and roses, and the oval rag rug and the black rocker, in that house at the dead end of a dirt road in a hollow in West Virginia. And it seemed to him some nights, lying alone in the parlor, that his whole journey as a lineman had led him there, and each tower he'd put up was a mile marker on the road to Lick Creek. For he felt instantly, mysteriously, comfortable in the company of Emily and Ada Jenkins, as he'd never felt before in America, as if a piece of him had been lost and found. He tried to think of a way to tell Emily this, but he couldn't explain it at all, not even to himself, even if he'd had the words, which he didn't. He knew it only as an ache.

Midsummer began. The smell of wild

bergamot blew from the meadows. His leg was getting better and his ribs, too, and his head had all but healed. His desire to return to work was tempered now with the increasing urge to stay put, to languish around Ada, who fed, lodged, cooked, and cleaned for him, who mothered him in a way he hadn't been since he'd come to this country; and Emily, too, whom he'd never have fathomed in his wildest dreams, with her reddish braids and green eyes, her freckled arms, the men's trousers and faded shirts, and her odor, which seemed like the smell of pine needles long laid under an August sun.

By the last week of June Ada fashioned a crutch from a hickory branch, with a quilted pad nailed to the top as a cushion, and in the mornings now he raised himself from bed and hobbled to the outhouse. He spent his days on the porch with his leg raised on a cane-backed chair, and more than once he shuffled to the woodpile and tried chopping stove wood, but Ada forced him back inside. At night now, instead of staying in the parlor, he'd limp to the porch and sit with Emily and Ada and watch the fireflies rise like methane from the earth; and after a while Ada would yawn and head inside and leave the two alone in the dark. They'd sit as night increased around them and the crickets started in the grass; and each night there was the same awkward moment when they went inside and Emily latched the screen door behind and squelched the lamp; and they stood in the palpable darkness, not knowing what to say, so near they could smell each other's breath, and she'd turn and head quickly to her room.

Afterward she'd lie awake in bed, troubled, confused, with the sound of his voice like an incantation in her ear. She wanted so badly to tell him about the Roncevert Hotel and Robert Daniels. She wanted to tell him about the revenge she'd planned, the sabotage, the blowing up of a tower, how he'd ruined it all by coming with his broken bones and concussion. How she'd wanted to hate him and still wanted to hate him. And she thought of telling him the next night or the night after about the skunk on the tower and the stolen beams. Yet when she lay in bed with her eyes closed, the echo of his voice seemed to soothe over the old angers, and she no longer thought of Robert Daniels or the Roncevert Hotel; she no longer even thought of Gianni anymore. Instead she imagined Joseph, the way he had looked the first night, splayed on the table with his naked torso, his pelvic bone exposed like a plate of china and the dark hairs spreading delicately across his chest. The house seemed soaked with his presence,

as if some strange honeysuckle were blooming in a corner of her room. No matter how
hard she tried, she couldn't ignore the odor;
she couldn't be angry. The thought of Daniels
seemed to fade entirely from her mind.

★   ★   ★

One afternoon when his leg had healed
enough, they walked to the high pasture,
Joseph on his makeshift crutch. His bandages
were off now, the black curls almost all grown
back over his head. The day was blanched
with clouds, the sky washed a Wedgwood
blue. He was wearing Delmar's trousers,
belted, cuffs rolled, a white cotton singlet
freshly bleached. Emily had put on a dress.

They walked slowly up the wooded path,
Joseph crutching his way, stopping every few
steps to rest.

'You sure you want to do this?' she asked.

'Of course,' he said.

They reached the top of the hill, and Emily
helped him over the stile. A meadow spread
before them, sloping gently toward woodland.
A few Angus grazed below, and they lifted
their tails and shat as Emily and Joseph
passed.

They went along the edge of the pasture
through orange hawkweed, keeping close to

the fence line. Piles of dried dung lay papery in the grass. They passed through an alley of tall spruces where the earth lay carpeted with needles; and they walked into sunlight again, into another meadow where a succession of ridges stretched for miles to the south, creased and crumpled like an enormous green quilt. Emily stopped at an ancient maple in the middle of the field. Joseph laid his crutch in the grass. She sat and pulled a stalk of orchard grass and stuck it between her teeth.

'This is the high pasture,' she explained.

'It is very pretty.'

'The height's good,' she said, 'but no matter how high you climb round here, there's always another hill in the way. I'd like to see the horizon one day. I'd like to see the ocean. It must be very clean.'

'Clean?' Joseph asked.

'Yes.'

He shook his head. 'The ocean is a very filthy place,' he said.

Emily shrugged. They sat in silence. The field sparrows started in the grass, then stopped, then started again. Shelia came sprinting from the spruce trees, and when she reached them she was panting and burrowed her head into Emily's lap.

'Git!' Emily yelled. 'Lord knows what you been rolling in.'

Sheila shrank away, circled, and sat, her tongue out, looking back and forth from Joseph to Emily.

'What kind of dog is she?' he asked.

'Border collie, but she don't act like one. She's not good for much but watching chickens and making trouble.' She glanced at the dog, who cocked her head. Tree swallows dipped low over the field, and the cows had disappeared from the slope. Emily said it looked like rain. Joseph peered at the sky.

'But it's too much blue,' he said.

She took the piece of grass from her teeth and tossed it aside. 'Don't matter,' she said. 'Rain's coming.'

'I don't think it will rain,' he said confidently, glancing at the sky.

'Look ... ' She pointed to some clover where they sat. 'See how them little leaves are closing up?'

Joseph peered at the clover and back at her. 'No.'

She shook her head and leaned back. 'What do you know, you aren't from here. You can't read the grass.'

He pulled a stalk of timothy and twirled it between his fingers. His head was near her lap, and he leaned over and tapped her on the wrist. After a few seconds she glanced down at him.

'What are you doing?'

'This is how you test a wire,' he explained.

'With a piece of grass?'

'Yes. It goes through the grass so you don't get stung too badly.' He tapped her wrist again and worked his way up her forearm.

'I'm not a wire,' she said.

'But you are alive, aren't you?' He looked up and grinned. She could smell the odor of his scalp. Just then the dog barked and looked down the field with her ears pressed forward. They could hear something screaming far away. Emily craned her head and listened a moment.

'What is it?' Joseph asked.

'Sounds like one of the goats.'

'The goats?'

'One's due any day now.'

They listened a moment longer. The sound was far off, and then it stopped. Sheila circled and sat once more, and Emily leaned back against the tree.

'It sounds like a person screaming,' Joseph said.

'It's her first time.' She shrugged.

'What do you do with these goats?' he asked.

'Not much. We got them when I was young,' she explained. 'My father saved this fellow's life in the mine by pushing him away from a mule cart, and the fellow gave him a goat as thanks.'

'A goat?'

'He was Italian,' she explained.

Joseph pursed his lips and nodded.

'That goat used to follow me round all the time, so we kept it. Then one day my father took me to the coal camp to get a billy so we could at least have some milk.'

'And?'

'Well,' she continued, 'the man who was selling it had a son who I became friends with. His name was Gianni. He worked in the mines, too. So we got the billy and brought it home, and from then on we had goats. People thought we were crazy, 'cause no one keeps goats round here. But it became a thing of pride with my father.'

'And this boy Gianni. What happened to him?'

Emily looked down at the grass and said nothing for a long time.

'He died, too,' she said. 'In the mine.'

'I'm sorry,' he said.

'Yes, I was, too,' she sighed and fell silent. After a moment she stood and flattened her dress.

'Well, it's fixin' to rain,' she said. 'We ought to get moving.' She held her hand out to help him up. Joseph looked at the sky and back at her. A breeze was beginning to feather from the south.

'I don't think it will rain,' he said.

'Well, I do,' she said. 'And I'm not sticking around for it, neither.'

He stuck the piece of timothy between his lips. 'As you wish.' He shrugged, and grabbed his crutch and pulled himself up. They walked along the ridge together, through the hawkweed and vetch, Sheila leading the way, looking back occasionally to see they were following.

'Tell me about New York,' she finally said.

'What's there to tell?'

'There must be something.'

'Well, there is no grass to read,' he said.

'No grass?'

'No,' he said. 'Just people. So many people, in winter they sleep in the streets.'

'In the cold?'

Joseph nodded.

'Nobody takes them in?'

'No.'

Emily stopped and shook her head. 'I don't believe that.'

Joseph shrugged. 'Why would I make it up?'

They came to the alcove of spruces. The branches soughed backward in the wind, and needles were sailing through the air. On the other side, they were out in the pasture again and the cows had lain in the clover. Joseph stood a moment and watched the wind harrow the hillside, and they heard the screaming again in the hollow.

'It sounds bad,' he said.

'They do that.' She shrugged. 'So what else about New York?'

He thought a moment. The goat was still screaming; it sounded as though someone were being tortured. He took the grass from his mouth.

'There are trains that run under the earth. People enter them in the morning to get to work and take them back home in the evening.'

'Like a mantrap.'

'What's that?'

'Like they have in the mines.'

'I don't know,' Joseph said. 'The subway goes very fast, though. There are stops all over the city.'

'A city with underground trains?'

'Yes,' he said. 'Many people work there, some selling newspapers, roasting potatoes, shining shoes. It's like a village under earth.'

'I'd like to see that.'

'It is very dirty,' he said.

They came to the woods and began climbing toward the house, picking their way slowly down the path. The sky had suddenly turned a dark, tenebrous green, and Emily glanced back at Joseph but said nothing. They heard the goat screaming again. The trees swished back and forth like brooms, and the smell of rain came from the road below. They made their way into the hollow and down to the pasture, and the cries of the goat grew louder.

'Do you hear it?' she asked.

'The goat?'

'No.' She made a face. 'The rain.'

He stopped and listened. The wind snapped around them; some leaves galloped out of the woods and flew past as if possessed. They could hear the rain like a waterfall rushing up the hollow.

'I don't hear a thing,' he grinned.

She rolled her eyes. 'Come on, hop-along,' she said. 'We're almost in it.'

They hurried toward the creek, the wind flapping. A scroll of Emily's hair lifted like a kite string, and her dress flew around her. She held it down with one arm and tried to help Joseph across with the other, but he slipped on the last boulder and had to grip her waist to keep from falling. He excused himself and turned red, but the first drops had reached them and they ran toward the barn for shelter.

When they'd gotten under the eaves they were out of breath, laughing, their clothes slightly damp. The smell of hay rose around them. The rain fell in a curtain from the roof, and the goat was hollering inside. Emily said she'd better go check on it, and he hobbled after her into the darkened interior.

It took a few seconds for his eyes to adjust, and when they did he saw Emily beside a black goat.

'Damn, Nanny,' she said. 'Why now, when I got my good clothes on?'

The goat was bleating, her back legs spread apart, and strings of blood and striffen were oozing from her rear. Two tiny black hooves, shiny as glass, stuck out of her birth canal, and the tissue around them was pink and swollen.

Emily bunched her hair in a knot, grabbed a milking stool, and sat astride the goat and tried to calm her.

'You go ahead to the house,' she yelled to Joseph, and turned back to the goat. 'Calm, Nanny, calm down.'

She was stroking the goat's stomach, talking to her in soothing tones. The goat arched her back and thrashed her head on the ground. Her kid had gotten stuck in the birth canal, but Emily didn't know how long it had been there. She knew the kid wouldn't have long to live once it had entered, and she tried to calculate backward, wondering how long it had been since they'd first heard the screams on the pasture.

Emily lubricated her hand in the rill of blood, talking to the goat the entire time. She looked behind and saw Joseph but said nothing. Then she gripped one arm across the goat's chest and slipped her other hand up the cervix. She followed the contour of the tiny leg, pushing her way inside, fingers first, then knuckles, easing up into the uterus, concentrating the whole time with her eyes closed. She felt the kid's fetlock, the knee, the forearm, then the tiny blade of its shoulder, and she pushed deeper, the warm fluid enveloping her wrist, her arm, and she worked her way along the small chest and found what she was looking for. The kid's neck was twisted backward, its head deflected off the brim of Nanny's pelvis, and that's where it had gotten caught, just as she had suspected.

Emily breathed deeply. The goat bellowed, kicked it's leg, and slashed open Emily's shin.

'Hush, Nanny,' Emily said, and gripped the goat tighter to her chest. 'I just got to turn its head around, okay?' She braced herself astride the goat again. Barn flies were landing on her face and neck. Joseph stood back, helpless. Emily regripped the goat's chest and held it tight against her body, and with her other hand she pushed deeper into the uterus so Nanny screamed anew. She found the kid's jaw floating in the viscous cavity and cupped it with her palm like a mask, then gently eased it forward, over the pelvic bone, back in line with the rest of its body. Then she waited a moment and slowly withdrew her hand, inching it out of the canal so her arm came out glassy and streaked with blood and afterbirth. Her fingers made a small suck as they left the goat.

Her face was bathed now in perspiration, her arm steaming with flies. Joseph had retreated to the shadows. The rain gusted on the roof. Nanny screamed again. Then the two hooves started to move, and Emily clutched them in her hands and pulled down gently as they emerged.

'Come on, Nanny, push!' she said. 'Push!'

The hooves emerged, then the fetlock, the black forearms, the contractions working. 'Push, girl,' she whispered. 'Push!'

The black nose appeared, the closed eyes, the ears and head, and then the chest slipped out, soaked in striffen; finally the whole body popped out and dove through the air. Emily wiped mucus from its mouth. The kid stood on the ground a moment, wobbly, its fur steaming, entombed in its own liquid, then it folded its legs and dropped into a ball on the dirt floor.

Nanny twisted around and licked its nose and mouth. Emily helped wipe liquid from its face. Then she stood back and watched one eye unstick and then the other. Joseph emerged from the shadows and stepped toward her.

'Can I — '

'Just stand there,' she said without turning. 'I'll be a minute.'

She dried the kid with a clump of hay. The flies hissed in a cloud overhead, the rain drummed steadily on the roof.

'I need to get iodine from the house,' she said. 'I'm sorry it had to happen today.'

Her arm was still glistening with afterbirth. Joseph stepped to her and went to touch her arm, but she shot it in the air out of reach.

'Don't!' she yelled.

'It's all right,' he said, 'I want to.'

She stared at him a moment in bewilderment, then slowly brought down her arm and he touched it with two fingers, wiping the blood, and he stared at the fluid on his fingers. Emily shook her head and walked to the barn door and rinsed her arms in a rain barrel, splashed her face and washed the cut on her shin. Joseph was watching her, the field a sheet of silver behind. She leaned out the door and caught rainwater in her mouth. Then she brought over a bucket of water and checked Nanny. She was breathing evenly, the kid curled beside her on hay. A barn swallow flew in from outdoors and circled above them. She piled more hay around the kid and stood to go.

They headed back through the rain, Joseph gripping the crutch, hopping on one leg, squinting through scaffolds of rain. He crossed the creek first and stopped on the other side and watched her. She was lifting her dress with one hand. The water had clammed the fabric along her hips and her hair was down and the cold had raised her nipples through the cotton so he could see them; and as she came toward him he wanted to touch her, to move the wet strands from her face, to taste the salt on her neck, the sweat above her lip, to embrace her. Instead he stood blocking her path, staring dully at her face.

'You were right,' he shouted.

She held up her hair and looked at him as if he were crazy.

'What?' she asked.

'About the rain. You were right. You can read the grass.'

The rain was sucking his clothes, too, his

shoulders and clavicle, the white singlet plastered to his skin so his chest hairs showed beneath like a nest of sticks. She wanted to get out of the downpour, but he wouldn't move. Then he stepped to her and his mouth was on hers, and she didn't resist. She was tired, his mouth warm and inviting. Her fingers seemed to move of their own accord, seeking the back of his neck and holding him to her, pushing him tighter to her chest, before she pulled away and stared at him a moment, slightly stunned but happy.

And then they were both sprinting back to the house, hunched through the downpour, she in front and he hobbling behind, faster and more agile than either thought imaginable.

15

He left the following week in a company truck. He wore a blue chambray shirt and a stiff new pair of blue overalls the company had sent over. When he came to say good-bye, he stood awkwardly on the porch, shuffling from boot to boot, avoiding her eyes. One of his crewmates was waiting in the truck. Then, before she knew it, he was off the porch and the truck door slammed. The engine groaned down the road, but she didn't turn to wave. She recalled the first time the electric men had arrived years earlier in a similar truck, with gold lettering and the lightning bolt. The specter of Robert Daniels rose in her head, and she sighed and entered the house.

The parlor lay empty, Delmar's shirts folded in a neat pile. Ada retreated to her room, and Emily went to her own and shut the door behind. The house seemed unearthly silent. She sat on the apron of the window and stuck a hand to the glass. When she took it away the imprint stayed behind, five fingers in the pane, waving out the window like a ghost.

Two nights later she woke to tapping and knew it was Joseph. She went to the window and pushed the sash and saw him standing in the moonlight, a canvas haversack on his shoulders.

'Joseph,' she whispered.

He stepped to the window and cupped a hand to the screen.

'What are you doing?' she asked.

'I want to show you something,' he whispered.

'Right now?'

He ran a hand through his hair and grinned.

When she came out of the house, he was waiting on the porch, leaning against the balusters, the haversack at his feet. She fingered hair behind her ear and nodded to his leg.

'How's the leg?'

'I can't complain,' he said. 'It got me here okay.'

'And the work?'

'The work?' He shrugged. 'It's not the same.'

'The same as what?'

'Before.'

'I expect you miss laying about in bed.'

He smiled and leaned against the railing, and they both looked at a raft of clouds just edging over the mountains.

'You want to sit?' she asked.

'No,' he said, 'I wanted to show you this thing. It's up there.' He pointed toward Keeny's Knob. 'It's one of the towers.'

She looked at him quizzically. 'A tower?'

'You told me you want to see far. You can see the whole horizon from the tower, and the view is very excellent. So, will you come?'

'At this hour?'

'It's best at night.' He grinned.

She looked in the direction of the towers but could see only the dark silhouette of the knob, high-crested and humpbacked like a wave shaped against the night.

'You're crazy,' she said.

'No, I'm serious.'

'Like I said, you're crazy.'

'Please,' he said, 'trust me.'

'Why should I?'

'Why shouldn't you?' He shrugged.

Emily laughed. 'I can think of a few reasons.' She stepped to the door and opened it a crack and stood in the instep. She looked at the knob again. A tissue of cloud covered the moon like a film of milk.

'Wait here,' she said, and entered the house. In her room she pulled on a wool skirt, a cardigan. She felt slightly giddy, like a schoolgirl, tying her shoes. Outside, Joseph was waiting, the dog now by his side. They lit off into the pasture. A breeze blew the smell of horses from the bottoms. The grass wet her ankles. They came to the fence line and entered the woods, and by the time they reached the towers, the moon had slipped from its clouds and the hills lay lacquered in a clear blue light. Joseph removed a metal canteen and handed it to Emily. The water was cold and tasted of tin, and she peered up at the tower.

'I don't know,' she said, 'it looks pretty damn high.'

She handed back the canteen.

'It is perfectly safe,' he said. 'You'll be strapped in a bosun's swing. All you have to do is sit and I pulley you up.'

He screwed the cap on the canteen, hooked it to his haversack, and began removing a leather harness and a lanyard. She watched as he set to work, tying a hitch and doubling it back over a D-ring on the harness. His singlet looked alabaster in the moon. When he was done he stood and held the harness out to her.

'So,' he said. 'Are you ready?'

She glanced at the tower again. The beams raked steeply into the night, and a bat was flitting between the bars. She pulled her hair back, tucked it behind her sweater, and let him wrap the harness around her waist. She could smell his perspiration, and she closed her eyes. When he was done he led her to the center of the tower, where a flimsy-looking bosun's swing hung by a rope.

'You sure about this?' she asked.

'Trust me.' He held open the canvas swing, and she climbed into it and gripped the ropes at her side.

'How's it feel?'

'Tight,' she said.

'Good.'

He explained that she'd go through an opening in a wooden platform near the top of the tower. The crew kept the platform for when they strung the cables. He told her when she reached the platform she should shout down for him to stop pulling. She tried to pay attention but kept looking up where the ropes disappeared like silver strands into the night. Each time she looked, she felt a little queasy.

'Okay,' he said. 'You understand?'

'I go through the opening, and then what?'

'You yell,' he said. 'Then I stop pulling and you wait for me to climb up.'

She nodded and looked at the tower once more. The bat was still flitting between girders. Joseph latched her safety to a ring on the swing and tested it. He removed a pair of gloves from his back pocket and pulled them on. Then he grabbed the tag line and doubled it around his waist.

'Ready?'

'Wait! What do I yell when I get up there?'

He smiled and winked. 'Whatever you want to.' He reached for the rope and yanked it down with all his weight.

When she lifted off the ground, she screamed. She hadn't meant to, but the swing twirled and she gripped the ropes tighter to her side. The dog was barking, Joseph hauling hand over hand. Then, as if suddenly weightless, she shot into the night and the crossbeams whirred by and the tower tapered close to her sides. Her stomach flew into her mouth. The treetops fell away. The land lowered below and the platform dropped into view, and she shouted at the top of her lungs. The rope stopped abruptly so she hung suspended, swerving, the swing rocking from side to side.

The dog was barking far off now. The wind lifted her hair. On the horizon some lights seemed to shimmer in a haze. She felt light-headed and slightly sick, surrounded by so much air.

A minute later Joseph came clanging up

the step bolts, and she could feel the tower vibrate with his movements. He swung one arm over the platform and then a leg, and it made her dizzy just to watch.

'Careful!' she shouted.

He stepped toward her, grinning, and took the ropes in his hands.

'Hold on.' He drew her toward his side and unhooked her safety. She didn't want to let go of the rope. She felt safer in the swing.

'Grab on to me,' he said.

'I don't like this.'

'Just hold my arm.'

She gripped his forearm like a life preserver as he led her to the side of the platform, paid out her safety, and latched it to an X-brace.

'There,' he said, 'you're hooked in. You may sit now.'

'My legs are shaking.'

'They do that,' he said.

'I don't like it.'

'Come sit. You'll be fine.' He helped her down. The sky seemed to swirl with stars. She let go of him, cautiously, and sat holding both hands to the wood as if balancing on a raft. Over the lip of the platform the land lay chalked in moonlight, the ridges charcoal and blue. She inhaled deeply and saw the creek flashing far away like a rill of silver cupped between hills.

269

'Look — ' She pointed. 'There's the barn.'

'Yes,' he said.

'And there's the road. And that's the McClung place.'

'Yes.' He nodded.

'Everything looks so small.'

She tried to lean back, but her legs were still shaky. She could hear katydids susurrating in the treetops and the dog still barking below. Joseph uncinched his haversack and produced two apples. He unlatched his pocket knife and cut a piece from one and handed it to her, but she shook her head.

'I don't believe I could eat a thing up here.'

'As you wish.' He shrugged and stuck the apple in his mouth. A small breeze sprang from the valley. She glanced at the steel girders above.

'So this is where you work?'

'This and a hundred towers like it.' He rapped the platform with his knuckles.

'The tower belongs to you for a while.'

'For a short time.'

'And then what?'

'And then it belongs to someone else,' he said.

'The company,' she said.

'Yes.' He nodded. 'The company.'

'And then you move on.'

He didn't answer. He put down the knife

and the apple and leaned back on his hands.

'You ever afraid up here?' she asked.

He pursed his lips and shook his head. 'What's to be afraid of? Most of the time I feel safer here than on the ground. Even with the electricity in the cables, you always know what is going to happen up here. But on the ground, well . . . ' He smiled. 'Anything can happen there.'

'Really?' she said.

'Of course.' He nodded. 'The linemen, they have this expression. It goes: It is okay to be electrified but deathly to be grounded.'

'Deadly, you mean.'

'Yes, deadly.'

'What does that mean?'

'Well,' he explained, 'if a person is not contacted with the ground, electricity can go through him without hurting him too badly. But when a person has his feet on the ground the electricity will pass through him on its way to the earth, and boom, it will kill him.'

'Just like that?'

'Yes,' he said.

'And that's being grounded?'

'Yes.' He nodded. 'But they are meaning it in another way, too. The linemen, you see, they believe it is bad luck to stay in one place for too long. It is in fact, how do you say, a superstition. You see, when a lineman has

271

built one thousand miles of power line, he must quit his job wherever he is, whatever the season, and he must go and travel for some time before returning to work again. The linemen believe if you keep at any job past one thousand miles, it brings bad luck.'

'Is that so?' she said. 'And you believe this?'

He thrust out his lower lip. 'Do I believe it? Well . . . ' She could see he was grinning. 'Not exactly.'

'So you're not afraid of staying in one place too long?'

He shook his head slowly and stared at her, and she looked over the platform and sighed.

'Well, I certainly am. I been sticking around this holler my whole life, and I'm afraid I might never leave.'

'Where would you go?' he asked.

'Hell, anywhere,' she said.

'Anywhere?'

'This is a dead place,' she said. 'Only thing a dead place is good for is dying in.'

'I see,' Joseph said, and looked out over the platform. Emily felt sad all of a sudden, as if she'd spoken some terrible truth and had ruined the party. The moon lay on the horizon, and she watched it sink into the hills and the clouds become marbled in gold. Below, the katydids drilled in the trees. Joseph wiped his knife on his pants leg and closed the blade. He inched closer and draped his arms over his knees.

'You know what happens,' he said, 'when you are grounded and electricity passes through you?'

Emily shook her head.

'It is a very messy thing,' he explained. 'You see, electricity is always trying to get back into the earth wherever it is, in a wire or in the heavens or in one of these towers, and it will use anything to get there. It will pass through a tree or the air or even through a person and use them like a bridge to get back into the ground. When it goes through a person, it goes in through their arm or the top of their head, and on the way toward the ground, the electricity runs through the heart. You know what that means?'

'You die?' she ventured.

'Not always.' He shook his head. 'Sometimes it just makes the heart skip.'

'Skip?'

'Yes,' he said. 'Even small amounts of electricity can do it. There is a word for it, ventricular fibrillation.'

'Sounds dangerous,' she said.

'It is.' He raised an eyebrow. 'It can cause derangement of the heart.' He was staring at her, the wind shaking the curls around his face. She could smell his warm, appley breath, so close, and the words *ventricular fibrillation* kept quivering in her ear like a moth. She felt dizzy all of a sudden, her legs shaky. He leaned toward her, but she turned aside and shut her eyes. When she opened them again she touched the cold ring on her harness.

'Well, I think I've seen far enough,' she said.

'You want to get down now?' he asked.

'Yes. It's late. I should be getting home.'

Joseph sighed. He rocked onto his ankles and stretched, then he began packing his haversack, and she watched him out of the corner of her eye. The moon was gone and the night lay blackened around them, and his arms flashed faintly as he worked.

'When do you reach your thousand miles?' she asked.

'Soon,' he said.

'So you keep track, don't you?'

'Of course.' He shrugged. 'We all do.'

'I thought you didn't believe in it.'

'I don't,' he said, 'but what's wrong with keeping track?' He winked at her and went back to packing his bag.

'Where will you go when you reach a thousand miles?'

'Who should know?' he said. 'One place or another. I could stay here and do maintenance work. They always need some linemen to watch after a new line.' He looked at her significantly, then yanked the cinch string of his haversack, and put out a hand to help her up.

★ ★ ★

When she reached the ground again her legs felt tingly. The earth seemed to sway as if she'd been on a boat. The dog kept leaping at her, and she tried to shoo it away. She unbuckled her harness and stepped out of it, then fingered the new holes he'd punched in the leather so it would fit her. He was already reeling in the ropes.

'You set all this up for me,' she said, 'didn't you, beforehand. Even the belt.'

He didn't answer. He was flaking the rope evenly around his elbow. Emily stepped toward him.

'How'd you know I'd come?' she asked.

Joseph shrugged. 'I didn't.'

She took his wrist and he stopped reeling the rope, and she kissed him on the mouth and stepped back.

'Thanks,' she said, and kissed him again. 'I have to go now.'

'Wait. Let me walk you back.'

'It's okay,' she said.

'You can't go alone.'

'I always have.' She was already moving

away, the dog bounding in front. He tried to get the rope off his elbow, but she could see he was tangled in it.

'Come by Sunday,' she yelled. 'Okay?'

'Wait,' he shouted.

'Around noon. Okay?'

'Yes,' she heard him shout. 'Okay.'

She waved once more but could no longer see him. Her legs felt sturdy once more, the air bracing. She began to jog, the dog leaping alongside her, as they sprinted down into the darkened woods.

16

Sunday, she waited for him at noon in the barn while she milked the goats. She wore her lemon dress and black rubber boots, her hair piled above with bobby pins. The day was hot. Barn flies swirled on her arms as she squeezed udders lazily, one at a time, the milk hissing in the bottom of a wooden bucket. She wasn't surprised when she heard him behind and felt his hands slip over her eyes.

'Afternoon,' she said, and kept milking, the squirts a lower pitch in the bucket.

Joseph took his hands from her face and laid them tentatively on her shoulders. She finished with the goat, opened the slat, and slapped it away. His face was freshly shaven, half-moons of sweat stained his shirt beneath the arms. She dipped a finger in the goat milk and drew a line of cream across his cheek.

'You look nice,' she said. 'Come, I want to show you something.'

He followed her through the pasture, her boots making sucking sounds. The grasshoppers parted in waves. She left her boots on the porch and held the screen for him. The house was cool inside, the curtains drawn.

She took his hand and led him barefoot to her bedroom and shut the door behind.

'Where's your mother?' he asked.

Emily didn't answer. She went to the window, pulled the curtains closed, and came back and stood in front of him. She took his coat and threw it across a chair and fingered a strand of hair from her cheek.

'She's gone,' she said. 'She's gone all day.'

Joseph started to say something, but she placed her forefinger to his lips.

'Take off your shirt,' she whispered.

He raised an eyebrow. Emily nodded. Her finger was still touching his lip. He looked down at his shirt and back at her.

'Go on.' She nodded.

He began to say something, but she pressed her finger hard against his mouth, then circled his upper lip, and the lower, and took her hand away. He began slipping buttons through holes, uncertainly, watching her the entire time, one button and then the other, until the front of his shirt hung open and she could see the dark nest of hairs on his chest.

A fly buzzed around them. She put a hand inside his shirt and ran her palm over his chest down to the flat of his stomach, then stuck her fingers into the waistband of his pants. She could feel the curled hairs, the moist heat of his pelvis. The sun was flitting through curtains; the clock clapped in the hall. She pulled out her hand, undid the last wooden button of his pants, and stepped back.

'Take them off,' she said.

Joseph glanced nervously at the door.

'Don't worry, she's not coming back until nightfall.'

He took a step toward her, but Emily stepped back.

'Go on.' She nodded. 'You first.'

He bit his lip and attempted a laugh. The fly landed on his arm, but he didn't wave it away. He slipped one suspender strap off his shoulder, then the other so they dropped to his hips. Then he pushed his pants down so they fell around his ankles. She stepped back and inspected his boxer shorts, his black knee socks, the short muscled legs, his penis already lifting through his underwear.

She waited a moment, still staring. Then she shook her hair free, bunched it above her head, and turned her back to him.

'Unbutton me,' she said.

He didn't hesitate. He slipped the horn buttons gently through their fabric hoops. She could feel his hands shaking slightly, his breath shortened on her neck. She closed her eyes. She was sweating, her mouth dry, her arms quivering. When he undid the last button she felt him spread her dress open and press his palm into the small of her back, and run his hand up her spine. She shut her eyes tighter and let the dress slip from her shoulders to the floor. She was naked underneath. She turned and stood before him, her nipples risen and her hair down, and she took his wrist and led him to the bed. She lay in the cool sheets and he crawled into bed and they made love hurriedly, awkwardly, in the heat of the afternoon, with the hot air coming through the curtains.

They listened after to the wind washing in the trees. A cuckoo clucked in the forest. The curtains lifted and fell. Joseph pulled off his undershorts and boots and lay back naked next to her. She traced a finger over his face, down his nose, across his lips, which parted as she passed them. He hiked his head on one elbow and took her hand and held it upward, above their bodies, and their arms stayed there, twining and untwining around each other, hers pale against his brown, and they watched wordlessly as if their limbs had taken on a life of their own. He pulled her arm down and pinned it above her on the pillow and kissed the ginger hairs of her armpit; then he entered her again, soundlessly, her eyes still focused on the place where their arms had been, until they narrowed and her lids closed, and he made love to her once again, this time slower and gentler and more relaxed, with no sound but the bedsprings and their foreshortened breath.

When they woke the bed was damp, the sheets tangled on the floor. A strip of gold lay on the opposite wall where the sun skirted through. Joseph reached down and brought a sheet over his back and covered them together as if in a tarpaulin.

'You're my tepee,' she said.

'Tepee?' he asked.

'Tent,' she said, and kissed him.

'*Palatkee*,' he said.

'What's that?'

'A tent, in Russian.'

'*Pa-lat-kee*,' she repeated, and put a finger to his lips. 'What are these?'

'In Russian?'

'Yes.'

'*Goobah*.'

She laughed and said, '*Goobah*,' and moved her hand to his nose. 'And this?'

'*Noss*,' he said. 'Like the English.'

She reached down and wrapped her fingers around his penis. 'And this?' she asked.

'*Putz*' — he grinned — 'in Yiddish.'

'*Putz*,' she repeated.

'That's right.' He laughed. 'It is not such a

nice word to call someone.'

She put her lips to his ear and whispered: '*Putz.*'

Joseph smiled.

'*Putz,*' she said again.

'Shhh,' he said. 'Enough already.'

'*Putz,*' she said.

She let go of him and he lay back, staring at the ceiling.

'Do you know how long I have dreamed of this?' he said.

'Of what?'

'This here with you.'

Emily shook her head.

'Since I first came here,' he said.

'Uh-huh. You were unconscious then,' she said.

'So? I could still dream.'

'I doubt it,' she said, and ran a hand through his hair, and laid her head on his chest. She felt light-headed and empty, as if she didn't weigh a thing. She could hear his heart beating, the wind in the trees outside. A dog barked somewhere far away, as if in another world. She rose on an elbow and started to say something but stopped. She thought she heard a noise outside. She lifted her head and turned toward the door.

'What is it?' he asked.

'I don't know,' she whispered. She listened

again. Joseph was silent. She heard a sound on the porch and froze, and then a screen door banged.

Joseph threw back the sheet, leapt from the bed, found his trousers, and fought them on.

'Quiet,' she hissed.

'Ada . . . Emee . . . ,' someone was yelling in the house.

It was Garvin. She put a finger to her mouth and glared at Joseph.

'Shhh!' she whispered. 'Be quiet.'

She could hear footsteps now in the house, the boards creaking in the other room. Joseph was standing rigid in the corner behind the door, his shirt unbuttoned, his trousers half on. A cupboard shut in the kitchen, then she heard Garvin moving about the parlor.

She lay still in the bed, the sheet pulled over her. The footsteps creaked. They waited, and then the screen door banged again, and the house fell silent. She didn't move. Joseph stood, panting quietly. The curtains lifted and sucked against the screen, and they waited another minute, staring at each other across the room.

'I think he's gone,' she finally whispered.

Joseph closed his eyes, and his shoulders slumped. Emily crawled out of bed and crept naked to the window and peered outside and moved quickly to the wall.

'He's in the garden,' she whispered.

Joseph joined her, crouching below the sill, keeping the curtain drawn. Garvin was walking among the rows, his hounds sniffing behind him.

'What's he doing?' Joseph whispered.

'How should I know?'

They watched as Garvin picked a tomato from a plant and bit into it, then he reached down for a cucumber, twisted it from the vine, and stuffed it in his shirt pocket.

'Hmm,' Joseph said. 'A cucumber thief.'

Garvin took another bite of tomato, then turned and opened his fly to piss.

Emily put her back to the wall and covered her mouth.

'I can't believe it!' she said. 'Right in the damn garden!' She turned back to look. One of the hounds trotted over, sniffed at the spot, and lifted a leg and peed. Garvin finished and buttoned and wandered off to the side of the house where they lost sight of him. They waited another few minutes before Emily stood.

'I think he's gone,' she said.

Joseph went to the bed and collapsed on the mattress. Emily took a last look out the window, then came to the bed and stretched. She stood over him, bunching hair above her head.

'You shoulda seen your face,' she said. 'You were white as a sheet.' She began to giggle.

'It's not funny,' he said.

'You looked like you were gonna pass out . . . '

'It's not funny.'

'You looked like a damn corpse.'

She was in hysterics now, bent over, naked, laughing. He took her arm and pulled her back down on the bed and pinned her to the mattress and kissed her neck. She was flushed, her face red, and they laughed until they made love once more; and when they roused again the afternoon was growing old, the room filled with a rose light, and mourning doves were making their small sounds from the eaves.

They left the house after through the back door. The heat had broken, and swallows were swooping over the field. They wandered up to the woods in a daze, the smell of each other on their hands. They held each other again while the sky burned red and the trees flamed, and they went on, into the higher wood, as evening came down like a curtain.

PART III

17

In the days that followed, she waited each week to see him. She met him Sunday mornings on the road below the house or beside Lick Creek or at the Crossroads beside Laird's store. He'd arrive some days with a bouquet of flowers he'd picked along the way, blue asters and Queen Anne's lace, bird's-foot trefoil, or boneset, or sprigs of hoary mountain mint. Sometimes he'd come with a drawing scrolled in his pocket, a pencil sketch he'd done from the top of a tower, or a portrait of himself. They'd pass the day in some secluded spot, in the covert of the woods or down the gravel road to the mine, choosing their places carefully so as not to be found. They'd lie under an amethyst sky, fingers twisted together, and they'd part in the lingering dusk until the following week, when they'd join each other again.

It seemed a new chapter had begun in her life, one filled with rich and uncertain possibilities. She began to pay attention to her clothes, her shoes, her hair. She began to take languorous naps in the late afternoons. For the first time in her life she craved carrots,

289

turnips, radishes, anything that rooted underground and tasted of earth; she'd eat them raw or half-cooked while her mother looked on with growing concern. Ada, for her part, tried to bring up the topic of Joseph several times, but Emily refused to talk about him. For beneath her excitement, her newfound joy, lurked a nervousness, a nagging suspicion that anything could go wrong, just as it had with Gianni, and to talk about Joseph, to even mention his existence, was to risk some terrible disaster.

As for Joseph, he went about his week on the towers as if he carried a secret in his pocket, something alive and burning, an ember he'd take out from time to time and breathe on to see it still aglow. He thought of Emily all the time. He had a hundred pictures of her in his head. He loved the stories she told him, all with a poker face: how if you suckled on a sow you could see the wind; or if you ate nine minnows, you'd cure a toothache; or if you were lost and found a daddy longlegs, he'd point your way back home.

No sooner had the crew quit work Saturday afternoons than he'd hurry back to camp, rub himself with castor soap, blacken his boots with motor grease, and hitch a ride to Talcat or Lick Creek, where she'd be waiting in the twilight. Sundays he'd do the same, and Monday mornings he'd drag himself to the towers half-asleep and find her hairs still clinging to his clothing, long reddish strands he'd tie into tiny bow knots and stick inside the bib of his overalls as keepsakes.

* * *

One Saturday during lunchtime he was napping against a packing crate. The crew had been stringing cable all morning, and they rested in the shade with their caps crammed low over their faces and their lunch boxes strewn at their sides. Clement Veerd, the elder groundman, was telling anyone who'd listen that all great empires from the ancient Incas onward were built on the foundation of caffeine, whether from the tea leaf or the coffee bean, it was all the same. He took a quaff of coffee from an oversize mug and held it above his head.

'Here's to the brew!' he shouted. 'The building block of our days and the juice of civilization!'

Ratliff opened one eye and stared across at Veerd. 'You want to know what the real juice of civilization is?'

'What?' Veerd said challengingly.

'Poontang.'

Veerd lowered his mug. 'How would you know?'

Ratliff nodded toward the packing crate. 'Go ask Joe,' he said. 'He can tell you.'

The crew looked up from their hats and a few snickered. Ratliff squirted saliva between his teeth and flashed an enormous grin. 'Ain't that right, son?' he said.

Joseph felt his face redden but said nothing. Hager meanwhile walked up behind and said if they were done with the bullshit, it was time to get back to work.

★   ★   ★

By late afternoon Joseph stood on the topmost section of a dead-end tower. The sun was glimmering on the New River hundreds of feet below, and Baird and Ratliff were working on the crossarms just beneath him. They'd already attached one aluminum cable to the chain of insulators at the end of the tower's crossarm and were working on the second cable on the opposite arm. Joseph, who was on signal, had to watch the lead rope carry the new cable from one tower to the next. The winch lay half a mile ahead across the river, where it pulled the lead rope, which drew the cable out of its enormous spool a mile behind. Joseph had to send a signal at just the right moment to the relay man on top of the next tower, and that man, in turn, passed the signal to the winchman half a mile ahead. If Joseph timed it perfectly, the lead rope passed through a wooden block at the end of the crossarm, but the delicate aluminum cable that it carried stopped within inches of the butt of the block.

The afternoon was clear and windless, the clouds the color of oats. The river flashed turquoise in its gorge. Baird hung on a ladder suspended below the crossarm; Ratliff perched on the makeshift platform jutted off the crossarm's end. A heavy chain of insulator hung beside Baird like a stack of enormous plates four feet high. And as the signals were given, Joseph watched the lead rope bob and jerk and the cable inch across the span. The rope slithered upward into the groove of the block and turned black with grease. Yet before Joseph had a chance to signal, the rope stopped on its own accord and the aluminum cable hung bobbing several feet shy of the tower like a strand of wayward tinsel. He heard the winch motor die in the distance, and Ratliff and Baird looked up from their perch below.

'What happened?' Ratliff shouted.

Joseph shrugged and peered across the

gorge to the next tower. He sent a sign that they needed more cable and watched the signalman on the next tower send the same sign along. A minute later the signal came back that there wasn't any more cable to give.

'They've run out of line,' he yelled to the others.

'Shit,' Ratliff shouted, and yanked off his gloves. 'Looks like the goddamn engineers fucked us again. I bet the reel's done run empty.'

Baird hooked an elbow over a ladder rung, pushed back his motor cap, and eyed the aluminum cable. It was suspended just beyond reach of the porcelain insulators.

'How much off you think it is?' he asked.

'About the size of my goddamn pecker,' Ratliff shouted.

'What, two inches?'

'Nah.' Ratliff spat. 'More like two feet.'

Joseph shook his head and descended to the nearest cross-beam. Baird craned his head upward.

'How far's it look to you?' he shouted.

'Why don't you give it a try,' Joseph said. 'It's better than waiting here.'

'Why don't *you* give it a goddamn try,' Ratliff yelled.

Joseph shrugged. Baird tightened the gathers of his gloves. Ratliff readied himself on the platform above, holding a heavy steel joint pin with which to make the hookup. Baird grabbed the insulators over his left shoulder, leaned out, and tried to muscle the porcelain stack upward so the eye hook at their end would line with an eye hook at the end of the cable.

'Forget it,' Ratliff shouted. 'It's too goddamn far.'

Baird eased back, the weight of the insulators pushing him against the ladder. Ratliff yelled to the groundmen that they needed a good foot or more, and the groundmen sent a runner with the message. Joseph sat again on the crossbeam and watched the groundmen scurry below at the foot of the tower and the river beyond glinting in the gorge. A breeze lifted the odor of pine to the tower. Some turkey buzzards tilted on updrafts; he watched the birds awhile, then lay back on a beam. The steel was warm through his shirt, the breeze light. He could hear the clink of wrenches from time to time, and fragments of Baird and Ratliff's conversation floating up to him, but he wasn't listening. He was thinking of Emily, how he wished she were there beside him, on the tower, with the view of the river and the sun on the beams and the buzzards lifting like paper kites above the gorge.

Ten minutes later the message returned by runner that the winch was up to nine hundred pounds and the winchman would give them one thousand pounds but no more. Joseph elbowed up and yawned. The turkey buzzards circled closer. He rubbed his eyes and shouted to Ratliff and Baird: 'Come on, let's get the damn thing over.'

Ratliff yelled to the runner that they'd take the thousand pounds and sweat for the rest, and Joseph ascended to his position. In another few minutes the signal came from the forward tower to ready.

'They're going to do it,' Joseph shouted.

Ratliff scrambled down the ladder this time and changed positions with Baird. Joseph peered into the lowering sun. When he saw the signal he shouted, 'They're rolling!'

The lead rope jerked to life. The motor droned half a mile ahead. The rope inched slowly through the wooden block, and the cable rose behind it. The block tensed and leaned with the strain. The sun dropped out of a cloud and bathed the tower in an orange glow so Joseph had to hold a hand over his eyes to mark the distance. The tower groaned with the increasing pounds of pressure, and the cable reddened in the light as it rose to the tower, a curve of metal lifting upward, filament-like, glassine. Ratliff was ready with the insulators held above his head, and Baird was shouting, 'Come on, come on . . . A little more . . . Come on.'

Finally Baird yelled, 'Now!' and Ratliff swung out with all his weight to reach the cable. He held himself nearly horizontal against the ladder, hooked only by his safety, the veins of his neck bulging, arms twitching. Three feet above Baird shouted, 'A little more! A little more!'

'Come on, you son of a bitch!' Ratliff yelled, and heaved with all his strength. Joseph saw the eyeholes line, and Baird shoved the joint pin home, and they heard the metallic clink as it caught. Joseph shot an arm in the air as the signal to cut the winch. Ratliff released the insulators, and they flew upward into a horizontal position, strumming violently like an enormous plucked string. Joseph sent the signal again to cut the winch, but the winch was still droning in the distance, the lead rope still pulling on the cable even though it was attached now to the tower. He sent the sign again and again with increasing urgency, yet the rope kept pulling onward, the cable stretching, the insulators moving upward. Then a hot, sickly feeling came over him as he realized something was wrong, that the message wasn't getting through, that they weren't cutting the winch.

He heard Baird shouting below, 'Cut the fucker! Cut the fucker!' And he started shouting, too, 'Shut the motor! Shut the motor!' But the lead rope kept pulling on the cable so it stretched the insulators beyond their capacity. Then the tower began to creak ominously, and the block stood completely erect. He heard a metallic groan like a ship keeling over. The rope began to fray below. Someone shouted, 'Hit the deck!' and he threw himself flat against a beam. The rope was ripping outward, pinging off the tower in ever-increasing violence. He heard a crack like a bullwhip above, and the block shot into the air and a burst of blood exploded over the gorge where the buzzards had been.

And just as soon there was silence. A dead calm, with only the creaking of the insulators on their kingpin and the river flushing softly in the gorge. The winch motor died in the distance, and Joseph pushed himself up warily and peered below. Baird and Ratliff were clinging to beams. The groundmen lay flat on the earth. Above the gorge some feathers floated and a pink mist fell where the buzzards had been. Joseph rose to his knees.

'Are you all right?' he shouted below.

Baird raised one hand in response. Ratliff cursed and began climbing the ladder. Joseph flicked sweat from his eyebrow and saw the cable still attached, the insulators holding as if nothing had happened.

They all converged in the middle of the tower on the makeshift platform on the third section and said nothing for some time. The sun was sinking now into the horizon, the afternoon gone gold. The two new cables looked like strands of molten glass stretched to each arm of the tower.

'I'd like to wring the neck of that goddamn engineer,' Ratliff finally said.

'And the winchman,' Baird added.

A breeze kicked up from the gorge. The evening was coming on. Then each of them spat off the tower and watched their saliva angle to the earth. Three white dots going down. Joseph shrugged and walked to the step leg first. He was suddenly eager to get off the tower, to see Emily again, to have his feet planted firmly on soil.

18

She was waiting for him later that evening beside the cattle gate. She heard his boots scraping gravel before he materialized on the road in a fresh chambray shirt and a pair of dungarees. She took his hand in hers and led him to the high pasture. The air was cool now; the wind pushed leaves past her feet. They entered a field of stars and stood in the center of its ink as the night pressed around them, the constellations canted above. Joseph was about to say something when she put a finger to her lips.

'Don't talk,' she said.

'What is it?'

'Just watch.'

They heard cows moving in the pitch, then saw them emerge, slow and cautious, sniffing air, drifting up as silent as smoke. One craned its head toward Joseph, huffed hot air on his shirt, and licked his wrist. He turned to Emily in alarm.

'What is it?' he asked.

'Salt,' she explained. 'They like the salt.'

He turned to the cow. He could see only the whites of its eyes and one glassy iris. It slobbered on his arm again, and Emily tried not to laugh.

'Had enough?' she asked.

'I think so.'

She raised a hand, and the cow jerked backward. Then she waved her arms and the whole herd thundered down the pasture.

Afterward they sat in the grass, and Emily pulled her hair above her head. She was studying Joseph with a contemplative look.

'Your electric line will be done soon, won't it?' she asked.

'A few weeks,' he nodded.

'And then?'

'And then they'll turn the power on.'

He pulled a piece of grass from the ground and twirled it in his hands. 'The company,' he said, 'they're having a big celebration when it's all done at some hotel. And then, well . . . I'll have to find another job.' He smiled at her, but she didn't smile back. A barred owl was hooting downhollow.

'There's a chance,' he went on, 'I could find work close to here. They still might need someone to do maintenance work. Who knows? The work is not that exciting, but I could find out anyways if . . . if you think I should.'

He glanced at her, yet she didn't respond, then he tossed the piece of grass aside.

'So what do you think?' he asked.

'About what?'

'Me working close to here.'

'Hell, it's your decision,' she said.

'Yes, I suppose it is,' he sighed. The katydids pulsed loudly in the trees. The cows had disappeared from view. She wasn't going to ask him to stay; if he wanted to, he just would.

'Anyway,' he said, 'I wanted to tell you about this company dinner. Actually, it's an inauguration ball for the new electric line. They've invited our entire crew, and we may bring a guest. I wanted to ask if you'd come.'

'It's at a hotel?' she asked.

'Yes.'

'Near here?'

'I believe so.'

'It's probably the Roncevert,' she muttered.

'Yes, I think that's the place.'

'Oh,' she said, and felt something collapse inside her. She hadn't thought of the Roncevert in weeks. Neither had she thought of Robert Daniels, and the mere mention of the hotel made her heart race.

'What's the matter?' he asked.

'Nothing.'

'Tell me.'

'It's nothing,' she insisted. She laid her head on her knees and sat without speaking.

A breeze sent the smell of cows up the pasture.

'You know that man Daniels I once asked you about?' she ventured.

'Yes.'

'Will he be at this dinner?'

'You know him, don't you.'

'Yes.' She nodded. 'He showed up right after my father and brother died, just before they started building the electric line. He came in one of your company trucks like he owned the place. He bought that right-of-way for your line, and . . . ' She looked down at her hands.

'And?' Joseph prompted.

'Well' — she shrugged — 'he kindly showed an interest.'

'An interest?'

'In me.'

Joseph let out a dry laugh. 'I am not at all surprised.' He smirked.

'No?'

'No. He is always trying to get one girl or another. They say he's a real ladies' man. You know what the men call him?'

She shook her head. She wished she'd never brought it up.

'They call him the Don Juan,' Joseph said. 'Daniels the Don Juan.'

'Oh,' she whispered, and felt her face

redden in the dark. Joseph was chuckling to himself, leaning back on his arms. She pulled the cardigan to her neck. She wanted, suddenly, to be left alone.

'So,' he said. 'Whatever happened with this Mr. Daniels?'

'Nothing,' she muttered.

'Really?'

'Yes.'

'And that's all?'

She nodded and looked sideways into the night. A star streaked overhead and died, but she didn't point it out. She felt completely deflated, as if someone had kicked her in the ribs. The name *Don Juan* kept buzzing in her ear. If only she could just tell Joseph and be over with it. If only she'd told him, weeks ago, months ago, it wouldn't have been that bad. Yet it was too late now, and he'd never understand besides.

Joseph laid a hand on her shoulder and began to massage her neck through her dress.

'So,' he said, 'you'll let me know about this dinner. I think we may have fun there, okay?'

She swallowed and managed a nod. He pulled her close so his mouth rested beside her ear. She thought of Daniels again, the Don Juan, the ladies' man. The owl hooted once more in the night. She felt Joseph's hands around her stomach, his breath warm on her scalp. Yet he seemed suddenly an impostor, someone she hardly knew, and she wanted him to leave now. She wished that night, for the first time ever, that he had never come.

★ ★ ★

Later, after they'd parted on the road, she wandered the pasture alone. The night seemed different now, cold, autumnal, the wind restless. A harvest moon was blooming in the east, and the first leaves of the year whispered in the grass. She wrapped her arms around her chest and felt chilled and confused. She realized the whole time Joseph had been in the house, she'd willed away the memory of Robert Daniels and the Roncevert Hotel. She'd buried her feelings underground like a bottle of cider on a basement shelf, and there they had fermented and grown more complex. But now, with the simple mention of the hotel, she found herself bubbling over with all the old angers and confusion, distilled now but as virulent as ever.

She paced up the porch in a trance. She realized it wasn't only Daniels bothering her, but Joseph, too, for soon he'd be gone just the same. He hadn't really asked to stay; he wanted *her* to make the decision, and she certainly wasn't going to beg. Perhaps it was too much to expect of any man, that they would want to stay, for all of them had abandoned her in the end, even Delmar and Gianni, even her own father. It was much easier to be left alone, to be angry, to hope for nothing — especially from a man.

She entered the house in a daze. The rooms lay darkened, the fire undone in the stove. She seemed suddenly uncertain of everything: her future, Joseph Gershon, and now this inauguration ball. What would she tell Joseph? How could she begin to explain?

She didn't bother to undress but crawled into the cold sheets and pulled a quilt on top. Her breath was sour and there was no trace of Joseph anywhere, no odor, no article of clothes, not even a gift to remember him by. And this is what it will be like, she thought, once he's gone.

★   ★   ★

She passed a night of terrifying dreams, dreams she could hardly remember. There was a man in a clown face in one, a golden fish in another, a wheel of fortune, and a crib filled with coal. Sometime in the early hours she dreamed her whole life had been a river whose waters ran to the sea, and she saw the

306

ocean flashing before her like a knife.

She woke with the taste of chalk on her tongue. It seemed she'd been asleep for many years, and she didn't know what day it was, what month, what season. It seemed the old days right after the mine exploded had returned and Joseph was just a dream she'd had one fleeting night, and she doubted he'd ever come into her life at all.

She jerked on a pair of pants and dressed quickly. Her head throbbed, and she felt slightly feverish. She passed through the parlor and left the house. Rain was falling over the hollow, the laundry drenched on the line, the bench of earth across the way so familiar that it seemed the frame and prison of her life, and a panic rode through her like a flame.

She fled toward the creek and found herself staring into water. She recalled something her grandmother had said about an augur, a way of telling, a hand run over the water, how you could see your future there; and she knelt on a brown boulder and placed a palm above the riffles. She saw nothing but gray creekwater, her palm empty, and she stood and walked on. She kicked along a goat path toward Garvin's, the trail stamped with hoofprints, a kind of cuneiform in the mud. She passed ancient harrows, rusted, overgrown with grass, old iron buggy frames, ribbed and skeletonized, wheels lashed with bindweed. Between the multiflora roses, spiders had woven their webs like doilies in the rain.

Garvin's hounds caught her scent uphollow. She turned to head back but heard him hushing them and continued on. His cabin stood at the head of the hollow, two stories of chestnut logs, crumbled chinking, a rusted tin roof unpainted for as long as she could remember. The cabin had been her grandmother's old homeplace, her father's childhood home, and as she came up the road it hailed into view, smoke chuffing from the chimney, and Garvin stood on the hardpack, shotgun in hand, peering into the rain.

'Hey,' she yelled.

'Emee?' he shouted.

A black goat regarded her curiously from the top of a chicken coop. A set of makeshift kennels lay hammered from scrap wood, and in front of each a hound strained and snapped at its chains. Garvin set the gun in a nook above the door. He wore a faded red sweater with patches at the elbows, leather braces loose at his hips. It was eight in the morning, but he already smelled of corn liquor.

'You want coffee?' he asked. 'I'm just makin' her.'

'No thanks,' she said. 'I'm out for a walk.'

He looked at her sideways. 'Aw, come on, Emee, looks like you could use a drop.' He raised both eyebrows and shot her a knowing glance. 'I ain't gonna take no for an answer.'

'Well . . . '

'Come on.' He nodded her into the house. The hall was dark and redolent of cat urine, a rag rug faded colorless. In the kitchen the stove smoked and the linoleum was blackened beyond recognition. He gestured her to a table strewn with dirtied dishes.

'Go on and make yourself comfortable, I'm just gettin' her built.'

She unbuttoned her slicker and paced uneasily beside unglazed panes. Outside, rain paddled the leaves of a lilac bush.

'You're in trouble, ain't you,' Garvin said from the stove. He was feeding a log into the grate.

'What makes you say that?'

'Only time you come round's when troubles chasin' you.'

'You don't exactly put out the welcome mat,' she said.

'You know you're always welcome, Emee.'

He stood and nodded at her feet. 'You're goin' to wear a rut in them floorboards,' he said. 'Go on and sit.'

She pulled out a chair. A glass salt shaker

sat on the table with a rusted cap, a guttered candle stub in a sardine tin. Garvin was shuffling about the kitchen, and she wondered why she'd come. Finally he set two chipped teacups on the table, wiped their insides with the tail of his shirt, and sat.

'So,' he said. 'How you keepin'?'

'All right, I expect.'

'What's the trouble?'

'There isn't any,' she said.

'How's that electric boy a yours?'

'Fine,' she said, and tried to change the subject. 'You selling much moonshine these days?'

His face turned suddenly serious. 'Whose askin'?'

'No one,' she said. 'I'm just wondering.'

'A right smart amount, I reckon.'

'What if I wanted a bottle?' she asked.

He raised an eyebrow. 'Things that bad?'

'I'm just asking.'

An orange cat leapt on the table and circled stiff-tailed around Garvin. She studied her uncle's face, his bushed and graying eyebrows, his unshaven cheeks. She could see the vague resemblance to her father, the pale blue eyes, the lines around his mouth; but her father had been far more handsome. Garvin grabbed the cat off the table and dropped it on the floor. Then he put his hands on his knees and regarded Emily from his chair.

'You sure you ain't in trouble now?'

'Yes,' she protested. 'I'm sure.'

The kettle began to whistle, and he raised himself to the stove. When he came back he tipped coffee evenly in the cups and poured some in a saucer on the floor, and the cat ran to it.

'Goddamn cat nearly drains me a coffee,' he muttered, and set the kettle on an iron trivet. 'You wantin' sugar?'

'No thanks.'

'Milk?'

She shook her head.

'Good, 'cause I ain't got neither.' He winked at her and sat heavily in the chair. The sun broke weakly through the windowpanes, and she watched the coffee swirl and helix in the light. They sat for a moment not speaking, the cat making little lapping sounds in the bowl. The coffee was strong and tasted of chicory. She began to relax for the first time since the day before.

'Emee,' he finally said, 'I ever tell you why your daddy went to the mine and not me?'

'Nope.'

'Your daddy ever tell you?'

She took the cup from her mouth. 'I always figured because you thought it beneath you.'

Garvin made a face and shook his head.

'That ain't the real reason,' he said, and sipped some more and looked out the window. 'See, your daddy and me were only a year and a half apart in age. One of us was supposed to leave the homeplace. Seeing as I was the youngest, your daddy went to work the mine first. I was supposed to be the one who let out of this place. They were wantin' to send me to school, but I didn't hold with the schooling, and neither did I with the mine. So I left. I ran that store down yonder at the Crossroads for a while, what's Laird's now.'

'I know,' Emily said.

'And then I come back and tried raising cattle here.'

'I know that, too. And then you tried pigs for a while,' she said.

Garvin smiled. 'Yes, ma'am, hogs, then sheep, then rabbits. But it all went to the bad. The land was of no account for the cattle, and the hogs and sheep, well, I reckon as I wasn't much at raising things, that was always your mother's side. For me, there wasn't a thing else but the makings and some ginsenging and what else with trappin' and such. The mines, well, you know the way I felt about those that run 'em, but it wasn't that, either.'

He looked across at her, one eyebrow

raised, then lowered his gaze to his cup.

'See, I wanted to work the mines just like your daddy and your granddaddy,' he continued, 'but there was a problem.' He shook his head and screwed up one eye, then took a sip of coffee and put it down again.

'When I was a boy, see, I went down there into one of them little old caves. I was with your daddy and granddaddy, and it was all fine at first. We was in about near twenty, thirty yards, and the tunnel got right small so you couldn't stand up, and then something happened inside me. I felt all light-headed and fuzzy, and then I couldn't move like my limbs were a-frozen. Your daddy and grand-daddy kept on goin' until they saw I wasn't there, and they turned on back and found me standing in the middle of that tunnel, a-shivering and shakin' like a hickory leaf, and they wondering at me what-all's wrong. I told 'em nothing at first and tried my damnedest to get goin', but I just couldn't. Each time I went to move in that tunnel I like to get all spun round dizzier'n a pill bug, and my legs just done shut down on me. They had to haul me out directly, hollerin' and a-cussin', and it done take a full day so as not to feel sick. The only ones who knew about it was your daddy and granddaddy, and I reckon your grandmama, too. Your daddy, well, he was such a tight-lipped son of a bitch, he didn't say nothing after, but I still swore him never to tell no one what happened. And you know what? He never done tell no one, and he never mentioned it again. Only thing he ever said was, 'Garvin just don't hold with the mines,' that's all he'd say. Am I right?'

'Yes, Garvin,' Emily said. 'He'd say that.'

'You see?' He shook his head and bit his lip.

'I never did tell a soul afterwards. You're probably the first I'm telling since. I went down to the doctor in Beckley, and he's the one who done told me what was the matter with me. Said I got the claustrophobias and there was nothin' I could do about it. Said I better hunt down some other occupation, or leastways stay outta the mines.'

Garvin took another sip and sat nursing his cup. He looked at Emily.

'Well, after the mine blew' — he shook his head — 'I couldn't help but think, and I still can't help it, that it oughta been me down in that hole that day and not your daddy. I know as you don't need to be hearin' it, but I need to tell it 'cause it's been burnin' me up ever since. It shoulda been me down there, what with him havin' the family and all. I just wanted to tell someone, and I'm sorry,' he said. 'I'm sorry it had to be you. It just shoulda been me. That's all.'

He chewed his lip and his cheek twitched a little, and she could see his eyes had gone moist. She exhaled and put her cup on the table.

'Hell, Garvin,' she said, 'it's not your fault.'

'I know it,' he said. 'But that don't make no difference.'

She shook her head and looked out the window. The rain was coming down again, the lilac leaves padding back and forth. The room had grown warm, and she felt sad and weary all of a sudden. Garvin leaned back in contemplation. Then he placed his hands behind his head and studied her from his chair.

'So, Emee . . . ' He managed a smile. 'You gonna tell me what the matter is now?'

'I told you already,' she said. 'Not a thing.'

He regarded her with one raised eyebrow. 'Well, if you ain't gonna tell me what's wrong, whyn't you tell me about that electric boy?'

Emily shrugged. 'There ain't much to tell.'

'He treat you right?'

She nodded.

'He do right by you?'

'Yes, Garvin.'

'Well, I'd be careful with them electric boys.'

'He's a lineman, Uncle.'

'Whatever he is. They're traveling types. Tinkers. I'd know their skin on a bush. You're likely to get yourself a shock.'

She shook her head. 'He's all right.'

'He might be all right, but I still won't trust 'em. Where's he from, anyways?'

'Russia.'

'He's a Russian?'

'No,' she said, 'a Jew.'

'A Hebrew . . . ' Garvin raised both eyebrows and picked up the kettle. 'Never knew one I liked.' He poured more coffee into Emily's cup. 'Never did know one, though,' he said, and grinned so his front teeth showed.

One of the dogs started barking outside. Garvin went to the window and peered out, and the dog stopped barking. He came back to the table and yawned.

'Well,' he said. 'Finish that up. I want to show you something.'

She looked at him curiously; there was a strange expression on his face.

'Go on,' he said.

She swigged the coffee and followed him through the hall. Outside, the rain was falling harder and they huddled around back to the root cellar. Garvin fished a key from under the eaves, unlocked a heavy rusted chain, and opened a batten door. Emily followed into darkness.

It smelled damp and yeasty. Garvin was lighting candles, one and another. When her eyes adjusted she could make out shelves of bottles and glass jugs, each labeled as if in an apothecary's office. In the candlelight the jars glowed and the liquid inside seemed lambent and gold. Garvin had gone to the corner, where he lit two more candles, and she saw the spent drippings from decades of candle stubs, frozen midfall and spread white and gleaming over the floor.

Garvin disappeared into a corner and came back with a cigar box, brushed off the top, and handed it to Emily.

'I've been meanin' to give you this for some time. It was your daddy's, all that's in there, he left in the homeplace.'

The box was gritted with dirt, streaked where Garvin's fingers had been. She held it a moment tentatively, judging its weight, then she stepped to a candle and opened the cover. She could see some marbles inside, cobalts, cat's eyes, a glass daguerreotype, script coins with holes punched in their center. There was a deck of playing cards tied with pastry string, a guitar plectrum, a jasper arrowhead. She picked up the daguerreotype and held the plate to a candle and saw a man with a

317

brush mustache and broad-brimmed hat.

'That'd be your grandfather' — Garvin nodded — 'you never did know him.'

She laid the plate back in the box and shut the cover. 'Please,' she said, 'you keep it.'

'No, ma'am,' he said. 'I've been keeping that thing long enough, it's time someone took it away.'

He shook his head again. His face looked sunken in the candlelight. She didn't want the box or what it contained. It was just another burden, a coffin full of dead things. Garvin was already blowing out candles. She felt a cold shiver as the lights extinguished around her, and she started, unsteadily, toward the door.

19

For the next few days she couldn't sleep at night. It wasn't Garvin's story that kept her awake or the cigar box she'd shoved beneath her bed. Instead she lay awake thinking about Robert Daniels and the Roncevert Hotel. Joseph, meanwhile, had begun working weekends for the final push at finishing the line. They'd meet after his work some nights for a few moments on the right-of-way, or beside a packing crate, or beneath a certain tower. Yet something had changed, in her and not him, and the less she saw him, the more desultory and unsatisfying their lovemaking became. During the days she moped around the hollow, listless, unmoored, adrift in a fog of her own.

October began. The nights turned cold in Lick Creek. In the evenings she'd hear the haunting of owls in the twilight. She'd stop dead in her tracks on her way to the outhouse or shutting the chickens and believe they were telling her that she would be alone, that this was the way her life would be. Just as puffballs turned to powder in fall, Joseph, too, would soon be gone.

* ★ ★

One Sunday she sat with him on the concrete anchor of a tower, their feet dangling over the edge. It was late afternoon, and an orange sun was sinking into treetops. He asked her about the inaugural ball again. It was two weeks away now, and he wanted an answer. He reached into his coat and drew out a piece of white linen folded in a neat triangle.

'Open it,' he said.

'What is it?'

'Go on' — he gestured — 'it's for you.'

She found inside a necklace, a silver chain with three stones spaced in the center. She held the chain to the sun and the stones glowed yellow, translucent, like kernels of old corn.

'What are they?' she asked.

'Amber,' he said, and pushed her hair to the side, took the necklace, and attached the latch. The chain was cold on her nape. He turned her by the shoulders to examine her. He was grinning hugely, pleased with himself, proud of her. She closed her eyes; she felt suddenly like crying, though she couldn't say why.

'They look wonderful,' he whispered. 'You will be the belle of the ball.'

A breeze shivered the curls of his hair; the

sun made a marmalade in the branches. She didn't know what to say. She hadn't the heart to disappoint him. She put a hand to her neck and felt the beads against her collarbone.

'So?' he asked.

'What?' she whispered.

'Would you like to go, to the dinner?'

She sighed and looked over the darkening hills. She felt defeated, blunt, a knife with no edge. How bad could the ball be, anyhow?

'All right.' She shrugged. She told him that she'd go.

★   ★   ★

The next morning she lay in bed, listening to goldfinches, wondering why she'd agreed to go. The morning was warm, the sun shredding through curtains, the finches chattering outside in a maple tree. In the outhouse she sat a Sears, Roebuck catalog across her knees and studied women in organdy and evening gowns of silk and taffeta. She hadn't paid the catalog much attention before, and half the pages had been tossed into the hole, but that morning she scrutinized women in khaki riding suits and coats of Poiret twill and flapper dresses of crepe de chine. She peered into the mirror on the door back, bunched her hair, and pictured herself suited in a gown of silk or chiffon, with a string of pearls cinched around her neck. Perhaps the ball wouldn't be so bad after all, she thought. Perhaps her mother could design a dress just like the ones in the catalog, with tiers of sheer fabric or oyster buttons in the back, and maybe even Daniels wouldn't recognize her.

Later that day she confessed to her mother about the ball and handed her the catalog. Ada was skeptical at first as she studied the illustrations. But slowly, page by page, she warmed to the idea of making a dress. She would get to sew again, at any rate, and the notion of stitching a dress for something as glamorous as an inauguration ball had its own appeal. Over the course of the following week Ada threw herself into the project with gathering force, ordering fabric at Laird's, setting up shop at the kitchen table, consulting with neighbors, piecing, pinning, and sewing while Emily looked on, anxious, unsure of what she'd started. It seemed some strange surgery was afoot and the dress itself was the one going to the ball and not her, which suited Emily just fine. Yet when the final stitch was sewn and the fabric ironed and the dress held on a hanger, Emily was crestfallen. The crepe de chine looked shabby, the stitching crude, the hemline longer than she'd wanted. To make matters worse, her mother had sewn a silk rosette along the waist of the dress — right below the heart — without even asking her. To Emily's eyes the rosette looked absurd, like a tissue someone had blown their nose in. Yet there was nothing she could do. The dress was already made. She'd already agreed to go.

Finally the day arrived. Ada rose early and built a fire in the parlor. A cold rain sifted over the hollow. Emily retreated to her room at noon, lit a table lamp, lowered the wick, and pinned her hair fastidiously in the glass. She felt like a schoolgirl before a class play who hadn't learned her lines and didn't even know what part she was meant to play. What if Daniels recognized her after all? What if they had to sit at the same table? What would she say to Joseph?

At three she pulled on a white garter and hose and climbed into the dress. Ada kept barging in with powder, lipstick, a bottle of old perfume, and Emily hadn't the will to resist. At four she stretched a pair of cotton gloves to her elbows and fastened Joseph's stones around her neck. Resignedly she inspected herself in the mirror. She looked ridiculous, she thought, like some city woman or someone trying to dress like one, and the lipstick made her look like a harlot. Minutes later she heard an engine outside and saw Joseph climbing out of a company truck. She felt something hot and lumpy inside her chest, like bread beginning to rise.

They drove through a drizzle down the Lick Creek Road, Joseph in a tuxedo, hair pushed to one side, shoes as shiny as glass. In White Sulfur the gas lamps glowed in their mantles, and a mist was falling in the streets. Guests wrapped in raincoats hurried toward the hotel. Her heart raced as they pulled into the drive and the guard in an olive uniform waved them on. Trees swung in the headlights; the hotel came into view. And she remembered it all then as if it were yesterday, the white columns and the hotel kitchen, the boxwood hedges and the statue of Hebe where she used to meet him. She remembered the crowds on the lawn and the band in Prussian blue outfits playing Sousa. And the events of that afternoon came back like a picture at a penny arcade: She saw a bar with a piano, a bottle of rum. She saw an office with maps on the walls and velvet curtains, a chair covered with chintz. Her hands began to heat up in her gloves. The lights on the dashboard swam like minnows. Why had she ever agreed to come? She felt a wave of nausea rise in her throat and thought she might get sick.

When she caught her breath she heard music. Faint strains of stringed instruments, light, fluttery, floating on the night. Joseph was holding the truck door open.

'Are you all right?' he asked.

'Fine.' She swallowed.

'You don't look so good.'

'I'm fine,' she repeated, and tried to smile. He helped her from the truck. She seemed better standing on the ground, but her legs felt shaky on their heels.

A minute later she was staring into a lobby filled with people, men in tuxedos, women in glittering gowns, some with stoles or minks or Russian furs wrapped around their shoulders. It seemed everyone was watching her. She felt exposed and underdressed. She scanned the room for Daniels, certain he was somewhere in the crowd. She wished she'd cut her hair or worn a head scarf or a hat, anything so he wouldn't recognize her.

They passed into a sea of cigar smoke and ladies' perfume. A blond woman was cackling, an egg-size ruby bouncing on her breast. Someone in the crowd had dressed as a lightning bolt. Another had come as Zeus. The Lightning Bolt wore a silver suit with a papier-mâché head also painted silver. He pranced from one person to the next, shaking hands, bowing, swinging his lightning bolt head so others had to leap out of the way.

She clutched Joseph's elbow through the throng. Everyone seemed to be talking at once. They entered an enormous ballroom where the lights were lower and couples were turning on a polished parquet. Waiters in white hip coats drifted this way and that. Some carried lighted candles, others trays of hors d'oeuvres. She felt Joseph's breath on her ear.

'Can I get you something to drink?' he shouted.

'Yes.' She nodded. 'Please.'

'Wait here. I'll try to find something.'

He squeezed her elbow and pushed into the crowd. She shrank to the nearest wall. She couldn't believe she was back in the hotel. She was sure Daniels was somewhere near, that any moment he might pop out of the crowd like a jack-in-the-box, and she wanted to spot him first. She searched the stage at the front of the room. A dais bristled with blue-and-white bunting. A banner hung with the company logo, and at the sides of the stage stood two ten-foot replicas of steel electric towers.

Out of the corner of her eye she caught sight of a tall man in a cream-colored tuxedo. He was leaning against the stage with a woman in a saffron dress. He blew cigarette smoke above his head, and Emily felt her chest go small. But just then the ballroom lights went dark and a drumroll thundered from the orchestra. A spotlight swung onto the dance floor, and the Lightning Bolt began a wild dance.

She lost sight of Daniels just as quickly as she'd found him. Her heart was pumping. She felt instantly hot and sweaty. She fought her gloves off finger by finger and shoved them in her purse. The Lightning Bolt was doing flips on the dance floor. Someone touched her elbow, and she nearly leapt. It was Joseph behind her, holding two crystals of punch.

'Jesus,' she muttered, 'you scared me.' She grabbed one of the drinks and jerked it toward her mouth. The punch was iced and sweet. Joseph was looking at her gravely.

'What's wrong?' he asked.

'Nothing,' she chirped. She tilted back the glass and finished her drink.

'Come,' he said. 'I found our seats.'

He took her arm and steered her through the crush of people. She watched a white balloon float to the ceiling; she watched a woman twist a tube of lipstick and press it to her mouth. The orchestra ended its tune, and people began drifting toward tables. She kept searching the room for Daniels, but he was nowhere to be found.

The linemen were all seated around one table at the far corner of the ballroom. Some had come with dates, but most hadn't, and they all stood as Emily approached. She recognized the Italian brothers, the foreman, the redhead named Baird, yet in their tuxedos they all looked somewhat similar. One of them was talking about lobsters, another about a power line over Lake Pontchartrain. She tried to concentrate on the conversations but couldn't. Joseph leaned over and touched her on the wrist.

'I see your friend's here,' he whispered.

'Who?'

'Mr. Daniels.' He nodded toward the dais.

She peered into the stage lights and saw Daniels sitting to one side of the dais, and she suddenly felt lightheaded again. She couldn't believe she'd missed him, that he was right there, in plain view, stockier than she'd remembered, his hair combed back, his forehead shiny beneath the stage lights. Joseph laid an arm around her chair and was about to say something when a bald man with a monocle rose to the podium and held up a hand for silence.

'Good evening, ladies and gentlemen,' he began, and the microphone buzzed. The ballroom hushed. The man welcomed the company employees, the politicians, the investors and stockholders present. He spoke about the history of the power company and about its growth. He spoke of the completion of the electric line. Then he talked of its inauguration and the lighting ceremonies planned for the following week.

'In just a minute,' he continued, 'we will get under way with our keynote address. I want to take a moment to congratulate all of you on being part of the Appalachian Light and Power family. And now it's time to enjoy your dinner.'

He smiled and waved from the podium, and the orchestra began a minuet. A steady stream of waiters issued into the room, wearing white gloves and carrying silver trays. The appetizer was served, hearts of palm in a mayonnaise sauce. A clear consommé followed. Then the main course arrived: a London broil with potato croquettes, boiled carrots, and sprigs of flowering thyme on the side. Emily hardly ate. She pushed her food around her plate and kept an eye on the dais. Daniels had already finished his meal and was talking to the man on his left. She saw him surveying the room, waving at certain people, waving toward her table. She thought she was imagining it at first but hazarded another glance and saw Hager, the foreman, standing and waving back.

Her heart began to thud. Daniels was strolling off the dais. Perhaps he was coming over to say hello. Perhaps he was coming to greet the crew. She stuck her napkin on the table and stood.

'I'll be right back,' she whispered. She didn't hear Joseph behind her. She was already moving past tables, past people eating, drinking, laughing. The exit seemed so far. The violins squealed in her ears. She wished she could just disappear into the crowd.

She rushed through the ballroom into the empty hall and searched for the ladies' room. She hurried one way but couldn't find it and headed back the way she came. Yet when she looked up she saw Daniels; he was standing in front of her with a broad grin on his face.

'Violet!' he said, and the hallway grew blurry, the chandeliers swooned. She saw a bed of fabric before her, thick and white, like a mattress of silk. She saw a hand on a windowpane, a trilobite, an annelid etched in trap. She'd forgotten about the name, the frilly hat, the tulle fan. A name from another lifetime. She'd forgotten about his odor, too, the smell like a haircut, and she lifted her eyes and saw his white teeth flashing, his sandy hair, the heavy jaw, a blue primrose shaking in his lapel. He fished a cigarette from a silver case and looked at her ruefully.

'I can't believe it's actually you,' he said, tapping his cigarette. 'You know, I went to the fountain for days, searching for you, but you never returned. You just . . . disappeared.'

He fired the cigarette and wagged his head. The blood was thrumming in her ears. He seemed so familiar, so jovial, so upbeat, as if nothing ever happened between them.

'So . . . ' He waved smoke away. 'Who are you here with, Violet?'

She didn't answer. She stood staring at his blue primrose. She couldn't tell if he was pretending or genuinely happy to see her.

'That's not my name,' she said.

'Pardon me?'

'Violet,' she muttered.

He looked at her with a perplexed expression. 'I don't understand.'

'It doesn't matter,' she said.

'Well' — he smiled — 'so who's the lucky man?'

'No one,' she uttered.

'You're here alone?' He raised an eyebrow and glanced at her shoes. 'Well, you do look as lovely as ever. How long has it been?'

She curled her mouth into a sneer. She wanted to say: not long enough, or something about Don Juan or Daniels the ladies' man, but she couldn't think of any words. The sound of applause echoed out of the ballroom, and he looked distractedly down the hall.

'They're starting the speeches,' he said.

'Wonderful,' she said.

'I'm sorry, I'm supposed to be on the stage now.' He searched for a place to put out his cigarette. 'Maybe we can meet sometime?'

'Maybe,' she said with sarcasm.

'I'm serious. How about after dinner? I'd love to catch up. I still can't believe it's actually you!' He pulled his jacket sleeve and checked his wristwatch. 'How about eleven-thirty? Things should be winding down then. We could meet in my office for a few minutes.' He dropped his cigarette on the marble floor, tapped it with the toe of his shoe. 'Of course, if you have plans I understand, but if you could, I'm in room 312. The door is always open.'

She stared at him incredulously. She couldn't believe his confidence, or was it obliviousness? At the very least she couldn't believe he was actually asking to see her.

'Well, I've got to run.' He flashed her a smile. 'We'll see you later?' A burst of laughter erupted out of the ballroom. He leaned down quickly and pressed his mouth to hers. She was so shocked, so flummoxed, she couldn't move or speak, and before she could think, he was racing down the hall, his leather shoes squeaking against the marble.

She wiped her mouth over and over. A great perspiration overwhelmed her. She couldn't believe he'd actually kissed her, that she'd let him. She wanted to run after him and smash a fist in his face. She wanted to spit in his eye, punch him, kick him in the groin, but he'd already disappeared into the ballroom.

She turned and stomped down the hall, found the ladies' room, rushed into the first stall, and stood pacing like a penned animal. She was furious at herself for doing nothing, for saying nothing, for standing there like an idiot. She put her hands to the amber beads and wanted to tear them off and flush them down the toilet. She was suddenly furious at Joseph, too, for bringing her back to the hotel, for coming into her life in the first place. At least Daniels she could despise, not like Joseph, whom she'd foolishly fallen for, but who'd be gone just the same. She wished she'd never met him. She wished she'd never met a single man in her life. They were all such disappointments. The only good ones were the dead ones, who'd never leave her, who'd never disappoint, like Gianni and

Delmar, like her father.

She lowered the cover of the commode and sat. She wanted to crawl through some hole, some chasm, and disappear just as all of them had. She longed to be back home in Lick Creek, in her house, her bed, anywhere but in that hotel. She thought of Gianni, Gianni with his bombs and schemes, his pickax and shovel; Gianni with the mules whose legs were lashed together, braying as they bottomed into pits.

The sound of a toilet flushing broke her spell. A pair of heels ticked on the tiles. A faucet gushed. She shut her eyes and slumped against the stall divide. It would all be over soon, she told herself. Only a few more hours. A few more speeches. Then she'd never have to come back. She'd never have to see any of them again. She could say good-bye to Daniels, to Joseph, to the whole damn electric crew, and crawl back into her catacomb, her life, and be done with it. She took a long, deep breath and flattened her dress. She checked her stockings, her garter, then stepped out of the stall to the sinks.

* * *

Back in the ballroom, the chandeliers had been dimmed. A bearded man was speaking

334

from the podium. At each table candles flitted beneath faces. She found her table again, slipped into her chair, and turned distractedly to the stage.

'Ladies and gentlemen,' the speaker was saying, 'I foresee a future when electricity will flow into every artery of our great nation; when, at the flick of a switch, our electric will bring relief to millions of women and men and that simple switch, that miraculous knob, will become essential to the very functioning of our society. Men will heat their homes with it. Women will cook and clean with it. Electricity will be our lifeblood, and with it we'll be able to perform both the simplest and most amazing of tasks.'

Joseph leaned over and touched her knee. 'Where were you?' he asked.

'In the bathroom,' she said.

'This whole time?'

'Yes,' she whispered.

'You didn't do anything else?'

She looked at him with annoyance; he had an odd expression on his face. 'What do you mean?' she asked.

'I saw you.' He jerked his chin toward the dais. 'I saw you with your friend Mr. Daniels.'

'The housewife will want an electric oven and iron, an electric toaster, hair curler, and heater, and then a washer and wringer, and the farmer will want electric milkers, brooders, and canners.'

'So what were you doing with him?' Joseph asked.

'Nothing,' she muttered.

'It didn't look that way to me,' he chuckled.

She screwed her face up and glared at him. 'What's that supposed to mean?'

'It means I saw you kiss him,' he said.

'You saw me what?'

'Kiss him,' he repeated.

'*I say the time to strike is now, for when every home is hooked up, when electrical appliances become indispensable, our nation will hum with the sound of electricity, and I want ours to be the electric company the nation comes to depend on.*'

'Are you going to say anything?' Joseph asked.

'There's nothing to say,' she muttered.

'Then why did you kiss him?'

She rolled her eyes; she almost could laugh. First Daniels, now Joseph. She picked up her water glass, took a sip, and slammed it on the table.

'I didn't kiss him,' she seethed. 'And what do you care, anyhow? You're gonna hightail it out of here soon as your job's over, so what's it matter to you who kisses who?'

'Emily? . . . '

'That's right.' She raised her voice. 'And I don't care what the hell you do. You can reach your damn thousand miles and move on and go straight to hell as far as I'm concerned!'

She slumped in her seat and glowered at the stage. Some of the linemen looked over. She wanted to raise her dress at them, overturn her plate, pull the cloth from under the table. Give them all something to talk about. Joseph sat glumly, staring into space.

'Already our power lines run from Bar Harbor to Birmingham, Washington to Wichita, like a great spiderweb spreading across the nation. We've tapped the coal fields of their riches and harnessed the mightiest rivers and streams to feed the ever-expanding appetite of our growing cities and towns.'

'Listen,' Joseph whispered. 'I'm not running away. I want to stay with you. I don't care about the thousand miles. All I want to know is what happened between you and Daniels.'

Emily shook her head. 'It doesn't matter what happened.'

'It does to me.'

'Well, that's too bad,' she said, and crossed her arms.

'So you did go out with him, didn't you?'

'Leave me alone,' she said.

'Soon electricity will run from our outlets as easily as water from the tap. We will all be linked in a great gridwork, all of us operating at the same voltage and current. By bringing electricity to the people, we are like Prometheus of old, who brought fire to civilization. We bring our fire in the modern form of alternating current, and we carry it not in kindling, but in kilowatts.'

'I'm asking you one last time,' Joseph whispered. 'Just tell me what happened.'

'For Christ's sake,' she said.

'Why can't you just tell me?'

She closed her eyes. She wanted to scream. She twisted her napkin into a tourniquet.

'All right,' she said, 'you really want to know what happened? You really have to know?' She threw the napkin on the table and faced him. 'I went out with him, okay? The Don Juan took me out. He got me drunk. That's right. Daniels got me good and goddamn drunk and ... and ... ' She couldn't finish the sentence. She found herself choking on the words. She stopped and turned to the speaker.

'I leave you with this final thought,' he said. 'For years scientists have pondered the nature of electricity, yet the keenest minds, from Franklin to Edison, have never understood its essential mystery. Now, I am not a man of science, ladies and gentlemen, but one of business, so let me submit to you my own definition. Electricity to me is not a mystery, not some genie in a bottle. When administered properly and transmitted from tower to utility pole, it is, gentlemen, pure profits. It is money in the bank. It is quicksilver moving at the speed of light. And investing in it is investing in the strength of our nation, in profit and progress, and the greatest good of American democracy. Thank you, ladies and gentlemen. God bless you, and congratulations on being part of our bright electrical future!'

The audience burst into applause. The orchestra broke into a march. Joseph was still waiting, and she turned to him now in exhaustion.

'Okay . . . ' She swallowed. 'You want to know what happened? He took advantage.'

'Advantage?'

'Of me.' She nodded. 'He took advantage of me when I was drunk. Do you understand?' she asked. 'I was drunk. Daniels, the Don Juan, your boss's boss . . . he took advantage. I didn't even know. He pinned me down . . . he hit me. I was drunk. Do you understand what he did? Are you happy now? Do you understand? Does it make you feel better?'

She'd never spoken the words before, not even to herself, and now with them out in the air, it seemed suddenly so real, so awful, that she felt the weight of it crash around her and thought she might explode into tears.

She was shivering all over, her fists clenched. The Lightning Bolt had run onto the stage and held the speaker's hand aloft like a prizefighter's. She was aware of bright flashes, small explosions of blue popping on the parquet. Then she bolted from her seat and fled past tables. She didn't know where she was headed. She needed to get out. She pushed a man aside by the exit and dodged down the hall past one room and another, but in each there were people sitting on sofas, drinking from fluted glasses, putting on coats and hats. She felt as if she were in some underground cave, with brattices and gob piles and tunnels that trailed one way and another, but none seemed to lead out into the open. She needed a door, a window, a way of egress. She found herself at the foot of a staircase and began climbing as if for air. She took two risers at a time, up one flight and another, the banister hot in her hand, until she reached a landing where she couldn't hear the orchestra anymore, only her own blood hammering in her temples.

Before her lay a corridor, gloomily lit, with

a wine-colored carpet and crystal sconces on the walls. A window on her left looked out into the night, the lawn extinguished in darkness save for a gas lamp lighting a piece of sidewalk, a boxwood hedge, an iron bench. Then a chill went through her like a ghost over her grave, for she knew instantly it was Daniels's hall. She remembered the carpet, the doors, the small framed prints on the landing, and she felt herself choking with a rage she barely knew existed.

She stepped forward, impelled as if in a dream. She had a sudden need to go back there, to see his room, to see his office, now that she'd told Joseph, now that the secret was out, now that she'd breathed life back into it. A deep cavern opened before her, a limestone crypt. She searched the doors for some sign, a letter, a word, some indication of which was his. On a brass plaque she saw the numbers *312* and read the words *Appalachian Light and Power.* She grabbed the knob. Just as he'd said, the door was left open.

★ ★ ★

How long she stood in the threshold she couldn't tell. She saw a green-shaded lamp burning on a mahogany desk. She saw some colored maps on the wall, a telephone table, a red leather sofa. She saw French doors leading into another room, dark-stained cabinets with deco doors and the curtains, crimson, murrey-colored, like underripe eggplant. Then the memory of that afternoon flashed like a fish in a creek, half-seen, shimmering, naked, and she closed the door and strode to his desk. She jerked open the first drawer she found, rifled through papers, and flung them on the floor. She wanted to unhinge his life as hers had been unhinged. She wanted to overturn the furniture, tear down the maps, set the curtains ablaze, carbonize the place in a great conflagration, just as the mine had been burned, just as all of them had gone up in flames. She searched for matches, a lighter, a flare, anything to set a spark. She wrenched open more drawers and ransacked papers, keys, manila folders, canceled checks. Then she recalled the shelf where he kept his liquor bottles, and she remembered a wall safe as well, and she hurried across the floor. She tried one set of doors and another until she found the shelf, shoulder high, filled with bottles, decanters, soda bottles with siphons. The safe lay behind, the small lever, the shiny cylinder, the heavy plated hinges. She checked the lever, but it was locked, and she scanned the room, trying to recall where he might have kept the key. It seemed suddenly very important. It seemed her whole life depended on it. If she couldn't burn the place down, she could at least steal something, violate him as he had her, defile his office, his sanctum, his safe.

She rushed back to the desk and rummaged through drawers, found a large brass key ring. A clock chimed the quarter hour. She had fifteen minutes before he'd arrive. She shoved one key in the cylinder, but it didn't fit. She fumbled with a second, a third, a fourth. She heard a light tapping on the door and heard her name whispered, and saw Joseph cowering by the door.

'What the hell do you want!' she snapped.

He stepped inside quickly and closed the door. 'I followed you,' he said.

'Go away,' she muttered, and turned back to the safe.

'I came to apologize,' he said.

'It's too late for apologies.'

'Emily, please.'

'Go back to your damn ball.' She picked up the brass ring again. She'd lost track of which keys she'd already tried and had to start all over.

'Look,' he said, 'I'm sorry about all the questions. I had no right.'

'Go away,' she repeated.

He came to her side and put a hand on the shelf. 'What are you doing?'

She didn't answer but continued with the keys.

'Emily, I think this is a bad idea.'

'I don't care what you think.'

'Come now, you're being unreasonable.'

'Am I?' she snorted, and turned to him for the first time. 'This is the most reasonable thing I've done since the day I met you. At least now I might get something out of your damn company.'

She turned back to the safe.

'Come on. I said I'm sorry. I'll take you home.'

She didn't respond. She wished he'd just go. She had several more keys to try. A clock gonged on the desk, then an overhead light flicked on and they both turned and saw Daniels in the doorway, looking as surprised as they were.

'Hello,' he said. 'What's going on here?' He stared from one to the other. His jacket was hooked over a finger. He surveyed the mess on the floor, and Emily glanced quickly around the room.

'We're having a party,' she said.

'A party?' he repeated.

'Yes,' she said, and lifted a soda bottle with a siphon and smiled. The ring of keys accidentally fell to the rug.

Daniels stared uncertainly at Emily a moment. He seemed genuinely confused. Then he glanced at the keys on the floor.

'What are those?' He nodded.

She nudged the keys with the toe of her shoe and shrugged. 'Some keys, I reckon.'

He eyed them suspiciously and shot Joseph a glance. Emily felt an immense calm spread over her, like a sail luffing after the last breeze of a lingering storm. Daniels touched his bow tie. He laid his jacket carefully over a chair and considered the room. Then he started across the floor, and when he knelt to pick up the keys she could see the white of his scalp in the lamplight and the outline of his undershirt along his shoulder. She brought the bottle down with a stunning crash, and he staggered a step before falling flat on the floor.

Her whole body went limp. A warm sensation flooded her face. She felt hot and cold all at once. Daniels wasn't moving on the floor. She wasn't sure he was even breathing. A piece of his hair had fallen into his face, and she could see his cream-colored hose and his exposed ankles where his pants had risen up his legs.

Joseph knelt beside him, feeling for a pulse. Then he stood and grabbed her wrist.

'Come on, he's passed out, let's get out of here.' He tried to pull her away, but she was transfixed by the sight of Daniels, his pale ankles, his sunburned neck, his silk cummerbund immaculate and white. There was no blood, no cut, and he seemed almost peaceful, as if he'd decided to curl up on the rug and fall asleep.

She set the bottle on the floor beside him. Her hands were no longer shaking. She reached into his pants pocket and fished out a set of keys.

'What are you doing?' Joseph asked.

She didn't answer, but hurried back to the safe.

'Come on,' Joseph hissed, 'there isn't time.'

She tried one key and another. She was focused now, singular. The third one seemed the right size, and the cylinder clicked. She could hardly believe it herself.

She found paper documents inside, a book of blank checks, a black ledger, and two stacks of bills. They were ten-dollar notes, chalky to the touch, cinched in the center with green treasury paper. She stuffed one into her purse and reached for the other, but Joseph tried to close the safe.

'You shouldn't take that,' he protested.

She elbowed open the door and nodded toward Daniels. 'He owes it to me.'

'It's stealing.'

'And they've been stealing from us for years.' She forced the second stack into her purse. Then she tossed the keys in the safe and slammed the door behind. 'There,' she said. 'It's too late to put back.'

Joseph looked at her in dismay. 'I'm leaving,' he said.

'Good,' she said, 'so am I.' She strode to the door and slipped the purse inside her dress. She took one last look at Daniels. His mouth hung open, and a puddle of saliva had darkened the rug beneath his face. Then she shut the overhead light and closed the door quietly behind.

★　★　★

They made their way down steps, quickly, furtively, Joseph a flight ahead. The hallways were all empty, the lights burning on the walls. They left the hotel through a back door at the lowest level. The night had cleared outside, the air was crisp. She smelled wet leaves on the lawn, wet boxwoods. The pebbles crunched beneath her heels.

Joseph reached the truck first and hurried her into the cab. He started the ignition and was about to engage the gear when he cut the engine.

'What's the matter?' she asked.

'This is very bad.' He shook his head.

'It'll be worse if we don't get out of here.'

He put his hands to his face and rubbed his temples. 'You have to give the money back,' he said.

'What?'

'He'll come looking for you if you have it. But if you return it, perhaps he'll leave it be.'

'You expect me to go back there?'

He took his hands from his face and shook his head. 'I don't know what to expect from you anymore.'

'Don't you see?' she said. 'They owe me this money. Not only me, but Delmar and my father and my mother.' She looked at him in exasperation, then checked the front of the hotel. The lights from the lobby cast long shadows across the lot. She thought any moment Daniels might appear at the truck.

'You're a very stubborn girl,' he finally said.

'I've been told.'

'This is not a compliment.'

'Let's just go, okay?'

He mumbled to himself and started the engine. They backed slowly into the drive and circled the lot. Leaves were skittering in the headlights. Privet hedges passed, white-painted trunks, the shapes of pine trees pressed darkly against the sky. Near the exit, an Appleton lamp burned beside the guard booth, and the guard sat silhouetted in his chair. Emily watched as he rose and stepped onto the road and raised his hands in the headlights.

'What does he want?' Joseph asked, an edge of panic in his voice.

'How should I know?' she said.

She wasn't worried; she was sure it was just some routine. The guard lifted his hands higher, so the metal buttons of his coat reflected back in the headlights. Joseph was saying something beneath his breath, a kind of supplication, and she glanced at him and saw his face filled with panic, lacquered in sweat, and before she could stop him he floored the accelerator. The tires squealed, the truck lurched forward. The guard leapt out of the way at the last second, but the side mirror slammed his head and ripped it open and a spray of blood exploded on the windshield. Emily screamed. Joseph was screaming, too. The guard went down behind them, and they saw him writhing on the ground, a geyser of blood reddening the beam of his flashlight.

Joseph gunned the engine. They skidded onto the main street and raced past darkened shops, past streetlamps, past cars parked for the night. Emily clutched the dashboard for balance. It had all happened so quickly, so unexpectedly, that she couldn't yet speak. They reached the end of town and the road darkened, and she turned to Joseph in disbelief.

'Why did you do that!' she shouted. 'You could have killed him!'

'You had a better idea!' He cursed and pounded the wheel. 'You shouldn't have taken the money! I told you not to take the goddamn money!' He muttered something she couldn't understand and glared at the road ahead.

She felt a sinking feeling in her chest. She kept seeing the guard flailing on the ground. She felt a million pins pricking her arms and legs. She glanced at the windshield and saw blood streaked in striations across the glass, then something flashed at the side of the road, and a pair of headlights appeared on the pavement behind.

'Who's that?' she asked.

Joseph turned and shook his head, but didn't answer.

She rolled her window down and stuck her head into the breeze. The headlights were coming on fast. Joseph jammed the truck into a lower gear, and floored the engine. They were climbing a hill now, the road banking into a series of curves. They cambered to the right, and the headlights popped up behind and sent a sheet of light into the cab. Emily pounded the dashboard.

'Can't we go any faster?' she screamed.

Joseph didn't answer. They crested a rise and hit the downhill. The road shirred in the headlights. The truck picked up speed. Fence posts flew by, a billboard for a soft drink. She tried to get a look at the vehicle but could see only the twin lights dogging them from behind.

Joseph hunched over the wheel and the engine whined. She could see a big barn in the headlights, a lantern in the bay. Then she realized where they were, the road familiar, the same one they traveled each autumn with the steers.

'Up ahead,' she shouted, 'right after the next curve, there's a road on the right. Turn into it. We might be able to lose them.'

Joseph looked behind and shook his head. 'I doubt it,' he said.

'Just try it!' she shouted.

She could see the curve nearing. Joseph checked the mirror again, then took the turn fast and braked at the last possible moment, so they almost overturned in the grist. Emily groped for the dashboard and extinguished the headlights, and the road went black before them. They were inside a field of corn, that much she knew. Joseph leaned into the windshield and tried to navigate in the dark. Rows of corn raced past, the road rutted and narrow. They climbed higher until the field ended and the night opened around them. Emily stuck her head out the window and saw dust tunneling behind, the corn retreating in the distance. The hard road was just visible beyond with no light on it, and no car anywhere in sight.

'I don't see them,' she shouted. The wind was batting her hair. She watched a while longer, and dropped into her seat.

'I think we lost them.'

'They could have their lights off,' he said.

'I don't think so.'

She scanned the road again but saw only their own dust feathered in the night, and she fell back in her seat and exhaled. The air was cooler now. She looked up through the windshield where the stars were slipping overhead like a thick fabric. She could smell cows and damp earth and dead leaves along the roadside. She could smell the hardening corn and the bur cucumber and bindweed and all the ripening earth flushed into the cab, so vivid and mineral that it seemed she'd never really smelled anything before, that her whole life had been lived without odor, and she felt momentarily invigorated and alive.

Then the image of the guard came back, the blood bursting against the window, and she shot up in her seat. What if they'd seriously hurt him? What if they'd killed him? Wouldn't they come looking for her? Wouldn't they blame her for knocking out Daniels, for taking the money? Wouldn't they blame Joseph, too?

She tried to dismiss the thought. Everything could be explained. Surely the guard wasn't hurt that badly. Perhaps he had a concussion or a black eye, a bloodied nose, a bad cut, probably nothing more. She tried to relax, but the fear returned as if someone had injected bleach into her veins.

Joseph pulled on the headlights, and the road blossomed before them. They were in open country now, on a road she didn't recognize. Cows huddled along a fence line, their eyes orange disks in the night. Emily sat in dazed silence, watching the road whiten in the lights.

'So,' Joseph finally spoke, 'what are we to do now?'

'I don't know,' she said almost in a whisper. 'Get to the house. Get to the holler. Get away from here . . . I'm sorry,' she glanced at him, but he was staring at the road under hooded lids.

'Do you have any idea what they do to

353

people like me for this?' he asked.

She shook her head.

'They put you on a ship,' he said. 'They send you back where you come from. They call you an 'undesirable alien' and deport you. They do it all the time.'

'It won't happen,' she said.

'This is easy for you to say.'

'It won't,' she protested, and lifted a hand to his face and felt his cheeks already roughened with stubble. 'Garvin will help,' she whispered. 'It'll be okay. I promise.'

He stared blankly at the road ahead. He wouldn't even look at her. She could smell his sweat through his shirt, pungent, vinegary, unlike the way he usually smelled. She dropped her hand from his face. She wasn't really sure anything would be okay.

★ ★ ★

And then they were driving in silence. The dash lights glowed in their glass bezels. The moon hadn't yet risen, and the night lay indigo all around, with a faint stain of pink from their tail-lights. They crossed into the pastureland around Dawson and then up into the hills, and the forests came down like cathedrals; and it seemed for a moment that she was in a foreign country, in another time

354

or place, that she'd crossed into some strange landscape she'd never known before. She thought of rivers emptying into each other, the Greenbrier, the New, the Mississippi; and she thought of harbors and men in bowler hats. She looked again at Joseph, his face doubled in the windshield, hard, reddish, almost devilish in the glow of the dash light. She wanted to curl up beside him and go to sleep forever, to forget about what had happened, to return to earlier that afternoon or last week or month and live it all again, but differently this time.

20

They took the long way around to Lick Creek, through Monroe County, keeping to the back roads past Addison and Arbodale. By the time they reached the Crossroads, the light hung over the eastern sky like a scar beginning to spread. They'd decided to hide the truck down the road to the mine and hike to Garvin's, where they'd figure out what to do.

They turned at Laird's up the Lick Creek Road, the houses silent in the dawn, the lamps yet unlit. Smoke chuffed quietly from chimneys. At the Two Mile Road the headlights luminated old asters and goldenrod gone to seed; and they bounced down the gullied lane, bottomed into a bench of earth, and splashed through standing water. Joseph gunned the engine and the tires rooted and sprayed mud. He gunned the engine again, and they dug in farther until he cut the ignition.

The dawn was blacker in the wood. She heard birds calling from the gloom, juncos, chickadees, others she once knew but now couldn't recall. Joseph brought a checked wool coat from the back of the truck and urged her into it. For the next quarter hour they dragged branches and downed limbs, covering the sides of the truck, concealing it in the woods, and when they were satisfied, they lit off into the dawn.

The day was breaking overhead, fog filtering through the trees. The jewelweed kept wetting her dress, and briers caught her stockings. Every few seconds the image of the guard entered her head like a bird alighting on the same branch, and she tried to chase it away. Yet the nagging feeling was still there, that nothing would ever be the same.

By the time they skirted up the hollow, the sky was pale blue and the top of Keeny's Knob lay sealed in a strip of gold. She heard Garvin's rooster below, her own responding a quarter mile away. She saw the moon in the south, pale now, mother-of-pearl, vanishing with the advance of day. She was cold and thirsty, her stockings torn. Joseph lumbered up the slope, shivering slightly, his face drawn. She took off the coat and handed it to him.

'You take it now, I better go talk to him first.'

She pulled the purse from her dress, took one stack of bills, and wrapped it in a handkerchief. Joseph dropped on a downed log and wiped hair out of his face.

'Are you all right?' she asked. She wrapped the coat around his shoulders and kissed him on the forehead. 'It'll be okay,' she said, 'I promise.' Then she started down the slope toward Garvin's.

★ ★ ★

His cabin lay that morning in a scrim of fog, the tin roof a dull sheen in the dawn. As she came out of the wood, she could see the entire hollow in the distance, the walnuts beside the creek and the frost just burning off the fields. She could see the ponies on the pasture hanging their heads to the grass, and beyond the acreage leading down to the McClungs and the Toothmans and the Loudermilks. She couldn't see her own house but knew it was up there, just beyond the curve of the creek, and knew too that her mother would be waiting, without having slept that night. And for the first time in what seemed like her whole life, she yearned to go back there, to the porch and the kitchen, to the dog and her room, to her life as it had been before.

She trudged through wet grass. A million thoughts raced through her head. She had to be strong. If not for her sake, then for

Joseph's. Garvin's hounds were howling below. The dander from the dried milkweed floating in the first light. She saw Garvin in the mist, gun in hand, dressed in a red union suit faded to pink, and she tried to compose herself. He stared as she approached, rubbed sleep from his eyes, and nodded at her dress.

'What the hell happened to you?' he asked.

'It's a long story.' She gestured toward the house. 'Can I come in?'

'I reckon.' He yawned. 'Lord knows it's early enough.'

The kitchen was cold and dank and smelled of rotting fruit. He lit an oil lamp and the flame danced in the greasy glass, yet it wasn't much to see by. She paced beside the skewed panes while he stirred embers in the stove.

'What manner of trouble you get yourself in now?' he asked.

'I need a vehicle,' she said.

He chuckled and shook his head. 'Oh, Emee. You're always needin' something when you come here.' He closed the stove door and regarded her for the first time, and she stared back, rubbing her arms against the cold.

'Hell,' he said, 'you're serious, ain't you?'

'Yes,' she nodded, and felt suddenly as if she were going to cry.

Garvin came over and sat her in a chair, and pulled a seat beside her. 'You want to tell me what happened?' he asked gently.

She shook her head. She was afraid if she opened her mouth, she might start to bawl.

'Come on, honey,' he urged. 'Whyn't you tell your uncle what happened.'

'I'd rather not,' she whispered.

'That kindly makes it difficult,' he said, and waited. The kindling caught in the stove and a pole of orange light danced from the open damper.

'Garvin,' she said, 'I don't have much time. I'd tell you what happened, but then you'd have to lie if anyone asked and I wouldn't want to put you in that position.'

'It's that bad?' he asked.

She didn't answer. She stood and walked to the stove and held her hands over the iron.

'Did you kill someone?' he asked.

'I don't believe so,' she said.

'You don't believe so?'

She shook her head.

'Well, that don't sound encouraging,' he muttered.

She pulled the handkerchief from her purse and walked to the table and laid it in front of Garvin. 'Open it,' she said.

'What is it?'

'Nothing that wasn't owed me.' She

360

nodded toward the bundle. 'Go ahead. It's for you if you can get me a vehicle.'

Garvin eyed the handkerchief suspiciously. He untied the cloth and shot Emily a glance. 'Where'd you get this?'

'You don't want to know,' she said.

He lifted the bills and fanned them with a thumb. 'You ain't goin' to tell me where this come from?'

'No, sir.'

'How you expect me to help 'lest you tell me?'

'Please, Garvin, I can't.'

He placed the pile gingerly in its handkerchief. 'Well, I expect you can one day, right, Emee?'

'Yes, Garvin,' she said. 'One day I'll tell you, one day soon. If you can get us a vehicle, I promise.'

'Who's us?' he asked sharply.

'Me and Joseph.'

'That electric boy?'

'Yes, him.'

'He get you into this?'

'No,' she said, 'I got him in it.'

Garvin leaned back and sighed. 'I expect you did,' he muttered.

The stove was heating up, the day growing brighter in the panes. Garvin looked at the money again.

'Does anyone else know about this?' he asked.

'I think the law might.'

'Good Lord, Emee,' he said, 'you are in trouble. Whyn't you say so!' He shot up in the chair and rubbed the stubble on his cheeks. 'Well, you can't stay here, that won't do. They'll be all over this place like flies on horse shit.'

'I know it,' she said. 'That's what I been trying to tell you. It's why we need that vehicle.'

'Damn,' Garvin said, and chewed his lip. 'Whyn't you just tell me what happened?'

'Garvin . . . '

'All right, all right' — he waved a hand — 'let me just think some.' He paced to the stove, opened the door, and closed it absentmindedly. He walked to the window, then back to the table. 'Well, I seem to recall this old feller down in Pence who was wantin' to unload a vehicle, and if not him, I can think of one or two other things . . . ' He scratched his neck and looked toward the window. 'I reckon I might be able to come up with something,' he said.

'You think so?'

'I can only try.'

She stood and walked about the room, trying to calculate where and how they'd meet and where she and Joseph might go. Everything had happened so quickly; she hadn't even thought of that yet. The idea of actually leaving seemed so abstract. Garvin was in his seat again, staring at the money.

'Good Lord, Emee.' He shook his head. 'What's your mama gonna say?'

'I don't know,' she said.

'You aim on seein' her before you leave?'

'It would make leaving hard,' she mumbled.

'It'd make it a lot harder if you didn't.'

Emily shrugged. The thought of her mother made her instantly weary.

'Well, I don't think it's a good idea to see her,' she muttered. 'And don't you go telling her a thing about this until I'm gone from here. Otherwise she'll come looking for me. Okay?'

Garvin nodded. The sun was beginning to pare through the branches. Some ocher leaves drifted outside. The room was warm now, and she felt sleepy all of a sudden, her lids heavy, as though she could take a nap right there. Garvin's orange cat came over and sniffed at her leg and walked away. Then a dog barked outside, and she shot up in her chair.

'Is someone coming?' she asked.

'Relax.' Garvin gestured her to sit. 'No one's coming. I can tell by their bark.'

She nodded at the pile of money. There wasn't any time to lose.

'Take what you need and give the rest to my mother,' she said.

Garvin shook his head. 'I don't want none.'

'You'll need it for the vehicle,' she said.

'No, ma'am. You'll be needing it more than me.'

She started to protest, but Garvin shut his eyes, and she knew there was no point in arguing.

'Well then, give it all to my mother,' Emily said.

'She'll be wantin' to know where it come from,' he said.

Emily raised herself and sighed. 'Tell her it's our compensation for the mine. Tell her it just took a while to get it.'

'Whatever you say, Emee.' Garvin nodded. 'Reckon I ought to get on my glad rags.' He stood and started for his bedroom, but she stopped him in the doorway.

'So where should we meet at?' she asked.

He thought for a moment, staring at the ceiling. 'How about up the Pence side of Keeny's Knob. You know that turnaround up there on that old loggin' road?'

'Yes.' She nodded.

'It's a right smart climb, but it'll keep you off the roads and out of anybody's business.'

'What time?' she asked.

'Sundown, I expect.'

'Sundown,' she repeated. She leaned up and pecked him on the cheek. 'Thanks, Garvin. I knew I could count on you.'

He looked around flustered a moment. The dogs were barking again. He shouted through the walls for them to hush, but they kept howling as Emily headed down the hall.

21

They hid in the woods all morning on a bed of copper leaves. The day turned clear and autumnal, a brilliant blue sky, billowy clouds the color of butter. Joseph dozed from time to time while Emily stayed awake, listening to the soughing of the trees and the creek below and a cow bellow occassionally from the pasture.

Around noon she heard the siren of a squad car. The sound diminished and echoed up the hollow in waves. Joseph woke, and she laid his head in her lap and they listened as the siren approached. A car door slammed down in the hollow, and the siren stopped. Ten minutes later the door slammed again, and the siren wailed away in the distance.

By three o'clock they were crossing old fields, through iron-weed and mullein, the two of them in their evening attire. They kept to the edge of the wood, the orchard grass gone brittle. They climbed split-rail fences rotted to red dust, old fields choked with rose bushes. A biplane passed overhead, its engine sad and distant, and they hid beneath branches just to be sure. They found a small mountain stream and washed their feet in the riffles. Cottonwoods shivered around them; the day grew cold, and they continued on.

By evening they'd circled to the Pence Creek side of the knob. Emily had hung her shoes around her neck and went barefoot, and Joseph did the same. They reached the logging road and threw themselves at the base of a tree. A dog was barking in the dusk. Emily heard a train whistle somewhere but realized she'd been dreaming. The night inked above. A quarter moon tipped to the north. They huddled together, hungry and tired, with the one wool jacket between them for warmth.

★   ★   ★

At nine they heard a vehicle below. Emily checked the road and looked to Joseph.

'Do you think it's him?' she asked.

He blew on his hands and shrugged. 'How should I know?'

She stepped toward the road. She wasn't afraid anymore, even if it wasn't Garvin; she was too cold to care. A pair of headlights appeared through the trees, bore up the incline until the lights fell on her dress and the car stopped in front of her. The engine rattled off. The lights went black. She heard

Garvin and closed her eyes in relief.

'I got good news and bad,' he said when he reached her. 'The good is she's all paid up and she runs right pretty.'

'What's the bad?' she asked.

He spat on the road and looked toward the car. He smelled strongly of gasoline.

'Now, don't go blamin' me, 'cause I didn't say a thing, she just kindly knowed it. She came to my place right after you done left. Said she got her premonitions back.'

Emily peered into the dark and saw someone in the passenger seat of the car.

'Damn,' she said. 'I told you . . . '

Garvin raised both hands. 'I swear I didn't say a word.'

Emily could see her mother now, climbing from the car, standing against the running board, holding a suitcase in one hand. She wore a white housedress and a sunhat, and Emily couldn't remember the last time she'd seen her outside the hollow. In the thin rays of moonlight, on that road at that hour of night, her mother looked so lost to Emily, so out of place, so frail and old and ridiculous in her sunhat, that it made Emily angry and sad all at once, and she wanted to rip the hat from her head and hold her and confess everything that had happened. But she knew there wasn't time.

Ada set the suitcase on the ground and clasped her hands together.

'I brought you some clothes to wear,' she said softly. 'There's some in there for Joe, too, Delmar's and such.'

'Thanks,' Emily managed.

Ada nodded toward the car. 'I fixed some sandwiches, too. They're on the front seat. Figured you-all'd get hungry.'

Emily nodded. Ada lifted a hand to her daughter's cheek, then dropped it to her side. They stood in silence while a whippoorwill called from the dark, quit, and called again.

'You got anything you wantin' to say?' Ada finally asked.

'No, ma'am.'

'Well, Garvin's got a car waitin' down the road, so I reckon I'll best say my good-byes now.' She waited for Emily to say something.

'I ain't gonna ask you about the money,' she continued. 'But I got my suspicions. And I'm not saying I hold with whatever you did, but I don't blame you for leaving. I promised myself years ago when the day came I wouldn't put up a fight, 'cause you been wantin' to leave as long as you were big enough to think about it. I just wish you'da picked a better way of doing it.'

Emily started to say something, but her mother cut her off.

'Let me finish,' she snapped, and fixed her gaze fiercely on Emily. 'I just want you to come home when all this clears. You hear?' she said. ' 'Cause I can't hold with the idea of being alone in that house and everybody good and gone. You hear? And I can't hold with the idea of not seein' my girl again. Okay? You let me know where you're at. Write to me or Garvin or somethin', I don't care how you do it, just do it. I just want to know.' Her voice was quavering, but she composed herself.

'Oh, hell,' she broke off again, 'there ain't no point in telling you things you ain't gonna listen to anyhow.'

Emily was shaking now. She tried to control it, at least so her mother wouldn't see. But then Ada stepped to her and crushed her against her chest, and Emily felt her mother shaking, too; and they held each other a moment, quivering, until her mother let go and stepped back to the car. Emily wanted to say something, that she loved her, that she'd miss her, that she'd be back in a day or a week or a month. But she was afraid whatever she said might not come true.

Her mother opened the car door and climbed inside. They would drive her down the road. It seemed to Emily that she was watching everything through the wrong end of a telescope and that her mother, Joseph, Garvin, and the car were all small and far away, as if she were alone on top of a tall hill, looking down on a land she'd once lived in. She had a vague sense of voices nearby, Garvin's or Joseph's. The whippoorwill was calling again in the night. Then something flew through the dark, a white wing barely visible, a luna moth or a bat, and a cold breeze blew across her chest.

Joseph touched her arm. The engine sputtered and hummed. Garvin was climbing into the passenger seat. It was time, she realized, though she wasn't ready, it was time for her to go.

22

They spent the night traveling a darkened country, down highways she never knew existed. She woke once in North Carolina and slept again and woke at a level crossing somewhere in the early hours of dawn. Boxcars were moving in the headlights, crossing bells banging, lights flashing red. She thought of her mother, where she'd be at that hour, back home alone, and she felt a hollowness inside, as if a rib had been ripped from her chest.

She drifted asleep and dreamed of streetcars, of music pumping out of a Victrola. She dreamed her whole life she'd lived inside a room and she was stepping into a world with no walls or hills to hold her, and she was afraid of falling through a bottomless void. When she woke again hours later, a streak of orange sun stabbed into the car. Joseph touched her cheek with the back of his hand.

'You're awake,' he said.

'Yes . . . ' She swallowed. 'I think so.' She rubbed her eyes and squinted into the light. The land was flat outside, the windshield powdered with a fine red dust. Some fields furrowed past like corduroy.

'Where are we?' she asked.

'Georgia,' he said, 'I thought you'd never wake up.' He took his hand from her face. 'You were snoring.'

'I was not.'

'You were.' He grinned.

'I don't snore.'

'Maybe when you're awake you don't.'

She made a face and stretched. The air was balmy, April-like. She felt rested and somehow restored, as if she'd taken some tonic in the night. They were coming into a town of whitewashed bungalows and brick buildings, advertisements painted on their sides. They passed a drugstore, a bank, a courthouse with flags. The Roncevert Hotel seemed so distant now, like a memory of something that had happened in a dream.

They passed under tangles of telephone wire and pulled in front of a building with a tin sign in the shape of a sandwich. The paint on the lettuce was peeling.

'What are we doing?' she asked.

Joseph set the parking brake. 'Finding something to eat.'

★　★　★

373

Bells banged on a leather thong as they entered. Three men at the counter regarded them briefly before huddling back over their cups. Joseph led her past a varnished counter to the back of the room, where they sat in a dark-stained booth with high backs and pads of red leather. She'd never been in a roadhouse before. She studied the men on the stools, their suspenders making three X's across their backs. A waitress in a hairnet handed them each a card covered in oilcloth and asked if they wanted coffee. Joseph said yes, please, they'd take two.

Emily looked at the counter. A cook stood over a grill. Above his head hung a greasy calendar of a cola girl holding a bottle, her skirts raised behind. The waitress returned with two steaming porcelain cups and fished silverware from her apron.

'Y'all know what you want?' she asked.

Joseph said he'd have a steak with scrambled eggs. The waitress turned to Emily, though she hadn't even looked at the menu.

'I'll have the same as him,' she said.

'Biscuits or toast?'

'Excuse me?'

'You want biscuits or toast? They come with.'

'I'll have biscuits,' Emily said.

Joseph said he'd have the toast, and the

waitress took the menus and shuffled behind the counter.

Emily yawned and blew on her cup. Joseph took small sips, his eyes half-closed, the steam evaporating around him. His cheeks were shaded with stubble, and he was wearing one of Delmar's large flannel shirts. She slid a hand across the table, hooked her pinkie around his, and held it a moment, as if testing him. He looked, she thought, like a fugitive.

'How are you doing?' she asked.

'Okay, considering.' He blew on his coffee and sipped.

'You know, I never meant to get you into any of this,' she said. 'We shouldn't have gone to the ball. It was my fault. I suppose I should have told you about Daniels, beforehand.' She pursed her lips. 'Can you understand why?'

'You could have left the money,' he said.

She unhooked her pinkie. 'And you could have not hit the guard.' She stared out the window. Some cars were passing on the highway. A filling station across the way displayed a pyramid of whitewall tires.

'So,' she asked, 'you're mad at me?'

'Not mad. You did what you had to. It's too late to be mad, besides. What matters is what we're going to do now.'

'Looks like we're stuck together,' she said.

'It appears so.' He picked up his cup and drank. She could see he was trying not to grin. 'So,' he said. 'What do you propose we do?'

'Find a place to sleep.'

'You have to be married to stay in a hotel.'

'Really?'

'Yes,' he said. 'All the motor courts and hotels have these signs, 'No Negroes, No Unwed Couples.''

'We can ask for two rooms, then.'

'They'll know.'

'So we'll sleep in the car,' she suggested.

'You can sleep in the car. You'll get tired of it after a few nights,' he said. 'Trust me.'

The bells banged on the door, and a man in a houndstooth motor cap found a seat at the counter.

'The way I see it,' Joseph said, 'there's only one thing we can actually do.' He put his cup down delicately in its saucer and laid his hands on the table. 'We have to get married.'

'Like I said, I'll sleep in the car.'

'Emily, I'm serious.'

He was staring at her under hooded lids, and she stared back across the table.

'What exactly are you serious about?' she countered.

'Getting married.'

'You want to stay in a hotel that badly?'

'No' — he shook his head — 'it's not that.'

'Then what is it?'

'It'll be easier that way,' he said. 'For us.'

She studied him a moment. The coffee steam was swirling around his face. She fingered the salt shaker and touched a grain on its tip, and rolled it between her thumb.

'So it's just easier?'

'No,' he said. 'Do you think that's all?'

'Hell . . . ' She shrugged. 'I don't know what to think. I think you're crazier than I ever expected.'

'Maybe,' he grinned.

The bells banged on the door again, but neither of them looked up. Then the waitress returned and plunked down two porcelain plates of steak and eggs, two bowls of steaming grits, and a basket of warmed biscuits and toast. She asked if they wanted anything else, and Joseph thanked her and said they had all they needed.

Emily ate slowly. She wasn't that hungry anymore. She kept glancing at Joseph to see that he was still there, that it was all true, that he'd meant what he'd just said. He was cutting his steak, forking pieces into his mouth, blushing each time their eyes met, as if they were on a first date.

She pushed aside her plate and toed off her shoes. She found his leg beneath the table, and ran her foot along his thigh and let her heel rest in the V of his crotch. She was smiling now. She couldn't help herself. He was grinning, too. The sun was coming in the window, the bells banging on the door. She raised her cup to him.

'Okay,' she said bravely. 'You want to know what I think? I think yes, we should. I will. I do.'

He smiled sheepishly and raised his cup, and they clinked. She pressed her toes deeper into his crotch.

★   ★   ★

They drove after to the courthouse in town. A clerk gave them the address of a retired judge who might be able to marry them. At the judge's home a housekeeper told them he'd be back at four. They climbed into the car again and motored out to the highway. The sun was slipping through clouds; the heat felt tropical. They passed a man selling watermelon at the side of the road. They passed a motor court on a lake with green-and-white painted cabins and a sign that read 'Vacancies.' In the afternoon they headed back to town as a drizzle began to fall from the sky.

A thin black man ushered them into the

judge's house this time and had them wait in a vestibule. A frosted-glass globe hung above them, the light jaundiced and pale. A curtained door led to the main part of the house. Emily could see herself doubled in the mirror of a walnut hall tree, and she tried to fix her hair. She felt nervous all of a sudden, giddy, and slightly sick. She could hardly recognize herself in the glass.

She heard a creaking in the hall and voices, then a door opened and a small elderly man caned his way into the vestibule. He had lively blue eyes and flaxen hair combed neatly across his scalp. He wore a plum-colored ascot and a pair of bifocals hung from his neck. He asked what he could do for them, and Joseph explained that they were on their way to New Orleans, where he had a job, and they wanted to get married. The judge removed a pocket watch from his sweater, popped it open, and read the hour.

'It's a little late in the day for a wedding,' he said. 'Wouldn't you agree?'

Neither of them answered. A clock was clapping in another room. Perhaps they shouldn't have come, she thought. The judge set his bifocals on the bridge of his nose and inspected Joseph as if he were appraising a piece of art. He turned to Emily next and studied her dress and shoes, then he made a gesture for them to follow.

They were led into the house, where a grand staircase curved upward to a landing and a long hall led to other rooms. The judge rested his fingers on the silver handle of his cane and turned to Emily first.

'May I ask, miss,' he inquired, 'where you are from?'

'West Virginia,' she said, then regretted telling the truth.

'I take it you're running away from home.'

'No, sir.' She shook her head.

'Do your people know about this marriage?'

'Yes, sir,' she said.

'Then why aren't you getting married back in West Virginia?'

She swallowed and scratched her neck. Joseph started to speak, but the judge held up a liver-spotted hand and said he was asking the young lady.

'Please,' he said. 'Go on.'

'Well, sir,' she explained, 'they know about it, but they don't rightly approve of it.'

'And why is that?'

'Well, they had another boy picked out for me,' she explained.

The judged raised one eyebrow. 'Another boy?'

'Yes, sir.' She nodded.

'How very old world.'

'It is,' she said, 'and that's not the worst of it.'

'No?'

'No, sir.' She shook her head. 'See, this boy's a terrible drinker, and he's bad-mannered and foulmouthed and mean as a weasel, and I couldn't very well spend the rest of my life with him, let alone one night.'

'So you ran away.'

'Well' — Emily gave a shrug — 'in a manner of speaking.'

'In your manner of speaking.'

'I'm sorry,' she said.

'I see.' The judge excused himself and removed a handkerchief from his back pocket, blew his nose, and stuck the handkerchief back.

'Now, miss,' he said, 'how old are you?'

'Twenty-one,' she said.

'Old enough to make up your own mind?'

'Yes, sir.'

'And old enough to know what you want.'

'I believe so.' She smiled.

The judge turned to Joseph and tapped him lightly on the arm with his cane. 'Which brings up you,' he said. 'You're a long way from home, son, aren't you?'

'Yes.'

'And where do you call home?'

'New York,' he said.

'And what is it that you do?'

'I'm a lineman.'

'A what?'

'An electrical lineman.'

The judge pulled a face. 'So you climb poles for a living?'

Joseph smiled. 'Sometimes.'

'And you bring lights to places?'

'Yes.' He nodded. 'Electricity and lights.'

'You know what the Latin is for 'bringer of light'?' he asked.

Joseph shook his head.

'Lucifer,' the judge said. '*Lux fero*, the bearer of light.' He winked at Joseph and smiled. 'You make a good wage at that pole climbing?'

Joseph said he did.

'You can support this young lady, at any rate.'

'Yes,' he said.

The judge's eyes were roaming over Joseph. 'Do you have any identification with you?'

He said he did and reached for his wallet, but the judge stayed him with a hand.

'And you, miss?'

'No.' She shook her head.

'Well, we'll just have to take your word for it. Can we trust you?'

She smiled and nodded.

The judge looked at Joseph. 'And Lucifer over there. Can we trust him?'

'I wouldn't take any chances.' She grinned.

'Fine,' the judge said, and gestured for them to follow. He caned his way over oak floors through a glass door to a study. There were bookcases all over the room, lampshades with silk tassels, a stuffed heron mounted on a table, a small bluegill in its beak. There were diplomas on one wall, gilt-framed portraits of bearded men long deceased, a music stand, a cello case on a chair.

The judge gestured them to a davenport covered in an Oriental throw. Emily sat first, and Joseph followed. The judge was peering at books in a barrister's case.

'I haven't done this in quite some time,' he explained, 'so you'll have to bear with me. There was a time I married near twenty people a week, ten on Monday morning and the rest Friday evening, seemed to be the most popular marrying times, and mostly in May and for some reason November, too. But I've gone out of that business, or it's gone plumb out of me.' He found what he was looking for, a large black ledger. He hauled it to a desk and switched on a lamp. His face looked waxen in the light, his lips trembling. He dipped a pen in a glass inkwell and held it above a piece of notepaper.

'What are your names again?' he asked. 'The lady first.'

Emily told him hers and Joseph his, and the judge penned them delicately onto the paper. When he was done he removed his bifocals and held them in the air.

'I'll be just a few minutes' he said. 'Make yourselves comfortable.'

They sat on the davenport, holding hands. The sky was growing dark in the windows, the trees flushed with rain. When he was gone five minutes Joseph began to worry.

'I don't like this,' he whispered. 'I think we should go.'

'It's okay,' she said.

'He's taking too long. Maybe he's calling the police.'

She squeezed his hand and said it was fine, that he wasn't calling any police.

A gust of rain rapped against the window. Water eeled down the glass. They heard the judge talking in the hall. Then he entered, this time wearing a black robe and carrying a book under his arm. The rest seemed to happen so quickly, with the judge asking questions and reading from the book and having them put their hands on the Bible and swear and the black man there as a witness. And when they were done signing, they paid the judge and he handed them a piece of paper, folded his bifocals, and said that was all there was to it, that it was easier than pulling a tooth.

★   ★   ★

They drove after to the motor court along the lake. The rain on the roof sounded dreamy, the gravel crunching under the tires of the car. To Emily it seemed she'd been suspended all day in some clear distilled liquid, something lambent and amber and utterly intoxicating, for she was waiting now to come down, to catch her breath, to find herself back in her life again, in Lick Creek, in Falls County, waiting for someone to tell her it wasn't real, the rain on the windshield or the white arrow pointing to the office door or the instrument knobs of the automobile inlaid with mother-of-pearl. She watched Joseph run through the rain, flip up his collar, and clutch his coat. He fought a screen door open and disappeared inside the office, and she listened to the engine idling, the wipers slapping back and forth, the rain like some music on the roof. She watched for several minutes the water curtain under an outdoor lamp and the trees sway like drunks; and she breathed the odor of the leather seats, the air so sweet and alive that she wanted to weep. At last he emerged from the office and hunched back to the car, and she realized, yes, it was all real.

'What happened?' she asked.

He ran a hand through his hair and whipped water off, then reached into his coat and fished out a shiny key.

'Number seven.' He grinned. 'It's on the lake.'

The cottage smelled of cedar. There were ladybug carcasses all over the floor, a white chenille spread on the bed. Emily opened drawers, closets, a desk; she cracked the window and let in a seam of cool air. She went to the bathroom and checked the toilet, the porcelain pull chain, a clawfoot tub. There was a faint odor of mothballs, and the walls were roughly paneled. She turned a nickel-plated tap and felt cold water turn warm, and she splashed her arms and face.

They didn't bother to bathe first but undressed in silence, Emily first, slipping off her dress, her camisole, her garter, piling them on the bed until she was naked with only the amber beads around her neck. The rain drummed against the windows. He came to bed already aroused, and she could smell the odor of his armpits. His chin was rough on her cheek, her neck, down her belly, along the inside of her thighs. He undid her hair so it fell along her back, and he turned her over and they made love with abandon, wildly, as if she were some other woman. She gripped the headboard and saw lightning stroke over the lake and heard the swish of trees outside, and she roused him again with her mouth, and they made love once more until they collapsed in exhaustion.

They lay in the emerald light as if on the bottom of some ocean. She watched flashes thrown against the walls and listened to the thunder peal and die. After several minutes she climbed on top of him and covered them in the cotton sheet. 'How's my tepee?' she asked.

He didn't respond. He was gazing upward, distracted. She ran a finger over his lips and made a circle of his mouth and kissed him.

'I have a question,' he said.

'Mmm.'

'What's Lick Creek?'

'What do you mean?' she asked.

'I mean the name. Where does it come from?'

She fell back beside him on the mattress and stared at the ceiling. The stucco was dark, the rain raking softly on the roof.

'It comes from the rocks.' She sighed.

'The rocks?'

'There's salt in the boulders along the

creek,' she explained. 'The buffalo used to go down there and the deer, too, and they used to lick the rocks because of the salt in them.'

'The rocks had salt?'

'They still do.'

'Like tears,' he said.

'I suppose.' She shrugged. 'Anyways, the buffalo were all hunted out and the deer, too, so not much licks at the creek anymore. When I was a girl I tried some of the boulders just to see what they tasted like.'

'You licked them?'

'I did.' She grinned.

'So what did they taste like?'

She propped her head up on an elbow and curled his chest hair with a finger. 'They tasted like rocks,' she said. 'They tasted just like rocks.'

Thunder growled outside. She winked at him, slipped into his shirt, and walked to the bathroom. In the metal medicine cabinet someone had left behind an old toothbrush, a scissors, a rusted razor. She returned to the bed, where Joseph lay splayed on his back.

'I want you to do me a favor.' She dropped the scissors on the mattress. 'I want you to cut my hair.'

He looked at her, perplexed. The light was angling in from the bathroom.

'I'm serious,' she said. 'In case someone

recognizes us. And besides' — she raised an eyebrow — 'a bob is very fashionable.'

He picked up the scissors and worked them open and closed. She lowered herself on the edge of the bed, gathered her hair in a ponytail, and turned her back to him.

'Go on,' she said. 'Just snip it right off.' She felt his hand press into the small of her back, then he kissed her left shoulder blade.

'I can't do it,' he said. 'It would be like killing something.'

'Christ,' she said, and grabbed the scissors and strode into the bathroom. Before he could stop her, she was working the blades across her hair, and thick clumps were falling on the tiles, on her shoulders, her breasts. She grinned at him in the mirror and continued to snip. Her face was flushed, freckled, bony. She looked, she thought, like a boy.

★　★　★

In Atlanta they bought matching gold bands at a pawnshop. They bought new clothes at a ready-to-wear, shirts of Egyptian cotton, socks, underwear. Emily bought wool jodhpurs and a gray flannel dress, aviator goggles, and a silk motoring scarf for the car. Joseph bought a madras shirt, a pair of khakis, a sports coat, and a felt bowler. With her shorn hair Emily felt liberated, lightheaded, her limbs loose. She wanted to smoke a cigarette. She wanted to wear men's trousers. She wanted to sprawl in the grass like a horse.

They stayed at the Tremont Hotel in Atlanta, a motor camp south of Anniston. They ate in roadhouses and diners. And on the long journey south she felt as if she'd entered another planet, with the long-leaf pines shirring past, the cane fields, the rust-colored roads, the rivers that ran black as blood, the belching refineries outside Birmingham lit up like jewel boxes in the night.

★   ★   ★

They arrived in New Orleans late in the afternoon, when the city was pink, the buildings pastel, a canvas of tropical colors thrown against the sky. The city smelled of diesel. She'd never seen so much traffic, so many people in one place. The river flashed between buildings like a coin.

Their hotel room had apple-green shutters, an ironwork terrace, brown caramel floors. She could see sprays of a palm tree thrust upward like punctuation. A woman sung scales across the street.

They existed those first few days in a world of their own, walking the boulevards beside the river, eating late breakfasts, drinking mugs of hot chocolate under striped awnings. It was the farthest she'd ever been, this city, unlike anywhere she'd ever dreamed of, with its plazas and pantile roofs and the arches along the arcades. They slept in the afternoon; she'd never known such luxury. They woke with bright bars of alizarin through the wood-slat shutters and the sound of voices in the hall; and there was something sad about those awakenings, the quality of the light, the street sounds so strange to her, the horsehooves, cycle horns, the scrape of a metal grating from a shop.

In the late afternoons they rode streetcars through the garden district, the warm Delta breeze blowing through open windows. She liked the names of the cars, the green paint, the wooden scroll blinds through which the striped light fell, the shower of sparks from the catenaries that Joseph pointed out and said: 260 volts.

She liked the streetcar bells, which reminded her of cow-bells, the ones they hung on their Angus up on the high pasture. As they rode into the verdant suburbs, she would mouth the names of the streets they passed — Menopeme, Caliope, Terpsichore — a guidebook on her lap, her hands in white gloves. Clio, Thalia. The names of muses ticking passed like pikes on a wheel of fortune.

'There's none for electricity,' Joseph said on one of the trips.

She shrugged and said, 'There's none for coal miners, either.'

When they reached the end of the line, she'd step off the rear of the car, the pattern of the straw seat imprinted on the back of her dress. They'd board the next car back, retracing their journey to Canal, the muses going the opposite way.

★　★　★

Sometimes in the afternoons she took a towel from the bathroom and hung it over the shutters so the light came in copper and muted, and she sat at the small portmanteau and wrote her mother letters. She told her everything. She described storefronts, the bolts of satin and crepe de chine, the dead pigs hung waxen in the windows, the steamed glass with trays of cooked crayfish, silver tea sets, crabs on ice. She wrote about their rented room, the milk carts she heard in the morning on their way to market, the glass bottles rattling like castanets in their cages, the horsehooves on cobbles, the hazy city waking. Or the sounds of river barges in the evening or the horn of a steamboat as it hailed into port. She told her about the skyline, how in the afternoon the city took on the tones of the sky and the buildings flushed flamingo pink and the blue of chickory flowers; and how once she walked along the river and saw coal barges coming down the Mississippi, a chain of them, and she knew they'd come out of the mountains, probably from Charleston or some other inland port, and how it seemed so easy now, as they drifted past, the coal banked in clean piles. She stopped and watched them and wanted to tell people lounging on the park benches that each chunk of that coal came from the insides of the earth and had to be hauled out by hand. She wanted to tell them, Look, this is what makes your city sing, your streetcars run, your lights, your lifts, your crabs on ice, and it is not easy, not a drift down a river, but a struggle, a war. She watched the barges sail into the evening and remembered what Gianni once said, that only miners knew what it was like to be dead, for they spent so much time underearth.

She wrote her mother this and more. She wrote about the seagulls, birds she'd never seen before, so large and noisy, reeling over the terrace, how sad their cries seemed, like the cries of a goat. She'd once read in the encyclopedia that the Greek word for goat, *tragos*, was where the word *tragedy* came from, because the sound of a goat screaming was so haunting. And she thought the seagulls had that cry, too, and the city seemed full of flying goats.

Usually she'd wait until Joseph left the room or was sleeping. And she'd write about people eating at all hours in restaurants and sidewalk cafés or tell her how Joseph had just started a job building a power line across Lake Pontchartrain, just like in West Virginia, only this time over water and not land; and that perhaps they would stay there until spring. And she told her of shopping in the market alone. The woman who sang across the street, the sound of the radio that seeped into their room. She told her too how at times she felt alone, like a fish out of water, when people couldn't understand her accent, and how, sometimes late at night, awake, she longed for the cold mountain air, for the smell of hardwoods, the hickories and oaks, the sound of the creek slurring past; and that the trees here were unknown to her and full of impossible blooms, the river not what she'd expected, either, but oily, with tires floating in it, dead fish, the water the color of coffee; and that she knew now what it was to be a foreigner in a foreign place, like Gianni, like Joseph.

When she pictured her mother back home, it was enough to make her cry, for she imagined her at a certain time in the afternoon on the porch, bundled against the cold, the sun slanting over the balusters, and she could taste the odor of the November air, thick with woodsmoke, and the dog there, too, and downhollow the McClung sisters and Ruth Loudermilk and Betty Laird. She loved them all now, even Garvin, especially Garvin, and though she didn't tell Joseph, and though she could hardly admit it to herself, she missed her home, her house, the hollow. She missed her mother, each day more and more.

She wrote all this in her letters. And afterward she'd cap her pen and screw the lid on the inkwell and put the letter in a paper envelope, address and seal it, and stick it in the drawer to send later, or never at all, for she was afraid they might get found or intercepted, and they'd find out where she was. And this was why it was so easy to speak to her mother in these letters, why she was so free to tell her things she wouldn't back home in Lick Creek; and why in her last letter she confided that she'd missed her period, that Joseph didn't know yet, that she was afraid to tell him, that she was terrified to admit it herself, but she thought — she knew — she was pregnant.

★　★　★

One afternoon she tucked the letter away as usual in the top drawer of the portmanteau and pinned a small navy hat to her head. Joseph was away at work, and she sighed as she checked the mirror, then locked the room and headed to the market alone.

Outside, the sun was shining in the live oaks. It was December, but the summer seemed never to end. She walked over cobbles and heard music, a soft anklet of sound she faintly recognized. She followed the thread of song. It was coming from an open window somewhere, and she turned a corner and the music grew louder, and she realized it was a song she knew, a song she hadn't heard in years, the opera Gianni used to play on the Victrola on Sunday afternoons. The wind was fresh off the river, and the music came and went, and she even remembered the opera, *La Traviata*. It seemed like a lifetime away, this thread of music. She began to hum it. She could see the store now across the street where the music was coming from, the ironwork out front, the sun boring into the brick, the awning red. The music grew louder, and she stepped toward it.

Addio, del passato bei sogni ridenti . . .

She remembered him hiking his pants and pretending to be a prostitute. And the sun came out and she could hear cowbells banging in the afternoon, her Angus coming to hay, a tinkling sound on the high pasture, this world she left behind.

Le rose del volto gia' son pallenti . . .

She didn't see the streetcar career and screech; she didn't see it coming.

A stone drops, and electricity travels along a wire at 187,000 miles per second; and the pain is so searing, it is like a fire blown through a house.

She hears only the music, faded now, as if spun on a slower rpm. Then she is aware of many different sounds all at once, sounds she can't categorize or find names for. She is on the ground, and the heat from the pavement is somehow seeping into her hands. People are leaping off the streetcar, but she doesn't see them come her way. She is aware of the music flowing over her like a wind, faces around her, but none she knows. The people crowd and push. Someone shouts and fences them back. An electric arc spills in sparks, and a man in a blue uniform talks to her, but his words come out like a rusty gate, a grackle voice, gnashing and inchoate. Maybe she was wrong about the opera after all, because she can't hear it anymore. Another sound intrudes, a jumble of notes, a blare of a trumpet. A brass band piping a slow tune with trombones and tubas, and she sees them flashing through people's legs, a parade of black men, somber and high-stepping, some with bow ties, others with neckties, all of them in suits, one dressed like a jester. She sees them passing on their way to the river, and they don't turn to look but keep marching, the large man in the rear with a bass drum lashed to his back. And she can't tell its beating from that of her heart.

The ambulance is white, a scarlet cross on the door, a little light in front like a pharos lamp. Through the windows she can see trees. Magnolias and spreading banyans, branches with tropical flowers whose names she doesn't know. They pass colonnaded sidewalks. She hears chapel bells chime, the wind high in the hornbeams. Two boys tap-dancing on a piece of rusted tin, pennies shivering at their feet. Once in a while they stop and she can hear the crackle and static of a radio and horns honking. She calls for Gianni, for Joseph. Then she enters a kind of cave, a well-lit place; it is a room in a house, and through the window she can see the ocean flashing bronze, but the room is too bright to behold.

A nurse waits in the corner. The gnomon of a wall clock circles in silence, then circles again. The world is white enamel. A doctor leans over her, a silver coin on his head, a tiara, a crown, and he whispers in low tones in a language she can't decipher.

Outside, the autumn sunlight slides through caged windows. An oak rustles against the glass. The rivers are going down to the sea, the Greenbrier, the New, the Ohio, the Mississippi. She can't tell the time of day. She doesn't know how much time has passed, days or minutes or weeks. She keeps turning corners and meeting them. They are patient and smiling, sitting in straight-backed chairs, hats in hand, wearing clothes they never wore in life. They've grown older, or maybe only wiser. Delmar has a scar she doesn't recognize. Gianni is wearing black priest's vestment, holding the sacrament in hand, flanked by his father and mother. Her own father is in a dark drill suit, but when they start to talk she hides before she can hear them.

When she wakes again it is night and a castor-oil moon spills through the bars. Joseph is there in the dark, sitting woodenly in a chair, and she is aware of his presence, like a blanket she once covered herself with; and she wants to comfort him now, for he is the one without friends here.

She sleeps and wakes. She sees minnows floating in a creek. Bluegills sparkling. The flash of pink trout. Delmar naked, covered in black. A fish trembling in the grass, her father waving on the road to the mine. They are dressed in new starched shirts, holding nets and seines and carrying angling hooks and tackle boxes. *We've been waiting,* Delmar whispers. We are fishermen here, we have learned this trade. A life on water to cleanse us of coal. This is what happens, he says, to those who die underearth. A special place by the sea. A constant ablution. Remember the donkeys I told you about, he says. How their legs snapped off when they're lowered in the shafts. They're here, too, he says. They carry our baskets of fish. They swim in salt waters. They eat honey and oats.

The sun comes up in skirts of gold and pierces the room. She feels a piece of life leaving her and remembers the fog she caught

in the mornings, the *malochim,* her parents'
walnut bed, the figures inlaid on the
headboard. The first time Gianni saw it he
said, Look, little *putti,* and she said, What?
and he said: Angels. She remembers also the
crack in the mirror glass, how she traced it
with her finger, saying, This is my country;
this wallpaper pattern of anchors and roses,
roses are for the land, her father said, anchors
for the sea; and the smell of his skin, all their
skin, encrusted with coal, as if they came out
of the earth ashed and kilned, spun on wheels
like walking pottery, the dark bituminous
caverns on one side and the kingdoms of
karst on the other.

We've been waiting, he whispers again. It is
Delmar. She can see him clearly now. She
understands at last why his name means 'of
the ocean.' Do you want to see the house? he
asks. He is patient, his hands clasped
together. She says yes and then no, and then
yes again. And he reaches out and touches
her and takes her by the hand. They turn up a
road and there is a big house on a bluff built
of new lumber, and she can see the bluest
ocean beyond, through each opened window
it shines; through the dormers and double-
hung panes, a light so magnificent and bright.
And there are people standing in the
doorway. Her father and Gianni and a host of

others. See? Delmar says. *We've been waiting.* There are nets and donkeys. Oars and rowboats. The sea is flashing blue, the waves cresting. He lets go of her hand and turns and smiles. Yes, he says. *We've been waiting.* We've been waiting all this time.

23

At eight the next morning a doctor pronounced her dead. The nurse swaddled her in a muslin cloth and wheeled her body from the room. An orderly arrived with a bucket and mop and began to scrub the floor. Joseph staggered out into the morning sun. Crows were hopping in the trees. A streetcar ground past. He sat on a curb and laid his head in both hands and wept.

Two days later he boarded a train north, the pine box placed below with the luggage, its sides stamped in ink with its destination: White Sulfur, West Virginia. And it seemed to Joseph that the whole journey passed in silence, three days shedding by like a film, the same scrap of landscape, over level crossings and rivers, through towns, through dark and light and dark again. He spoke to no one. He ate no food. On the third day he entered the Alleghenies. And on the fourth he reached Lick Creek. It was late December in the mountains, the hills barren and brown, the country raked by rain. Puddles lay along the Lick Creek Road, and the cows were bedded on the hills.

The ceremony was small, with only a few neighbors. The minister read Psalm 88 and the Lord's Prayer, and no one sang. A cold wind whipped off Keeny's Knob and kept blowing the minister's cornsilk hair across his scalp, while Ada clutched her collar, unable to speak. Joseph wore the same stiff black suit he'd been wearing all week. His beard had grown in thick. Before the first shovel load fell, he walked to the edge of the grave, tore his shirt, then ripped a handful of hair from his scalp and let it drift in the hole.

* * *

He stayed for a week, haunting the high pasture, the goat barn, the towers, the places in the woods they used to go. The crews had all gone, and the right-of-way had grown back with new greenbrier. Up on the hill the towers held voltage, and he could hear the cables buzzing in the snow.

Days later he drifted west. To Houston, then Colorado. He traveled north to Oregon and Washington State. He found line work where he could, and all along he held her in mind, like a spur that kept him moving. The years passed, and the names of the companies he worked for became a litany of utilities: Gulf Light and Power, Denver Electric,

Pacific Electric Light, Puget Public Service. He built transmission towers across the Sierras and up into the Cascades. In the Second World War he constructed communication lines in Burma. He was thirty-four when he remarried. He had two children and still later three grandchildren.

In his older years he retired to a house in a town just north of New York City, along the Hudson River, and he'd sit of an evening on a small concrete patio, listening to the sounds of the commuter trains coming and going, the look in his eye sad and distant. He never spoke of West Virginia or Lick Creek or Appalachian Light and Power. He never mentioned the name Emily Jenkins. He was seventy-eight years when he died.

★   ★   ★

Years later, I found his lineman's belt in the cellar of his house. The leather was macerated and greenish with mold, the hardware pitted and rusted; it left a fine powdered dust on my hands. Hidden beneath the boxes of glass insulators and bell wire was a shoebox tied tightly with a lamp cord. Her letters were inside, her handwriting beautiful and rounded, all the envelopes addressed to 'Ada Jenkins. Lick Creek, West

405

Virginia' with no post code or street address and no stamp affixed to the corner. I could see where the blue ink had gotten wet and run and where the ghost of the glue once sealed the envelopes and where his finger-prints had left their patterns like a pentimento on the paper.

Why he'd kept them, and not Ada, was a mystery I never fathomed, and how much my grandmother knew was a mystery, too. Perhaps she understood something of his youthful romance, as the box was not well hidden. But I imagine him heading down to the cellar every year and taking out the box and rereading the letters by a bare lightbulb and putting them away until the next time he had the need to visit Emily Jenkins again.

As for me, I have read them over and over, trying to glean everything of her life. The pages are as brittle as old napkins. I read them and slip them back into their paper sleeves. And each time I think of Emily and Gianni and Ada. I think of my grandfather Joseph, too, and I wonder how things could have been otherwise, and how the world is so much rounder and more magnetic than ever we might dream.

Acknowledgments

I would like to thank the following for their kindness in helping create this work: the Hambidge Center, the Virginia Center for Creative Arts, Villa Montalvo, the Williamsburg District Historical Foundation in Williamsburg, West Virginia, Appalachian Power Company, Greenpoint Light and Power, Wood and A and the farm; Jeff in the white house; Glenn, Stuart, and Isabel Kessler; Billie Fitzpatrick, Stephen Hubbell, David Murin, Susan Wheeler, Harvey Shapiro, Maggie Paley, Janet Coleman, and Jill Ciment. Special thanks to Betsy Lerner for her passion and Nan Graham for both her vision, and for revealing what matters most. And Dona, finally, for living it.

We do hope that you have enjoyed reading this large print book.

Did you know that all of our titles are available for purchase?

We publish a wide range of high quality large print books including:
Romances, Mysteries, Classics
General Fiction
Non Fiction and Westerns

Special interest titles available in large print are:
The Little Oxford Dictionary
Music Book
Song Book
Hymn Book
Service Book

Also available from us courtesy of Oxford University Press:
Young Readers' Dictionary
(large print edition)
Young Readers' Thesaurus
(large print edition)

For further information or a free brochure, please contact us at:
Ulverscroft Large Print Books Ltd.,
The Green, Bradgate Road, Anstey,
Leicester, LE7 7FU, England.
Tel: (00 44) 0116 236 4325
Fax: (00 44) 0116 234 0205

Other titles in the
Ulverscroft Large Print Series:

STRANGER IN THE PLACE

Anne Doughty

Elizabeth Stewart, a Belfast student and only daughter of hardline Protestant parents, sets out on a study visit to the remote west coast of Ireland. Delighted as she is by the beauty of her new surroundings and the small community which welcomes her, she soon discovers she has more to learn than the details of the old country way of life. She comes to reappraise so much that is slighted and dismissed by her family — not least in regard to herself. But it is her relationship with a much older, Catholic man, Patrick Delargy, which compels her to decide what kind of life she really wants.

COME HOME TO DANGER

Estelle Thompson

Charles Waring has come home to Queensland to attend his mother's funeral and his remark, intended only for a family friend to hear, is inadvertently overheard by several other people. The chain of events which follows convinces Charles that his mother was murdered because she knew a terrible secret from someone's past, and he finds himself in a deadly game of cat-and-mouse as he tries to unravel the mystery. Meanwhile, he must face the certainty that someone among those he has come to care about poses a cruel threat.

SUMMER OF SECRETS

Grace Thompson

When Bettrys Hopkyns' alcoholic sister Eirlys committed suicide, Bettrys was determined that Eirlys's baby daughter Cheryl — the result of Eirlys's secretive summer love affair — would stay with her. Still yearning for Brett, her former lover, Bettrys sets herself a challenge: to find Cheryl's father. Her search takes her and Cheryl to a small seaside village in west Wales; to a close-knit community seething with secrets. Befriended by the cheerful Gordon, who falls in love with her, Bettrys is quickly drawn into a web of deceit and is forced to face the terrifying possibility that Brett might be a murderer . . .

A MORTAL AFFAIR

Stella Allan

Frances Parry seemed to have it made. She was married to a Harley Street consultant, she had a beautiful home, wealthy friends — including the fascinating Bernard, her husband's friend since undergraduate days — and a creative job. But suddenly Frances's world was turned upside down; her home was sold, her sideline job became a vital means of livelihood, and Bernard, who had become her lover, was exposed as a criminal. And then Frances found that she herself was indulging in criminal activities in a deadly duel with the law.

EVERY GOOD GIRL

Judy Astley

After twenty years of marriage, Nina had offloaded serial philanderer Joe and was happy coping alone with their two demanding daughters. But some disturbing elements began to appear in her new, carefree life. A flasher had been accosting young girls on the nearby common. Home no longer felt so safe. And Joe, during one of his oh-so-civilised monthly lunches with Nina, revealed that the new love in his life, power-dressed Catherine, had decided that she now required a baby. But babies, Joe told Nina, were what he did with her: a remark that Nina found oddly unsettling . . .

A FANCY TO KILL FOR

Hilary Bonner

Richard Corrington is rich, handsome and a household name. But is he sane . . . ? When journalist Joyce Carter is murdered only a few miles from Richard's west country home, his wife suspects he has been having an affair with her, and forensics implicate him in the killing. But Detective Chief Inspector Todd Mallett believes that Joyce's murder is part of something much more sinister and complex. There have been other deaths; the senseless killing of a young woman on a Cornish beach, another in a grim London subway . . . And somewhere on the Exmoor hills a killer waits. Stalking his prey. Ready to strike again . . .